THE FETISH CHEST

ULTIMATE UNDIES

EROTIC STORIES ABOUT UNDERWEAR AND LINGERIE

THE FETISH CHEST

ULTIMATE UNDIES

EROTIC STORIES ABOUT UNDERWEAR AND LINGERIE

EDITED BY RACHEL KRAMER BUSSEL
AND CHRISTOPHER PIERCE

© 2006 by Alyson Books. Authors retain the rights to their individual pieces of work.
All rights. reserved.

Manufactured in the United States of America.

This trade paperback original is published by Alyson Books,
P.O. Box 1253, Old Chelsea Station, New York, New York 10113-1251.
Distribution in the United Kingdom by Turnaround Publisher Services Ltd.,
Unit 3, Olympia Trading Estate, Coburg Road, Wood Green,
London N22 6TZ England.

First edition: August 2006

06 07 08 09 a 10 9 8 7 6 5 4 3 2 1

ISBN 10 15583-961-4
ISBN 13 978-1-55583-961-1
An application for the Library of Congress Cataloging-in-Publication Data is on file.

Cover photography © Image Source / Punch.
Book design by Victor Mingovits.

CONTENTS

INTRODUCTION: WHAT LIES BENEATH

RACHEL KRAMER BUSSEL

When it comes to underwear, I just can't get enough. I have enough bras and panties to fill several drawers, and am always on the prowl for more. There's just something so alluring about clothes you put on that nobody else will ever see unless you choose to share your private treasures with them. Underwear and lingerie cling to our most private parts, and can be our naughty little secret under a business suit, or a bold statement when worn provocatively. Underthings can taunt, tease, stroke, or caress. Sometimes a glimpse is all you need to reel you in, to make you want to feel what's happening right below the surface of those boxers or that camisole.

Our underwear goes places no other item can reach, curving, bending, moistening, as we do. It feels our arousal before anyone else, knows precisely when we start to get wet or our cocks swell. Our underwear is a barometer for our lust, enhancing our pleasure by teasing us with its presence. For some, it's a cornucopia of underwear that we love, diving into a pile of soft, sensuous materials. For others, it's one specific passion, one kind of frilly plaything that gets our attention, and we, or our lovers, must wear that item before we can get off. The fabulous book *Panties: A Brief History*, by Sarah Tomczak and Rachel Pask, gives a history of the rise and breadth of these playthings.

Underwear can be a private luxury for you to treasure alone, or something that you let peep out from your jeans or shirt, luring the viewer in, making them picture you naked … almost. A puckered nipple pressing against the sheerest of fabric, or a stiff cock barely contained by the fabric trapping it.

The authors in this volume understand that what goes on inside our underwear is something to be valued. Stroking a hard dick or a wet pussy through someone's underwear is a tease—you're so near, yet so far. You can pinch and stroke, fondle and jiggle, offering the promise of fingers slipping beneath a fold but still holding out. Our underwear moves with us, and is usually the last thing we remove before getting totally naked—if we even do at all. Characters like those in Lynne Jamneck's "Never Take It Off" understand the allure of keeping our undies on, even during sex.

With the stories we've collected for you, we strived to offer a range of undergarments, from boxers to thongs, silk to strap-ons. These writers know that sometimes almost-nude is the hottest look going on. "Better than bare," Teresa Noelle Roberts writes in "Burlesque and Answered Prayers" as she describes the twirl of a tassel as a dancer teases her audience into a frenzy. These characters use their underwear to tease their lovers, and sometimes to surprise them, whether it's the confident cross-dresser in Alison Tyler's "Whose Panties?" as he saunters around in her favorite black pair or the athletes who have their own secret winning tactic in "The Sniff Test." Sometimes, the person doesn't even have to be wearing the given object for it to incite the most rapturous lust. For the "Dirty Little Boxer Boy" in Ryan Field's story, shorts speak louder than either words or actions.

These men and women know that underwear can be our signature style, our trademark, the thing that our lovers will remember us by all those years later. The last item we take off before bed (sometimes) and the first we put on to get dressed. There are so many kinds of underwear—boxers, briefs, crotchless panties, thongs; add in lingerie and you've got even more to choose from. So many of us rip our underwear off in the heat of the moment without taking the time to appreciate just how many secrets your underwear has heard, how much panting, writhing, and just plain lusting it's seen.

For me, underwear simply says sex. I have friends who walk around every day without panties, whereas for me, I'd feel simply naked, and not in a good way. Wearing my little secret close to me all day, knowing that someone special may get the chance to run their fingers up, up, all the glorious way up to press them against my panties, to ask permission to go inside, or to simply press them against my sex until I can't stand it anymore, is one of the most divine rituals I know of. Sometimes my whole day's mood is set based on what bra I'm wearing. We try to decode our lovers' personalities by the undies they wear, and sometimes we're right. Getting there, where you're almost naked, where your desire can be seen through the most intimate of apparel, is a journey worth taking. Read on, and take that journey with us again and again.

THE MAGNIFICENT TEASE (AN INTRODUCTION)

CHRISTOPHER PIERCE

When I was about fifteen years old I was still having sleepovers with my best buddy. We'd been spending the night at each other's houses since kindergarten, it didn't occur to us to stop—even though we were now horny teenagers. We would watch movies and play Atari (yes, it was the eighties) and then fall asleep side by side on the hide-a-bed hidden within the couch. There seemed nothing odd about this to either one of us.

Very early one morning, with the sun streaming through the window, the unimaginable happened. As I lay there, eyes closed, floating between asleep and awake, I felt my buddy's hand between my legs. Frozen with shock, I kept my eyes closed and hoped I had imagined it.

But I hadn't.

Taking my lack of reaction as a sign I was still asleep, my friend got braver and felt my cock through my underwear (tighty-whitey briefs). My penis stirred awake, seemingly of its own volition, and hardened under his touch. My buddy began to experiment with different ways of touching me, first cupping my balls in his hand, then gently rubbing the length of my stiffening dick, and squeezing them gently, all through my underwear.

My Christian upbringing would have been dialing 911 if it hadn't been for the simple fact that *it felt so fucking good* to be touched by him in this way. Encouraged by my cock's rigidity and the rest of my body's apparent slumber, my friend grew even more brazen. He lifted the waistband of my underwear and slipped his hand inside it to actually touch my cock and balls, skin on skin. Figuring I wouldn't stay asleep for long, he jerked me off until I came.

It took about five seconds.

After I'd squirted my load, my buddy slid his hand out and tucked my cock and balls back snug and tight in my underwear. Then he rolled over, facing away from me, and went to sleep. Do I have to tell you that we had many more sleepovers, until we turned seventeen and our parents put their collective feet down and said no more?

Needless to say, my erotic fascination with underwear (my own and other men's) began that morning. Although the sight of a handsome naked man is as hot to me as to any red-blooded American gay boy, there's something about a dude in his underwear. We're all fiercely protective of our "family jewels," and for me the first step of protection is *underwear*. I hate having my cock and balls flopping around inside my pants, I like them snug and tight inside my briefs, trapped between skin and fabric.

There, I know they're safe.

When I see another man in shorts, boxers, briefs, bikini bottoms, the shape of his cock and balls under the covering is a magnificent tease—a hint, a taste, a preview perhaps— of a real or imagined sexual encounter with their owner. So of course I jumped at the chance to co-edit a collection of stories about that magnificent tease, and have been richly rewarded by the stories that came pouring in from the submission call. I was also taken on a further frontier's journey as I learned from my co-editor and the many female contributors the secrets and pleasures hidden within a *woman's* undergarments.

I hope that the assemblage of tales in these pages will be as exciting, rewarding and eye-opening as it has been for me. The pleasures that await you include…

Breathtaking erotic sincerity in Justin Tyler's "Fate and Gravity." Neil Plakcy's "Elephant Jock" brings every frustrated boy's locker-room fantasies to vivid life. A flash of stocking on a windy city street is hotter than any steamy bedroom in "Practice Makes Perfect" by Kristie Helms. Tenille Brown's "Things Between" and Julian Tirhma's "On the Bias" show that intimacy can be a powerful aphrodisiac. Aching nostalgia flavors "The Wash Line" by Lew Bull and just plain raw fucking heat makes "The Banana Dash" a certified one-hander.

Enjoy the stories!

PANTY-OF-THE-MONTH CLUB

MILA WHITELEY

I am an underwear addict, a lingerie junkie, a "panty-aholic." Let me explain. I have a drawer full of silks and satins, bras and panties, camisoles and negligees—a rainbow of underclothing to make the heart leap and the groin grow wet with want (of the select and lucky few who get private viewings). I like to run my fingers in this drawer, to choose what I will hide beneath my sophisticated suits. *Should I wear the emerald green velvet panties beneath the black pinstripe? Or perhaps a red satin set, trimmed in lace.*

I love my lingerie collection … except for the pieces that have bad connotations. Nightgowns worn with ex-lovers. Underclothes worn during out-and-out fights. Panty sets worn during breakups. Now, when my fingers fall upon the sapphire Oscar de la Renta underwire bra, I think only of Tami, and our last night together on the beach. Our last night before I found out she was sleeping with my ex—best friend. Another favorite, my lavender peignoir, was one of my most prized possessions, until Lulu left me while I had it on. I wore only white cotton panties when Jerusha and I were an item. She liked the good-girl quality of them; she liked pulling them down from under my red plaid skirts when I was a bad girl. She had a thing for white cotton. Since we broke up, I can't stand the sight of them.

But what to do with these unwearable pieces? No one wants used underwear, and throwing them out meant I'd have an empty drawer. Then, one evening, while paging through a magazine, I came upon an advertisement for the "Panty-of-the-Month Club." This amazing company delivers a new set of fancy, frilly, fantastic panties (and bras if you pay a bit more) every month. I signed up immediately.

And a strange thing happened. Each month, when I collected my new set from my mailbox, I'd get a supercharged, feline feeling inside. An "I'm ready to take on the world" feeling—or at least, the drop-dead gorgeous bartender at the club down the street, if not the whole world. And each month, wearing my new lingerie set beneath my normal outfit, I'd stalk my prey and win her over.

The bartender, Alison, who hadn't given me a second look in the two months I'd attempted to woo her, brought drinks directly to my table, her phone number written in bold ink on the napkin she placed beneath my white wine. We spent a heavenly night making love on her balcony. In the morning, I collected my clothes ... but was unable to find my panties or bra. *Bizarre*, I thought. *They must have gotten tucked in her bedding*. But when I searched the sheets, they were gone.

The next month, I received a pair of white satin panties trimmed with lace, and a matching bra. I wore both, beneath a black suit, to a birthday party for one of my dear friends. At the party, a coworker I've lusted after for two years took me by the hand and led me to the master bedroom. "I've got a thing for you," she said, softly. "I haven't been able to sleep at night, visions of you plague me so."

We made love like animals, fucking and humping on my friend's designer sheets. When it was time to return to the party and eat our cake, smug smiles on our faces, I could locate neither the panties nor the bra. I hoped my friend wouldn't find them and know what had happened. But somehow I was sure they'd never appear again.

When my third box arrived, I decided to put my theory to the test. I called up my ex-lover, Jerusha, the one I'd never gotten over. The one who said she'd never sleep with me again. Of course, I put the brand-new white cotton bra and panties on before I placed the call. And, of course, I stood naked except for those well-cut pieces as I waited for her to answer the phone. When she did, I said, "Jerusha, I miss you."

In the past, she's hung up. This time, she finally said, "I miss you, too."

"Will you come over?"

Another hesitation, before she said, "Tonight. Maybe we can talk."

I pranced around all day, thrilled to death. I couldn't believe my luck, that I would actually have a second chance with her, my one true love. When the bell rang, I answered the door wearing her favorite of my outfits, the schoolgirl plaid, with the magic panties underneath. Within minutes, we were bumping and grinding on the sofa, just like old times, her hands stealing beneath my skirt to pull down my panties, her mouth against my cunt, her warm, hungry mouth bringing me all the pleasure it had in the past. And even more, the remembered pleasure, the buildup of wanting her, cascaded through me and brought me to climax after climax, like never before.

My panties did their trick, and I'm sure you're wondering whether they disappeared after. They did, but that doesn't mean we're through. Because when Jerusha arrived at my house, when I peeled off her black skirt and her hose, she was wearing a pair of magic panties of her own. And I know that our mutual desires, working together, will make love last this time around.

SNIFF TEST
JAY STARRE

It began innocently enough. Gavin was changing in the dressing room before his hockey game when he looked up from his seat on the bench by the wall. Brian, in his underwear, stood directly beside him. The tall, lean hockey player's crotch was at Gavin's eye level and he couldn't help but stare at the bulging package hidden beneath the clean white tighties encasing them.

Gavin was so close to Brian in the crowded changing room that he could actually smell those white cotton briefs. A fresh, just-washed scent assailed his nostrils as he drank in the sight of that fat bulge behind the white cotton.

Although he couldn't see through the material, the underwear appeared almost brand new. He could see the outline of a lengthy snake lying comfortably in a diagonal across Brian's belly below the snug waistband.

Time stood still as Gavin stared. He soaked in every detail he could make out and whatever his fertile imagination could conjure up. Was that the outline of the flared head? Was that full lump Brian's ball sac? From the corners of his eyes, Brian noted the way the waistband clung to Brian's lean, smooth waist and stomach.

The thick snake moved! It jerked under the tight underwear and it grew longer! Gavin caught himself just in time to prevent a moan escaping his pursed lips, drool threatening to pool there before he hastily licked it up and glanced upward.

Gavin dared to glance up, but Brian looked away before they could make eye contact, then the hockey player hastily turned around to pull down his underwear in order to dress in his hockey gear.

Now, Gavin was face-to-face with a tight, pale ass. The

snug jockeys slid down Brian's lean thighs and over his feet as Brian gawked at the smooth butt cheeks and deep crack right in front of him. Between Brian's parted thighs, a tantalizing glimpse of balls and fat, dangling cock teased Gavin just before his teammate pulled on his jockstrap and then his bulky hockey pants.

Gavin came out of his fog and looked around. No one else seemed to have noticed his moment of fascination; his teammates were all dressing up for the game as usual. As if everything was entirely normal. It wasn't. Not for Gavin. That moment had changed his life forever.

That was the beginning of his obsession, the episode he would continually return to in his fantasies and relive and relive, sometimes changing the scenario so that Brian pulled out his fat cock and whipped it across Gavin's cheeks before stuffing it between his lips. Or Brian would bend over with his underwear still encasing those beautiful butt cheeks and shove his ass in Gavin's leering face, smothering him with the scent of the clean underwear—or other variations on the theme of Brian and his tight white briefs.

That moment of gawking revelation may have been what initiated Gavin's fascination with tight white underwear, but what cemented it was the following few weeks in the locker room. Days and days of teasing glimpses eventually culminated in a wild sexual romp that he would never forget.

Gavin was a sophomore in college, and Brian was two years older, a senior. They weren't friends outside of their hockey team, and in fact rarely spoke except during the course of the game itself. Gavin noticed that Brian had other friends on the team who hogged his attention. But after that initial stare into Gavin's tighty-white crotch, the older hockey player began to alter his behavior toward Brian.

If Gavin was in the locker room before Brian arrived, the senior would move directly to drop his gear beside Gavin and change in front of him. Gavin made sure he always arrived early enough so he could drink in the sight of Brian's underwear before every game and practice. Brian didn't say much, merely nodding and smiling now and then, while he pretended to ignore his younger teammate as he changed.

Brian always wore pristine white jockeys. Either he had an endless supply of the new underwear or he recycled his best pair to wear to hockey games. The smell was always the same: clean and fresh. Brian made it a practice to quickly strip off his shoes and pants, then take his time with the rest so that he was in his underwear much longer than really necessary, right in front of a gawking Gavin.

The fat fuck tube often swelled visibly beneath the ivory-white underwear as Brian's crotch faced Gavin's surreptitious stares. And Brian would take much longer than he needed to pull down those tight undies when he turned around and offered Gavin a view of his solid jock butt. That ass was encased in white before being revealed in all its flesh-pink glory, as the college senior slid the tight underwear down to his feet and pulled it off.

Gavin's own cock was stiff and dripping every time, and he had to work at hiding it as he undressed and put on his street clothes. Fortunately, most of the other players weren't as interested in checking out naked crotches as he was.

Two weeks of the same had Gavin in a state of perpetual sexual excitement. No matter how often he beat off at night thinking of Brian's underwear and Brian's cock and Brian's ass, he was still ravenous with lust when it came time for their hockey games and practices.

It was a lucky chance during the third week of that rapturous hell that circumstances pushed Gavin past the point of no return. Even though he was always in a rush to get to the changing rooms early, that evening Gavin was late.

Frustrated at the snowstorm that slowed the buses and caused his tardiness, Gavin rushed into the rink and headed for the changing rooms. He paused at their regular dressing-room doorway and noticed Brian wasn't there among his other teammates, who were hurrying to get ready, most of them late as well, because of the inclement weather. Gavin sighed—the object of his obsession was not going to show—so he moved to the next dressing room to change alone in martyred gloom.

To his delight, Brian was there, alone. The senior must have just shown up, too, because he was still in his street clothes and was fiddling with his hockey bag, apparently not in a rush to strip. He turned and nodded to Gavin with a smile, exactly as he normally would.

"Too crowded in there tonight," he murmured in his husky drawl as he began to take off his clothes, exactly as he usually did. This time they were alone.

Gavin was breathless from his rush to reach the rink, as well as from the opportunity to bask privately in Brian's presence. He sat close to his teammate on the bench by the wall, even though there was plenty of space in the room. Brian didn't object, his pants and shoes already off, and the tantalizing underwear teasing Gavin to a state of extreme lust, and fear.

Gavin could barely contain himself. He wanted to lurch forward and bury his face in the underwear, to mouth and suck on the fat cock underneath with the fresh-smelling cotton against his tongue and lips. He was frightened he would actually do something so stupid, when he realized that Brian had taken off his shirt and was standing still, directly in front of him.

There was a moment of absolute calm. Neither moved. Gavin sat on the bench, Brian stood facing him. Brian's cock lay lengthwise across his belly under the embrace of those tight white jockeys. Gavin stared, his soft blue eyes intense as he watched for any sign of movement, and was rewarded. The cock jerked, and swelled, and began to tent the underwear. Gavin couldn't help the moan that escaped his parted lips. The covered cock twitched again, stretching the cotton material as Gavin's eyes grew bigger too.

"Hey dudes, practice is about to start. Get a move on," a voice from the hallway shouted to them.

The moment was dispelled, all Gavin's hopes crashing as Brian immediately turned and did what he always did, slowly slid down his underwear after offering Gavin a short view of his underwear-encased jock butt.

Both hockey players had to rush then, and neither looked at the other as they hastily donned their gear. Out on the ice, practice proceeded as if everything was completely ordinary, but Gavin was flushed with excitement from the moment of privacy he'd shared with the object of his obsession, and a dawning and frightening plan to satisfy his lust started to form in his mind. He left the ice ten minutes before practice ended, rushing to the locker room and stripping off his gear in a frenzy, tossing it everywhere. It was as if he was in a panic to get naked.

Once he was stripped, his cock rising up to stiffen and jerk against his belly, he did the unthinkable. There were no lockers in the dressing rooms, and the hockey players left their clothes in their hockey bags or on the benches or hooks behind them. No one ever disturbed another player's personal belongings.

But Gavin had conceived the plan during practice, and just couldn't stop himself. He had a few minutes to do the deed, and with trembling hands he rummaged through Brian's pile of clothing and found what he was searching for.

Gavin snatched up the snowy-white underwear. His hands were shaking so violently, he thought he would drop them, but he didn't as he did the only thing he could think of. He pressed the jockeys to his nose and inhaled.

Bliss!

Gavin snorted in the smell of fresh laundry, the distinct hint of crotch enhancing the odor of his teammate's jockeys. Gavin rubbed the underwear all over his face, breathing in deeply, imagining the cock and balls that had nestled beneath the white cotton material only an hour and a half earlier. He imagined the deep crack and taut butt cheeks that had pressed against the seat of the underwear, the flat belly the waistband had gripped and then slid down over as Brian pulled them off and revealed his naked goodies in all their glory.

Gavin was so intensely focused on the underwear pressed against his face that he didn't hear the door behind him open, but he did hear it bang shut. Facing away from the door, he prayed he had time to hide the underwear in his hands before he was caught.

A hand on his shoulder made him freeze, and he couldn't just toss the jockeys away like discarded trash. Not those precious tighty-whities! His cock lurched up even stiffer, slapping up against his belly without a hint of remorse as he craned his head around and saw Brian standing at his shoulder, his deep brown eyes boring into his.

"Put them on. Over your face."

The husky drawl was a low whisper in his ear. The fingers on his shoulder gripped fiercely. The eyes never left his. Gavin shook from head to toe as he followed his teammate's command. With trembling fingers he fumbled with the cotton underwear, turning and twisting them in his hands until he had them open and then with a disbelieving look into Brian's implacable amber orbs, he raised them up and pulled them down over his face.

Crotch wrapped his nose and chin. That delicious scent surrounded him. He forgot his fear for that one moment as he reveled in the feel of cotton surrounding his scalp and face. Then he remembered Brian was standing right behind him. What must he be thinking?

Brian didn't say a word, and Gavin was too excited and too stunned to dare speak. The hand on his shoulder moved away, and through the material of the cotton briefs around his ears, Gavin heard Brian stripping off his hockey gear.

"The door is barred. I can fuck you without anyone barging in."

What? Had Gavin heard right? He found out as hands

pushed him down to the floor, spreading him naked over their hockey bags, his thighs wide open and his ass crack exposed. A heavy body, all muscle, pressed down over him. A lengthy, stiff cock thrust up between his parted butt cheeks.

"Sniff my underwear while I fuck you good, Gavin."

The whisper in his ear was followed by a tongue stroking it, the material of Brian's underwear between that wet appendage and Gavin's flesh. Gavin shivered and bucked backward, willing his tight asshole to open for the blunt cock head stabbing against it. A moment of tension and held breath was followed by penetration and loud gasps from both of them.

Gavin snorted air in through the crotch of Brian's underwear as cock pushed past his sphincter and into his guts. As more cock drove in, more weight pressed down on him. Brian moaned in Gavin's ear, apparently enjoying the feel of a tight butt hole clamping over his probing cock.

Light filtered through the white cotton, but he couldn't really see anything. All he could do was smell and feel and hear. He smelled crotch and cotton; he felt firm hot cock push deep inside his asshole, he heard the grunts of his teammate in his ear and his own low animal moan as Brian fucked him up the ass with his own underwear over Gavin's face.

The fuck was deep and furious. Pent-up desire on both their parts had them thrashing around over their combined hockey gear in a frenzy. Gavin pushed back against the thick cock impaling him, while Brian pounded in and out while wrapping his arms around Gavin in a fierce embrace that did little to keep them both from flopping all over the floor.

With every deep thrust of Brian's cock up Gavin's tender butt hole, the college sophomore snorted in the smell of cotton and crotch. The feel of those tight undies surrounding his face, the taste of them on his lips and tongue, the muffled world around him through their white material, all combined in one intense experience. He was blubbering incoherently while Brian was nipping at his ear through the material of his own underwear and grunting like a pig in heat.

Gavin felt his own orgasm ripped right out of him. He shot a load all over their hockey gear. Brian was caught by the convulsing spasms of Gavin's asshole around his pounding cock and was forced to join the younger hockey player in his release.

He pulled out and spewed all over Gavin's naked ass cheeks.

Now the smell of fresh spunk joined the scent of clean underwear and crotch. Gavin was still moaning when Brian pulled his underwear off the sprawled jock's face. With a big grin, Brian slowly put them on over his come-dripping cock. The previously clean underwear had spit spots on them from Gavin's mouth and tongue, joined now by come-spots.

Gavin stumbled up and began to dress himself, shoving his gear in his bag, regardless of the jizz splatter on it. He attempted a feeble smile, but he was far too stunned to relax like Brian apparently had, who was smiling and humming now that the intense fuck was over.

In fact, Brian slapped him on the shoulder before he departed and winked at him. "I can't wait to do it again, dude."

Gavin only wished Brian had thought to give him those underwear as a present. They were his first, the first pair he wore while getting fucked up the ass, and ones he would never forget.

The next time they managed to be alone, in another dressing room after another game, the same scene was repeated, with Gavin sneaking in early to sniff Brian's cotton skivvies like a freak, shaking all over as he anticipated Brian coming in to catch him, and then the inevitable as the senior did just that. The fuck that followed was just as wild, but lasted twice as long. Brian's tight white briefs covered Gavin's head and face as the senior's cock pounded his ass long and hard. Rapture for Gavin.

This time when it was over Gavin asked for the underwear in a breathless voice.

Brian laughed out loud. "Okay. But I can't give them all to you. This pair is all you're getting."

It was enough. After an awesome season of getting drilled by his older teammate, while inhaling cotton undies from the inside, it ended. The senior graduated and left town. But fortunately Gavin had a pair of the lean jock's tight white underwear to remember him by.

And a fetish he would treasure for as long as he lived.

CHOICES
RACHEL KRAMER BUSSEL

Amber lingered at La Petite Coquette, her hand reaching out to stroke all manner of silk and lace in all the most beautiful colors. She studiously avoided the price tags and the other shoppers at the high-class Greenwich Village store; her eyes were solely on the luxurious merchandise, the bras scalloped with flowers along their artfully stitched edges, the camisoles that promised to caress her every curve, the panties that offered her tight but imperfect ass the promise of supermodel stardom. She put one hand on her belly and with the other dove into a drawer full of lace, innocently fondling the material as she imagined how her body would change in the coming months. Right now, it was imperceptible, her own little secret, and she was free to pretend she was just another sweet young thing, pretty as a peach, looking for the perfect item to enhance what was an already perfect body.

She declined the salesgirl's offer of help, preferring to do the browsing herself, with her eyes and her fingers, weaving through the potpourri-scented wares and trying to block out the jostling customers—flirtatious couples, uncomfortable men, a girl who had to be in high school, with A-cup boobs to match—until she came upon her own little slice of heaven. It wasn't the sexiest thing in the store, certainly; there were no cutouts or special effects, nothing to draw even more attention to her weighty breasts, still high and firm, simply the most gorgeous blue, a turquoise worthy of a peacock, woven with delicate bits of lace. It was a slip, but so much more than a slip. She couldn't imagine wearing it under her clothes; not only would she be way too turned on, but a slip like this, at a price like that, deserved better, and Amber was going to give it exactly what it deserved.

She paid for her private treasure, watching the sales-woman delicately wrap it in pink paper, leaving the store with a smile tricking about her lips. She went home and took a long, luxurious bath, the hot water finding its way into every spot she'd known was sore, and many she hadn't. She had plenty of time before Nick got back from the game, and used it well, lying around in bed with their biggest, fluffiest white towel wrapped around her like a cocoon.

She tried to read but found her mind wandering back to the slip, to the way she had held it as it threatened to slip from her grasp. She finally got up, reluctantly replaced the towel on its rack, then smoothed raspberry-scented lotion up her long, newly shaved legs and onto her arms and hands. She looked at herself in the full-length mirror. She was bare, freckles dotting her cheeks, tousled red curls framing her face. And still lean, with those proud breasts, and the still-flat stomach housing her most magnificent work yet, a tangle of ruby pubic hair hiding what lay beneath, strong legs keeping her up, toes sparkling with silver polish. She smiled at herself, the kind of smile intended to warm viewer and viewee, the kind that starts in the mind but in the act of raising the corners of one's lips makes itself known, demanding an answer. Then she grinned, her smile morphing into something not forced but fully felt.

And, grinning, she slipped into the two-hundred-dollar slip, the one she'd been too anxious to try on in the store. A cramped dressing room was no place for her body to be introduced to such a luxury. No, here in the privacy of her own bathroom, she let the silky turquoise fall against her, let the lace caress the tops of her breasts, her nipples threatening to peek through the mesh pattern. Somehow, the slip managed to straddle the line between elegant and sexy, between upper-class wife and downtown whore, quite perfectly. She put her hand on her hip, moaning aloud at the slippery perfection of this fabric against her skin. She'd bought a tiny matching pair of panties, ones that just spanned the curves of her ass, but she decided to forgo them. Standing, the slip's deliberately distressed hem grazed the tops of her thighs, the zigzagging lace pattern drawing attention upward.

Though she was generally prone to modesty, topped with a good dose of body-image issues, the sight before her was so sexy that Amber couldn't help bringing her fingers under its hem to stroke her own creamy folds. The additional hormones floating through her body combined with her joy at surprising Nick, and herself, was too much for her, and she knew she needed to come right then and there. While she watched in the mirror, looking on as if viewing a live-action peep show, which in a way this was, her hand dipped under the glorious silk, crushing it to her stomach as her fingers climbed their way to ecstasy, first meandering along her juicy slit, then pushing deeper, seeking more. She made herself keep watching, even when she longed to close her eyes and float away on the sensory overload of probing fingers and nipples pushing against silk, of hard and soft, bending, hiding, seeking, all joining together. From this angle, she couldn't see everything, and that was okay. It was enough to watch her first two fingers disappear inside herself, emerging wet and gleaming before plunging back in. She stepped closer, so she was touching the mirror, her fingers fogging it up, humping it almost as her body writhed against the hard surface, the slip the third player in her little game. The slip was so light, it had felt like nothing when she'd taken the bag from the clerk, but it was that lightness, that delicate touch that she had to focus on, to feel, and that kept her going. With her free hand, Amber rubbed her body, rejuvenating her self-love, the kind she remembered from rolling around in the grass of her backyard as a child.

She rubbed herself aggressively, wrapping the turquoise around her slim body, teasing her nipples by pinching them in turn between the softness as she got wetter and wetter. She longed to lift the slip above her head and slide it between her legs, let it sop up the wetness she'd been building, but she waited for Nick, even though with part of her knee she was ruining the garment with her clawing and grabbing. She didn't care, and as her breath fogged up the mirror even more, she leaned against it for comfort, coolness, support, fucking herself twofold as she finally shut her eyes and relented, gave herself up, wholly and fully, to her own urges, no one else's. She forgot about the baby, forgot about her husband, forgot about the store and the weather and dinner. All Amber knew was the ache deep inside, the raw need to be filled, full, fucked, and she crammed a third finger inside, maneuvering her thumb to get at her swollen clit.

"Yes," she whispered, then said it louder, her lips brushing the mirror as she spoke, the tiny word growing bigger, bolder, having greater purpose the more she spoke it; her "yes" traveled from her lips on down, resounding along her flushed chest, her proud nipples, past her stomach to where she needed it most. The "yes" seemed to slip onto her fingers, to become something more than three little letters as she kept saying it over and over as her fingers merged with her flesh, wet and urgent until they homed in on what they needed. "YES," she finally cried out, the noise coinciding with the crash of the open door as Nick walked in. He heard the final cry, but couldn't quite figure out what it meant.

Meanwhile, Amber sank down onto the ground, her bare ass against the pink carpet, her back to the cool tile wall as her hands lay at her sides. That's how Nick found her, the foggy window and his beloved with a look of half bliss, half exhaustion across her face. He was about to ask if she was okay, but then wondered if she might be asleep. Her eyes were closed, but he'd heard her exclaim only moments earlier. Then he noticed the slip, and while he was still a typical man, stunned into submission by shiny objects, his brain lost in a fog of femininity, this time he did see what his wife had just bought, both the object in front of him and what it had done to Amber. He shut his mouth and leaned down, picking her up, cradling her in his arms. She was back to being his dreamgirl, the one whose image woke him in the middle of the night with a pounding heart and a hard cock, the one who he'd fallen for all those years ago. He carried her fireman style, her body splayed out before him, the slip's ragged edge landing just above the thick layer of hair greeting her sex. His dick throbbed in his pants as she opened her eyes, lazily looking up at him, saying all she had to say with that gaze. This time, he didn't place his hand on her belly, didn't touch her like she might break.

He spread her legs wide, letting the slip ride up on her hips. He quickly stripped off his clothes, rubbing his cock against her slickness, then leaning forward to suckle one extended nipple, taking in the lace as he did. His tongue flickered against her raised pink bead, the lace suddenly not as soft as it pressed urgently against her bud, merging with it while he twisted her other one between his thumb and forefinger. Amber's neck came up off the bed, straining, bending back, her legs widening as he pushed her from solid to liquid, melting her until she was all his. With her nipple trapped between his lips, he opened his eyes, gazing up at her enraptured face, her hands above her, gripping the headboard, her body primed for him. He could feel her urging him inside, her straining, asking, wanting him. He knew she'd already come without him, knew she'd had her private magic moment, and he smiled as he pictured her wearing just the slip, her panties on the floor, wet, useless. When she cried out, opening her eyes as if in shock as his teeth sank into her already-tortured skin, he pushed his way inside her, entering her with his entire cock. He buried his face between her breasts, burrowing into the warmth of her as her arms came down to stroke his head. He raised and lowered his hips, feeling her nails digging into the back of his neck while the slip was the only layer separating them.

When she wrapped her legs around him, clutching him tight, he knew he was a goner. He lifted his head from its perch and slowly removed the slip, raising it over her head, stroking it against her cheek as they met again, skin to skin, raw, pure, as needy for each other as they'd been when they first met. Needier, in fact, after all they'd been through. Just the two of them, for a little while longer. He took the slip and placed it half in her hand, half in his, holding her hand with the bundle of crushed silk and lace between them as he pounded into her again and again, grabbing for her other hand as his weight crushed her. He raised his hips just so, in that way he'd learned was her favorite, grinding himself through her tight tunnel until he simply couldn't hold back any longer. "Amber," he said, his voice low, husky, filled with so much more than simply her name. He repeated her name as his come surged forward, coating her as he thrust a few final times. He reached down to push against her clit, his thumb pressing it deep against her bone, right where she needed it, and she exploded again, this time ricocheting back against Nick, letting him catch her as she trembled. When she was done, she turned to her side, shoving her face into the balled-up wad of luxury that had started it all.

She thought of all the racks showcasing other possibilities—ones rimmed with fur, with crystals, with ties and bows, tiny buttons and helpful wires. She pictured herself rolling around on the ground, naked, as Nick threw each new sensuous garment onto her until she was buried in a pillow of lingerie, letting it cover her entire body. She saw all the colors and styles she hadn't picked pass before her mind's eye, and Amber knew—she'd made the right choice. In the store, and in her heart. She kept the slip on as she curled against Nick's bare chest, and he put his hand on her back, his fingers resting against the lace. He didn't even show her the surprise he'd gotten her, one he'd been sure would be the perfect treat; she was already wearing it.

THE ELEPHANT JOCK
NEIL PLAKCY

If there's anything in life more embarrassing than waking up to find yourself hungover, curled up by the side of the road, and wearing only a jockstrap, then I don't know what it is.

Oh, wait. How about if the person who finds you was the captain of your high school football team, out for his morning run? A guy you had a crush on as a teenager, who barely knew your name back then?

If I could have just stopped breathing entirely, I probably would have. Especially after Jim Kane said, while eyeing me up and down, "Morning, Sutter. Looks like you've been working out."

Instead I had to say, "Morning."

I wasn't any kind of football player stud in high school. Nope, I was the wimpy gay kid who fumbled every ball he was thrown. I used to cower in the corner of the locker room when the jocks romped by, trying to hide the hard-on they gave me with their butt-slapping nudity, their muscles rippling in the shower, their tight workout shorts, wrestling singlets and tank tops. And their jockstraps.

Man, their jockstraps. I used to jerk off at home just thinking of those jockstraps. My freshman year, I stole one from Jim Kane. It was sweaty and stinky and I used to hold it up to my nose while I wrapped my fist around my dick, eyes closed, fantasizing about Jim or one of those other big, beefy studs.

By the time I got to college, my hormones had calmed down enough that I could work out at the gym and take a shower without popping a boner. I found that I liked lifts, squats, bench press, aerobics, cardio—all those things I hated in high school. And what I loved even more was perfecting a ripped body that made me a hit at any gay club.

I guess I was pretty cocky. I thought I was hot shit and any guy would be lucky to suck my dick. At my twenty-fourth birthday, earlier that month, I'd picked up a guy named Louis who had turned into something of a stalker—at least that's the way I described it. He said I broke his heart, and he was determined to get his revenge. He knew I was a cop, though, so I figured he'd be too scared to do anything serious, and basically I ignored him after our one night together.

The night before, I'd been at my favorite bar, Cruisers, and Louis had come in with a bunch of his buddies. I was so sure Louis was no threat, that I'd let them buy me shots, and then—shit, I wasn't sure what had happened, except I'd ended up by the side of the road with a hell of a hangover, wearing only a skimpy jockstrap.

It wasn't even my jock. At least I didn't think I had a red silk jock with thin black straps. Oh, and instead of a normal pouch, this little item had tiny plastic eyes, two flaps of red silk that looked like big round ears, and a long tube for the penis. Did I mention that the whole apparatus was meant to look like an elephant? Louis was sure as hell making me pay for not returning his phone calls and ignoring him at the gym.

"Rough night?" Jim Kane asked.

I nodded, and the motion made my head hurt like hell.

It was just past dawn, and the sun was rising. I lived down near the beach in the small South Florida town where I'd grown up, but from my surroundings it seemed like I was pretty far west, almost to the Everglades. Even so, there was a main road just a few feet away. The only thing sheltering me from a bunch of early-morning commuters was a low hibiscus hedge, vibrant with red-and-yellow flowers as big as plates.

"You can't stay out here forever," Jim said. "And you sure as hell can't walk around looking like that." He pulled off his University of Florida T-shirt and handed it to me. "Come on, get up, and wrap that shirt around your waist. I'll take you back to my place and get you some clothes."

I tried to get up, but I got all dizzy and fell back down. Jim reached up and hoisted me up under the arms. I could barely keep my balance, and flopped up against him.

Man, he smelled great. Lemon and sweat. And his tanned, beefy body bulged in all the right places—biceps like coconuts, pecs like beach balls, and a dick, I couldn't help but notice as it pressed against me, as stiff as a palm tree. Awkwardly, he wrapped his T-shirt around my waist. I still couldn't stand, though, so with a baritone grunt he lifted me up and threw me over his shoulder in a fireman's carry.

I threw up whatever was left in my stomach—fortunately missing his bubble butt, encased in sweat-soaked shorts. He turned around and started jogging slowly back the way he'd come.

To keep my arms from flapping around, I grabbed hold of the waistband of his shorts. My head was somewhere around the small of his back, my groin pressed into his shoulder, my feet whacking him in the chest as we bounced along. I hadn't thought it would be possible to feel any worse—but I did.

Mercifully, his house wasn't far away—a little bungalow on an acre of land about as far west of the Turnpike as you could get without alligators nipping at your ass. He kicked open the front door, walked through the living room, and deposited me on his bed. "Try not to throw up in here, okay?"

I mumbled something incoherent as I landed. I must have dozed off, because the next thing I knew he was sitting next to me on the bed, lifting me up and propping me against the pillows. He reached over to the night stand for a cup of coffee. "Drink this," he said.

I took a mouthful and nearly spit it out. "You don't like my coffee?" he asked.

"You'd never make it at Starbucks," I said.

"Drink it anyway."

I focused on his cut, shirtless chest instead of the coffee's bitter taste, and managed to choke it all down. "Shower next," he said. "Can you stand up yet?"

"I think so."

He stood and I swung my legs over the side of the bed. The room spun for a minute, but then it settled down, and I stood, tentatively. As I slipped, he grabbed me. "I'd better go with you," he said. He frog-marched me into the bathroom, and opened the door of an extra-large shower stall.

He reached in and turned the water on, then lifted me inside, still wearing the goofy elephant jock. He was right behind me, having kicked off his shoes and socks. He was still wearing his nylon running shorts, though, and as the water cascaded down I could see he was wearing a jock underneath. A regulation one, though.

I had plenty of those at home. I'd turned into a real underwear fetishist, collecting different types of jocks, hard cup and soft, x-type and thong, in varying colors and fabrics.

Standing in the shower there, with Jim Kane's body so close to mine, all those memories of high school came flooding back to me, and I popped a woody. My worst fears came true. As if Jim Kane ever had been unsure that I was a cocksucking, butt-fucking faggot boy, I was removing all doubt.

I felt my face go six shades of red and tried to turn away toward the wall. "Somebody's finally coming back to life," he said. When I looked at his face I saw that he was smiling.

Then he reached over and jerked the goofy elephant jock off my crotch, though the black straps still gripped my ass. Under the shower spray, he kneeled down and took my stiff dick in his mouth, and I leaned back against the wall for support. Well, damn, wasn't this a high school fantasy come true?

He sucked for a couple of minutes, then stood up and kissed me, wrapping his beefy arms around my back. The bitter taste of the coffee was still in my mouth, but it mingled with toothpaste and salt water. His tongue penetrated my mouth and I leaned back to give him access to all of me. His hands massaged my ass, his pecs pressed against mine, and my dick smacked against his shorts.

I was starting to feel a whole lot better. I reached over and pulled his shorts down, leaving his jock on, then kneeled in front of him. The dick that was outlined before me would have done any elephant proud—long and thick, with a circumcised head clearly visible against the cloth. I started licking it through the rough fabric of the jock, reaching around behind him to massage the globes of his ass. I grabbed a bar of soap and lathered up my hands, and then poked a soapy finger up his ass. He shivered, and spread his legs more, to give me better access.

I licked and sucked his dick through the jock and finger-fucked his ass. I figured it was the least I could do for him, after he'd rescued me from the side of the road. And besides, it was something I'd wanted to do since I was about fifteen. He started mumbling something—over the sound of the shower I couldn't tell the exact words, but I knew what they meant. His dick started heaving and spurting inside the case of his jock and his whole body shook.

I stood up, and we kissed deeply again. Then he grabbed the bar of soap, lathered up his fist, and started jerking me off as our tongues entwined. It didn't take me long to erupt, my body sagging against him as he steadied me with his free hand.

My hangover was feeling a hell of a lot better by then. I pulled down his jock to expose his fat, limp prick, beads of semen stuck in his pubic hairs, and made sure to rinse him down carefully with soap and water. And then he turned the water off and opened the stall door. He grabbed a couple of towels from the rack and dried us both off. Then picked me up again, but this time in his arms, not over his shoulder, and carried me back to the bed.

You've got to understand, I'm over six feet tall, close to two hundred pounds of mostly muscle. And Jim Kane carried me like I was nothing more than a sack of potatoes. Man, I could really fall for a guy like that.

I was thinking about falling for Jim Kane—and I'd promised myself I'd never go crazy over a guy—as he lay me down on the bed, then climbed in next to me and spooned his big beefy body up against mine, his fat, happy dick nestling against my ass.

It's a good thing it was Sunday and neither of us had to go to work, because we fell asleep like that, his strong arm sprawled possessively over me.

By the time we both woke again, it was after noon, and I was ravenously hungry—for something more than tube steak. Don't get me wrong; I'll pretty much suck a dick any time it's presented to me. But a boy's got to get his nourishment, too. I think maybe it was my stomach growling that woke Jim up.

"You want something to eat, elephant man?" he asked, yawning.

"Jesus, don't call me that," I said. "I still don't remember anything after about the fifth shot last night."

"You don't know who did it to you?"

I frowned. "I know. At least I know who had the motive, the means and the opportunity."

"You talk like a lawyer," he said, laughing. "Or a cop."

"Not surprising," I said, standing up and stretching. "I am a cop. I got my degree in police science. This is my second year on patrol."

He started to laugh. "And I'm a criminal lawyer. Funny we never ran into each other before." He shook his head. "Man, you are lucky I found you. Not some old lady who'd call 911."

"You know what they say," I said. "Dial 911. Make a cop come." I yawned. "About that offer of food ..."

He stood up. "Let me get you some clothes." He opened

a drawer and pulled out a jockstrap like the one he'd been wearing, another pair of running shorts, and a clean T-shirt from a surf shop up the coast.

"I'll take the shirt and the shorts," I said. I reached over to the pile of dirty laundry next to the bed and rooted through it. "But I'm wearing this strap." I pulled one out, lifted it to my nose and inhaled. It smelled just like Jim.

"You are one perverted son-of-a-bitch," he said, laughing. "Where the hell have you been all my life?"

"In the locker room, sniffing your jock," I said. "Just waiting for you to notice."

We dressed and walked out to the kitchen. He scrambled up some eggs and fried a couple of rashers of bacon, which we washed down with about a half gallon of orange juice.

By the time we finished eating, it was about two o'clock. "I use your phone?" I asked.

"Go for it."

I knew the number for Cruisers by heart. When one of the bartenders answered I asked, "Hey, anybody turn in a set of keys for a Toyota pickup?"

"This Tony Sutter?"

Jesus, I thought. Did the whole bar know? "Yeah."

"We've got your wallet, your keys, your clothes … man, you must have picked up a hell of a trick last night."

"You could say that," I said. "I'll come over in a little while and get it all."

After I hung up, I turned back to Jim. "I trouble you for a ride over to Cruisers? They've got all my stuff there, and my truck's in the lot."

"I don't know," Jim said. "What's in it for me?"

And just like that, my dick popped to attention and saluted. I stood up, dropped the running shorts Jim had lent me, and bent over his kitchen table. I left the jock on, the white straps framing the round globes of my ass.

You didn't have to make an offer like that twice to Jim. "Hold that pose," he said, and he took off out of the kitchen.

A moment later he was back, holding a condom and a tube of lubricant. As he started to drop his shorts I said, "Keep the jock on, all right?"

"Kinky bastard," he said, smiling, but he did, pulling his fat, stiff prick out the side and suiting it up with the condom. He squirted some lube up my ass, wiggled it around for a minute with his finger, then plunged his dick inside me.

I yelped as pain radiated out from my sphincter.

"Take it like a man, Sutter," he said, grabbing hold of my hips and starting to piston-fuck me. Very quickly the pain was replaced by a sense of euphoria. My jockstrap rubbed against my dick as the pouch of his rubbed, banged, and scraped against my ass. I felt every single point at which our bodies touched as if each were an electric socket.

His balls leapt free of the jock's pouch and started slapping against my ass as he pounded me. "You were watching me," he grunted as he fucked me. "All the time. In the halls, in the locker room. You were scoping out my body. You stole my jockstrap, didn't you?"

"You knew?" I panted.

"I knew. And I watched you when you weren't looking. But you were such a little wimp then. Not like the hard body you are now." The last few words came out in gasps, until, with the word *now*, he shot his load into the condom's reservoir.

He pulled out of me, and I felt so empty. Empty like I'd never felt before—like I'd never be whole again until I felt his dick inside me once more. He was panting and his chest was heaving, but he reached down, flipped me over, and brought me up to him. We kissed, and tears welled up at the corners of my eyes. Jesus, next thing you knew I'd want to be picking out curtains with him.

"You're really going to owe me for this," he said, in between kisses. "Your ass is mine for the foreseeable future."

"As long as your cock stays hard, it's got a home in me," I said.

"That won't be a problem." Even then, I felt him

stiffening against me.

"Jesus," I said, backing off and swatting at him. "My ass isn't the Holland Tunnel, for Christ's sake. Give your dick a rest, give me a ride to Cruisers, and then we'll talk."

He reached around to grab the straps of my jock—the jock of his that I was wearing—and snapped them against my ass. "Tony," he said, "we're going to do way more than talk."

WHITE T
GENEVA KING

"Still studying?"

I shrugged casually, as if I wasn't bothered. Tara wasn't even trying to keep the smirk off her face now. "I've been going hard all night. There's another section I want to go over and then I'm giving up. If I don't know it by now, then—oh well."

Tara dragged a chair beside the bunk bed and climbed up, and then rested her arms on top of my blanket. She peered at my paper, trying to read my notes by the clip light.

"Umm, Char, I don't think you've gotten that conversion right. I'm pretty sure the units … are supposed to be Joules."

Tara's damp curls fell out of her clip. My brain shut down as the gentle scent of her shampoo invaded my nostrils. I watched her face, pretending to listen as she pointed out my mistakes. Her face scrunched up when she was thinking, the freckles on her nose seemed to twinkle. Okay, not really, but I always felt poetic when she was near me. I caught myself drifting into yet another daydream about her.

"I see the problem," she said, poking me in the forehead. "You're not concentrating. You need to relax." She brought her face close to mine. "And I know just the way to help."

Tara raised her arms and pulled off her shirt, revealing the white tank T she always wore underneath her clothes. Beaters, we called them—ribbed, sleeveless shirts like the rappers wore on TV. Tara's had faded to a dull white. Taut, unrestrained nipples poked out toward me. Mere shock kept me from caressing them like I wanted.

"Well, are you gonna help me up?" She grinned and stretched her hands toward me.

I scrambled to my knees, pulling her onto the bed with me. Our heads bumped the ceiling, but I wasn't paying much attention to anything but Tara's body, inches away from me. The white from her beater stood out against her smooth brown skin, and this time I did reach out for her, anxious to feel her body against mine ...

"Hey, are you paying attention?" Her voice cut sharply through my reverie.

I blinked. "Yeah, thanks. I just need to go over it to make sure I have it straight in my mind."

Tara looked at me oddly, then handed me my pencil. "No prob." She hopped off the chair, her small tits bounced sharply as she landed. In the full light below, I could see the dark spots of her nipples under the thin, worn fabric. "Do you mind if I do my nails? I know you hate the smell, but they look something awful."

I shook my head.

"Thanks."

She plopped on her beanbag and pulled her supplies toward her. I turned my head back to my book, determined to get back to studying. My imagination quickly put an end to that goal.

"Don't take it off," I begged, as she started to lift the hem of the shirt. "Leave it on a while longer."

Confusion flitted over her beautiful face, but then her easygoing smile returned. "If that's what you want." She pointed to her baggy sweatpants. "Can these go?"

I giggled, although it wasn't really funny. Nerves must have been getting the best of me. "Toss 'em."

Toss them she did, after making a big show of taking them off. Finally, she got the pants to her ankles and kicked them onto the floor. She twirled to show me her undies. "You like?"

The boy shorts hugged her ass beautifully. I stroked the round hips gently, fighting the urge to sink my teeth into the soft flesh. Instead, I pushed her forward and plunged my fingers deeper between her legs. Her cunt was astoundingly warm. I thought about how it would feel to be in her and my body quivered. She moaned—something must have been to her liking. The only other thing that turns me on more than the feel of the girl is hearing the sounds she makes when I'm touching her.

Before I could go further, she pulled herself away and turned, looming over me. "I'm supposed to be helping you relax." Tara eased onto my lap, slinging her arms over my shoulders. She brought her face closer to mine, her shiny lips parting. "Char ... Char!"

I jumped. "What?" I looked down in annoyance.

Tara held up two bottles of paint. "I asked you which color you thought was best. Geez, you couldn't have been that deep into the assignment." Now she looked amused. "What were you thinking about?"

"Nothing important," I replied, rather shortly. I was a bit upset she'd interrupted just when we were about to kiss. She looked taken aback, so I relented. "I like the gold better."

"You don't think it's too ... brassy?"

"Nope, it's perfect."

She went back to her nails.

I watched her for a moment before picking up the pieces of my daydream: Okay, I was fingering her, and then ... yeah, there we go. Her soft lips touched mine, her tongue eased inside my mouth. Most French kisses felt too sloppy, but hers was more controlled. She stroked my tongue with hers and I pulled her closer to me.

She broke away, but before I could protest, her hands covered my breasts and she started feeling them through the shirt, her thumbs rubbing circles over my tightening nipples. I whimpered and wriggled, hoping she'd realize I wanted her to pull my shirt off. I needed to feel her hands on my bare flesh, the soft fingers pressed against my skin. I hoped she realized how much I wanted her to touch me, but I couldn't bring myself to tell her. So instead I moaned and arched my chest into her palm.

Her eyes twinkled, and for a moment, I thought she was

going to stop, but then she grasped the hem of my shirt, pulling it over the top of my head.

"Wait here."

I opened my mouth to protest, but she'd already swung over the side of the bed. Disappointed, I lay back against the pillows. The heat from her kiss still lingered on my mouth and her scent had settled into my sheets. I found my clit with one hand, and started rubbing my body in a desperate need for release.

"I'm back! Hey——"

Tara grabbed my wrist. "No way, I do that." She drew my finger into her mouth, sucking it slowly. "I'm not gonna help you if you keep trying to ruin it."

I nodded. "Sorry," I whispered.

"Char, how does it look?" Tara held her feet up for my inspection. "Good enough?"

"Brilliant. I'll have to do mine sometime."

"I can do it if you want. Tomorrow, after your test. We can do a mini-spa." She grinned. "Nice way to blow off steam."

"Can't wait."

"It's okay." Tara placed my hand back gently on my belly and held up a small bottle. "Massage oil. I thought it'd help."

"Help me or tease me?" My voice was already raspy. I wasn't going to last much longer in this state.

"Both," she chuckled. "Now lift your arms up ... yeah, like that."

Quickly, she pulled off her tank T. I wanted to complain, but the sight of her swaying breasts stopped me. Tara pulled the shirt around my wrists and deftly tied them together. She leaned over and ran her tongue along my neck before finding my mouth. "Damn, you taste good."

I felt something cold drip over my ribcage and I jumped. Before I could say anything, I felt her hands rubbing the now-warm liquid over my skin. She worked her way over my waist and breasts, down to my legs, and in between my thighs. My breath caught in my throat. I wanted her to make me come so badly I was almost shaking from it, but I was afraid if I moved, she'd snatch her hand away.

Tara's fingers sifted through the hairs covering my pussy before finally finding my nub. She rubbed it, almost lazily, until I couldn't take any more.

"Dammit, Tara, do something!"

She didn't say anything but instead moved her head down. Then, so lightly I thought I'd imagined it, her tongue darted over my clit and started massaging little circles around it.

I thrust my pelvis up toward her. "More," I demanded.

Her mouth covered me, sucking more intensely as I bucked beneath her. Something was missing. I realized I needed to feel the heat of her against my face, to taste her creamy cunt on my lips. So, as much as I hated to, I stopped her.

"Take off your panties and turn around."

If she was surprised, she didn't show it. She quickly stripped and followed my orders, until she was hovering over my face. I guided her back until her pussy was right above me. Her scent hit me, and I raised my head to the swollen lips, licking and sucking until she trembled in my hands. Tara managed a few licks before she stopped, but I didn't mind. Her obvious pleasure fed mine, and I kept suckling until she came, like a shower jet on my face.

I wriggled my hands out of the shirt and eased her body off mine. "Good?" I asked, rubbing her stomach as I snuggled beside her.

"Shit, yeah."

"Char! How much longer are you gonna study? You'll forget everything if you go too long." Tara had climbed back up beside me and stared at me, a concerned look on her face.

I brushed a curl absentmindedly off her shoulder. My body still cried out for release. "I'll be finished soon."

She yawned. "Great, then I'm going to bed."

Tara jumped down, peeling the white T over her head. She threw it in her laundry hamper.

"Night," she called. I caught a last glimpse of her brown nipples as she climbed into bed.

Heart pounding, I waited until I heard her snores before I retrieved the beater and massaged it between my fingers. Just a white shirt, nothing more. And yet, I could see the dimples her nipples had made in the fabric. I trailed the garment down my stomach to my little button, the rough material rubbing against my wetness.

Tara continued fondling my clit, kissing me softly as my pelvis ground itself against her hand. Finally, I came, sighing contentedly against her mouth.

"All relaxed now?"

I couldn't say anything, so I just nodded. My fingers traced a path along the edges of her shirt.

When my legs stopped shaking enough for me to walk, I stashed the shirt in a safe place, where I could grab it the next time I needed to relax.

CROSS-DRESSING CONFESSIONS

ZACH ADDAMS

I cross-dressed for the first time when I was eighteen.
I had left my conservative hometown to go to college at a
small, liberal college with a reputation for being a party
school—and it was a well-earned reputation. I had never
had a girlfriend before, but I fell right in with the decadent
environment of the dorm where I lived and quickly hooked
up with a girl who was, to me, incredibly wild. Her name
was Jodie. She was bisexual, experimental, and, compared to
me, very experienced. She had had five girlfriends and three
boyfriends, which to me made her a woman of the world.
She had also spent a lot of time in her hometown hanging
out at the local *Rocky Horror Picture Show* every Saturday
night. One night while we were talking, she said that even
though she dressed kind of boyish and wasn't much of a
girly-girl, she found men in black lace to be incredibly sexy
and thought that Tim Curry in *Rocky Horror* was about
the hottest thing she'd ever seen.

I sheepishly told her that I liked the idea of dressing up
like a chick.

"*Really*," she said with prurient emphasis. "You think
you'd really do it?"

"Oh, not in public," I answered with a quick, nervous
giggle. "I don't think I could ever do that. Ever."

"Who said anything about doing it in public?" Jodie asked
with a little smile and a smolder to her eyes that told me
exactly what she was thinking. I immediately got hard and
felt this wave of heat go through me. Jodie kissed me and
we made love—one of the most intense times I remember,
just from that one little suggestion.

Little did I know it would become much more than just a suggestion, especially after she asked me if I thought about being with a man or a woman when I thought about being dressed up like a girl.

Blushing, I said "I don't know." She pressed me, and I finally admitted it.

"Both, I guess," I told her.

I was still a little embarrassed, maybe unsure, about going through with it, even when Jodie came back to the dorms after a trip into town one Saturday afternoon. She came over to my room—luckily my roommate was out of town for the weekend. It was early in the afternoon but I was still asleep—with all the noise and partying in the dorms, I tended to sleep late. But Jodi had been up early that day, performing a naughty errand.

I never locked my dorm room door—these were simpler times—and she came right in without knocking and locked the door behind her. She stirred me with a kiss, then slipped off all her clothes and slid into my single bed, nude against me. There wasn't much room in there, and I immediately got turned on.

"Aren't you going to open it?" she asked me.

"Open what?" I asked. I hadn't noticed the small gold box she'd placed next to me on the pillow. With a smile I opened it—I think I was too sleepy to know what was coming, but I figured it out pretty quick. Actually, as I unwrapped the skimpy black lace panties from their white tissue, I thought for a moment that the sexy pair was for Jodie—something much lacier and sluttier than she would normally wear. Then memories of our erotic conversation of a few weeks before hit me like a heat wave, and I realized that I was the slut. The panties were for me.

"Like them?" asked Jodie as I held them up for her to take a look at. The panties—tarty, revealing things, mesh. and lace in the front, skimpier lace on the sides, cut close in the back.

As if receiving her answer before I could say a word,

Jodie's hand curved around my quickly stiffening cock.

"I think so," I said, my voice shaking a little. My mind hadn't yet caught up to my body's intense arousal.

She smiled at me as my cock reached full hardness. Then she laughed. "You think so?"

"I like them a lot," I admitted.

"Then put them on," she said breathlessly. "Put them on for me."

Sheepishly, I slid out from under Jodie's naked body and held the lace panties up nervously. They felt awkward in my hands—I was used to undressing Jodie, who always wore plain cotton panties. But as I stood nude before Jodie, I saw the ravenous look on her face—she was as turned on as I was.

I stepped into the panties, sliding them up my hairy legs and tucking my cock into them. My cock was so hard that there was no way it could be contained by the lace garment; the head of it poked out over the waistband. The panties were exactly the right size, but they were built for a woman—they felt strange on me. The strangeness turned me on even more.

Jodie reached out, slid her hands down my panties, and adjusted my cock to the side so that it stretched through the lace. Then she tugged me onto the bed and began making love to me.

"You're going to be my girlfriend," she whispered as she nuzzled my ear, rubbing her bare crotch against my lace-enclosed cock. "I'm going to be your boyfriend."

I couldn't believe Jodie had never done this before; she knew exactly what to do, how to tweak my fantasies so that I really believed I was the girl. Something about that little change—the panties, clutching me in their lace and mesh embrace, made me believe it when she said it, as she tugged my cock out of the panties, spread her legs and slid my cock into her—as she said. "I'm entering you."

Then she pulled a maneuver that made me just about lose it. She was a petite girl, and pretty flexible. While I was inside her, she was able to slide her legs together and coax mine open, so that as we fucked her legs were inside mine. Almost as if she were the one fucking me—as if she *were* my "boyfriend," just like she'd said, with her boyish little tits and hard, lithe body standing in for that of the man I could tell she was fantasizing about being. We both came hard and fast—Jodie actually came twice—and afterwards, as we cuddled together with the black lace panties all sticky and soaked, she asked me how it was.

"Incredible," I said. "I've never been so turned on."

She kissed me and smiled.

"You know, maybe next time you can come with me," she said. "We can buy you a whole outfit. Pretend we're shopping for me."

"We're different sizes," I said breathlessly. "Won't people know?"

"What if they do?" she asked. "Maybe they'll like the idea."

That was the first time—the first time I did it like that, cross-dressed, even if it was a humble beginning. More important, it was the first time I realized how lucky I was. Every time I think about that first experience, I thank fate that I Jodie and I somehow found each other. There were plenty more cross-dressing experiences to come—and Jodie would share them with me.

YOUR GIFT TO ME
ANDREA DALE

The salesgirl thinks we're just friends. She probably wouldn't have let me accompany you into the dressing room if she knew we were lovers. They never let guys in, anyway; I found this out when I was dating men and brought them lingerie shopping with me. Then, I had to go into the stall by myself, and only if the rooms were in an enclosed area in the back of the store could I open the door and show him.

The salesgirl doesn't have to worry about much, really. I'm not going to touch you. You know it, and I know it. The wanting, the needing makes it even sexier.

You've never been one for fancy underthings. You've always been perfectly happy in your gray Jockey For Her separates. God knows I'd find you sexy in a sackcloth, so I never complained. But you knew, didn't you? You saw my wistful gaze when the Victoria's Secret catalogue arrived. I didn't mean to sigh aloud.

I know you've never felt your body was worth expensive, frothy scraps that revealed more than they showed. I hope our relationship has helped you with that. The mere fact that you're in this dressing room, with its pale pink walls and framed photos of models in bustiers and camisoles and semitransparent robes trimmed with marabou, is a big step for you.

I give you a long, lingering kiss. You cling to me, just briefly, before I sit down in the ornately carved armchair with the fuchsia cushion in the corner.

You were a little overwhelmed when we got to the store. Too many choices. You paused just inside the door, blinking as if you'd just stepped into bright sunlight.

The salesgirl was a huge help. She had a good eye for what would best suit your coloring and body type. You've got a luscious hourglass figure: filmy camisoles and shortie chemises would just hang off you.

And, of course, technically it's my gift certificate. You put it in my Christmas stocking. Curled up together in front of the fire, mulled cider by our sides, we dove into our stockings with gusto, but you paused when you saw me open the embossed envelope.

You cleared your throat. "You get to pick the lingerie—for me. Whatever you want me to wear. Then we'll come home and ..."

At that point, you just looked wicked. You might be shy about dressing up, but you're not shy in bed, not at all.

"And I'll unwrap my present," I finished. I couldn't wipe the grin off my face, or stop the frisson of arousal that pooled between my legs.

I thanked you and kissed you, and you kissed me back, and we knocked over our cider when we ripped each other's clothes off, but we didn't care.

You turn away from me now, hesitating before picking up the first outfit. I'm not surprised you picked the plainest of the offerings first: a bra-and-panty set in royal blue satin.

When you turn around, I can see the outline of your erect nipples, no fancy lace or pattern to hide their obvious, proud need. Hell, I can even see the crinkle of your pubic hair through the smooth fabric below.

I shift restlessly in the chair. It's getting warm in here. If you're getting as aroused as I am already—and it seems you are, given the state of your nipples—we might have to buy every panty you try on.

You move on to more sets. A deep burgundy set catches my eye—it's elegant, not flashy. Lace overlays the silk beneath. There's a tiny single drop pearl at the center, between the breasts, and a scattering of pearls in a flower pattern at the front of the panties. A set to be worn for showing off, not for every day.

I can see you like the boy shorts, even the stretch lace ones. I figured you would, just as I figured the thongs would make you uncomfortable. Too exposed, too different from what you're used to. That's okay. Ditto the black bodystocking—a bit much, this time. Maybe later.

The emerald green satin teddy looks good on you, especially with that little ruffle at the edges. I enjoy watching you shimmy into it, adjust the straps. You're getting more comfortable, and I'm just getting more aroused. At this rate, I'm going to have to buy a fresh pair of panties myself.

I can't help it. I get up, pull you into my arms. My fingers skim up and down your back, enjoying the feel of the slick satin. You grab me, holding on tight, channeling all your nervousness into the kiss.

Nervousness, and excitement as well. My leg insinuates itself between yours, and I can feel the heat from your crotch. Thrilled, I nip at your lower lip, and you moan, long and low.

The salesgirl chooses that moment to knock on the door and ask how we're doing. You look horrified at first, but I merrily sing out that we're fine, just having trouble deciding, and she goes away. You and I break down in giggles.

In the end, my choice is clear. I pick the garnet-red merry widow, with matching stockings and a ribbon to tie around your neck. I saw your face change when you looked in the mirror. You saw how it displayed your breasts, how the lacy panties teased your ass, rising up just high enough to reveal the lower curve of your cheeks.

I pick this because you feel beautiful in it.

The fact that I want to press my lips to the pouting sliver of flesh that the panties highlight above your thighs is just an added bonus.

(When you're not looking, I give the salesgirl the royal blue satin bra-and-panties set and a few of the stretch-lace boy shorts to ring up as well.)

"Do you want to grab something to eat?" I ask as we leave the store, figuring this would give you time to relax a little.

But you cuddle up close next to me, clutching the fancy bag containing our purchases, and whisper, "No. I want to go home and model for you."

The eagerness in your voice nearly makes me come right there.

When we get home, you banish me to the kitchen to pour us each a glass of Chardonnay while you get ready. My hands are shaking; it's hard to cut the foil, much less get the corkscrew in straight. Thankfully, I'm not actually holding the full glasses when I hear you softly say my name.

I turn. You're in the doorway, wearing that incredible confection. Bouncing just a little on your toes, as if you can't stand still.

To hell with the wine.

I lead you to the standing mirror in the corner of our bedroom. It's an antique, one of the first things we bought together, polished mahogany wood and turned posts. You duck your head, but I gently encourage you to look at yourself. To see what I see.

"You look stunning in this," I tell you. "And you know it, too. See how it hugs your beautiful, curvy figure. Look how your breasts are just begging to be worshiped."

I stand close behind you, cup your breasts in my hands. I stroke the lace over your nipples with my thumbs. The buds are barely visible, almost the same color as the fabric, but I find them easily because they're tight and hard with excitement.

You gasp and press back against me.

"See how wonderful lace is?" I say. "How good it feels when it rasps across your sensitive nipples?"

I glide my hands down your waist, along your hips, murmuring endearments as I go. Then, I just can't hold back any longer. I move one hand forward, dip into the panties.

You're drenched.

Your eyes flutter shut as I find your clit and start to stroke.

"No, keep them open."

You try. You try so hard, but in the end, you can't. You

can't even stand up anymore, so it's onto the bed with us. I lie next to you and kiss you and keep sliding my fingers across your clit until your thighs tremble and your pussy pulses and you explode. I keep my hand there, feeling your shuddering subside.

You reciprocate, lips and hands, teasing my nipples, kissing your way down my stomach. Then your fingers are inside me while you use your tongue to flick at me, and just before I come I look down and see you kneeling there, your curvy bottom in the air, and I have to fantasize again about those brilliant-red lace panties, because I forgot to play with them before, and then I can't think straight at all.

Later—much later—you see me smiling, and tease me gently, tracing the outline of my lips with your forefinger. You think I'm smiling because I'm happy, because I enjoyed this so much, because I'm sated.

You're mostly right.

What you don't know is that for Valentine's Day, I'm getting you a gift certificate to that sex shop over on Division Street. You can pick out any toys you like.

And that night, you can use them all on me.

A STORM OF ME

JOEL A. NICHOLS

Day 7—I got my first transmission today: a packet of e-mails I can't respond to, a news report, a mission update (of course); I spend hours and hours monitoring the seedlings and still have hours and hours to stare out the portholes at the curving, blue halo of Earth or into the black. I wish I'd brought something other than *Ulysses* because even though I have nothing else to do, it's still practically unreadable. I should have brought the collected Steven King. There's another problem developing, too: I'm as horny as I've ever been and there's nothing to do about it. I spent most of day two jerking off and except for the novelty of come sluicing through the capsule in zero gravity, all that's happened is that I've rubbed myself raw and am still painfully hard. I got an e-mail from a couple I'd fucked around with, people who lived in my building, that had naughty innuendo but nothing really sexy. I fantasized about the last time I was with him, with the guy eating out my ass while I fucked his girlfriend. And soon enough I was poking out the front of my flight suit, my cock pointing straight out halfway between the two thick nylon straps. If only there was room for porn on board.

Doesn't capsule command realize that astronauts have needs, too, even horticultural science astronauts like me? One hour of radio range every forty-two hours? And then only to talk to the operator?

•

Day 16—Today one of my seedlings, a tiny vine, succumbed to the radiation I was giving it and sprouted a mutant-growth nub. I spent almost the whole day on that,

43

having to set up the lead shielding and radiation control, and then the relative excitement of something to do. But now it's a long wait for more plant growth, and I won't get another transmission for five days. I've even been skipping around in *Ulysses*, and smacked my dick off to Bloom in the bathtub. Twice.

●

Day 34—Have discovered that I can see a good reflection of myself in a porthole if the right lights are on behind me. I spent more than an hour making faces at myself, and it wasn't long before I was rubbing my dick, watching myself in the reflection. The image of my hand slipping up and down was imposed on a starry field, and I twisted my hips to get a profile view. I had opened the front of my flight suit, and my boxer-briefs were tangled down around my ass. I came fast, spraying droplets against the glass.

I pulled my underwear back up, pulled my still-big cock and tingling balls up into the pouch, and laid my palm over the top of it. I watched myself stay hard, then pumped my hips, making my bulge quiver. In a second my dick got rock-hard again, and slowly rubbed the head through the stretched-out gray fabric. I'm supposed to change my underwear once every ten days, and they sent me with nine pair: four briefs and five boxer briefs. My first three pairs are stiff with come. I wonder who does the laundry when I get back?

●

Day 53—I'm so bored I've read *Ulysses* the whole way through, and thought up and forgotten limerick after limerick after limerick. I'm still waiting for the plants to grow and waiting for a transmission—the news has gotten to be quite an event for me.

I've abandoned my flight suit altogether because the

heating system is turned up too high and when I'm facing the sun I start to bake. So I've been stretching out in patches of direct sunlight by the portholes, in my briefs. For a while I couldn't even jerk off because nothing got me hard, but then I ran out of boxer briefs: I found that feeling my cock and balls crammed together inside the tight white briefs has me half hard all the time. In the porthole, I watched my bulge grow larger and larger, and imagined it was somebody else, that we were reclined by a pool. I could see how his dick head was swollen, and poking to the left. I imagined it was Adam, the guy from the couple. We'd met up alone a few times, and traded blow jobs. I thought of Adam kneeling between my legs, slurping down my cock, licking the head and then the shaft. He'd reached up inside my boxers to grab my balls from behind, pressing his knuckles against the base of my ass crack. He squeezed my balls and swallowed my dick, over and over again. Here in the capsule, I had my eyes closed and my palm flat against my cock, growing warm through the cloth of my briefs. I started to slap at my cock through the fabric, lightly, and then squeezed my balls, holding the cloth around them tightly. It felt as it has with Adam, and I opened my eyes to see how my shorts were tenting.

I floated closer to the porthole, and watched as my straining briefs grew larger and larger. I pressed my dick up against the glass, and pumped my hips back and forth. The glass was cool against the underside of my shaft, and I thrusted against the surface. I closed my eyes and thought about Adam and Vanessa. I thought about how I'd pulled her thong strap aside and tongued and licked her ass while Adam had swallowed me. I crested on that image, clenching and unclenching my thigh muscles. I reached back and put my hands on my own hips, and pressed my cock against the porthole. The awkward positioning and feeling fingers pressing against my briefs almost felt like there was someone else there with me. I licked my lips and tried to lose myself in those fantasy images, in the feeling of the fabric pulled tight over my balls. As I held my muscles rigid, a load of come dribbled out and soaked the front of my shorts. I gave my balls a squeeze, and floated around to wipe my hands on the leg of my flight suit.

I couldn't afford to use up a new pair of briefs yet—I had decided to change them on transmission day, and that wasn't for days—so I let myself dry off in front of the air circulator, trying to ignore how the breeze tickled the hair on my balls, even through my shorts.

•

Day 71—Yesterday I got a transmission, a packet of e-mails and the week's news, and was relieved to read one from Adam and Vanessa. It said that they'd watched one of the home movies the three of us had made, and I wondered if it was the one in the pool and shower or the more vanilla one we made in their bed. My dick has been raw for days, and I have resolved to take as much time away from it as possible. I was even wearing two pairs of underwear—one of my soiled pairs of boxer briefs underneath my new briefs, because I thought it would keep me from easy access. But then I read the message from Adam and Vanessa, and started thinking about the pool party and how we'd each taken turns holding the video and training it on our favorite spots: Adam had taken my dick in Vanessa's mouth, I'd shot his cock filling her pussy, and she'd shot, near the beginning of the movie, the two of us with our trunks tented out, rubbing up against each other while we ate and licked her pussy together.

Inside my double layers of stretchy cotton underwear, underneath my flight suit, my cock stirred. I held on to one of the handholds riveted into the capsule and swung my legs forward and apart. I didn't want to add any pressure to it, to make my problem worse. I'm in my seventy-first day, and when I talk aloud to record research notes, my voice sounds strange—I'm only in range to talk to base for an hour every forty-two hours, and a lot of the bandwidth is taken up by the automated computers talking to each other. I get a minute or two of small talk with the radio operator, but my orders and updates come in the transmissions. How did I think it would be enough?

Even though I tried to think about the seedlings and my new data, I couldn't take my mind off my dick. I looked down and saw how my flight suit was bulging. My balls were hot and heavy, and my dick was pushing against them as it swelled up. I cupped the bulge with my hands and when I couldn't take it anymore I unzipped my flight suit. The stained Y-flap of my briefs flopped out, my half-hard dick in a lump. I reached for my balls with my other hand, snaking it down inside the boxer briefs. I rubbed the head of my cock slowly, using my other hand to pull the layered underwear tight up around my balls and ass. I think about Adam, licking toward my ass, grabbing my straps and pulling me against him, and I shoot again, my come floating around in the capsule in a storm of peculiar droplets—a storm of me.

PRACTICE MAKES PERFECT

KRISTIE HELMS

Waiting for the light at Fifth Avenue and Forty-seventh Street, Marcy turned to adjust the seams of her stockings. Heels planted firmly on the Manhattan curb, she pulled a leather glove off her right hand, leaned back at a slight angle, lifted the hem of her black wool winter coat with the back of her hand and with the edge of one newly manicured nail, ran her finger down the length of her back thigh until she found the wayward spot just behind her knee. She gently pinched the thin silk material with the tips of her fingers, being careful to keep her nails from nicking the fabric, and tugged the seam of the right leg's stocking back toward the inside of her leg so that it perfectly curved along the line just behind her knee. Her new, calf-hugging, three-inch leather boots kept bunching that stocking around her knees.

All of the morning commuters at the corner of Fifth and Forty-seventh were dressed in some variation on Marcy's corporate appropriate attire. Black wool winter coats wrapped around with scarves that were red or blue or even plain black. Marcy's scarf was a light pink. Just a little off from the others. Always just a little off.

Marcy was fully aware that the two men behind her had stopped their conversation recounting last night's Knicks game to stare at her seam. That seam. Marcy always made sure they saw that seam. She ran her smooth, white fingertip back up that thin black line and traced the edge back up to just under her skirt, pausing for just a beat before letting her coat and skirt fall back into place.

Mary adjusted the seams in her stockings the way other

women flipped a length of hair out of their eyes. Walking up subway steps in the middle of a rush-hour crush, she could straighten her seams with just enough subtlety that the Wall Street investor behind her saw only a flash of skin, a single black strap, and the small amount of plump thigh covered in a sheer black stocking that showed between the tops of her boots and the edge of her skirt. "Practice makes perfect," it is said, and Marcy practiced this maneuver so often that it had become just another of her unconscious habits. Like tucking a loose strand of hair behind her ear or sucking on the ice cubes that remained at the bottom of her cup at the movies. Straightening her seams always made her feel a little better. More together. She was a little more settled knowing that her seams were securely in place.

The "walk" light flashed and Marcy's heels clicked efficiently along the crosswalk. She never turned around to see that the two men who had witnessed her morning production were left rooted to the curb, their Bergdorf loafers unable to take a step after what they had witnessed.

Walking to work, Marcy liked to look up at the buildings and pretend she was a tourist from Omaha. She imagined all tourists were from Omaha and she knew that they all looked up at the giant steel skyscrapers. Those concrete monuments that were draped in windows with views all the way out to New York harbor. You could see forever from those corner offices.

Marcy knew she wouldn't be working much longer in one of those tight, low, three-walled, gray-carpeted cubicles that came standard issue with a boss standing over one of the walls. Bosses always seemed to think they were being charming and approachable when they leaned over Marcy's cubicle to inflict themselves on her "to do" list.

Marcy wanted a corner office of her very own. She wanted her own "to do" list. She took all of the night school classes at Manhattan Community College that her overworked credit card would allow. She packed peanut butter and jelly lunches to save money for student fees. She studied thick economics books over morning coffee, and she had been digging her way out of the temp pool for the last five years.

Marcy finally had a spot as an executive assistant, which required proficiency in maintaining budget spreadsheets, being able to set up a letter merge for mailings, and putting up with pats on her ass from the firm's oversexed, overpaid vice presidents. Even with their Ivy League educations, they still dropped by to ask Marcy's opinion on which mergers and acquisitions would bring in the most money for the company and fatten their wallets with quarterly bonuses.

Today was the day that all of this would come to an end.

Marcy had spent the past two months eyeing the one vice president who didn't lean over her cubicle, who let her keep her own "to do" list, and who never once patted her ass. She had seen the way his eyes widened slightly whenever she slipped off a pump and let the edge of her toe slide down her crossed leg while answering the phones outside his office. He had actually said "thank you" when she had brought the binders of color slides that he had forgotten to ask her to put together for a board meeting in his hurry to secure approval for a new project. After that meeting, she had quietly requested that she be an assistant only to him. He had approved it.

Evan was a gentleman, opening doors for her and allowing her to order first whenever she accompanied him on client lunches. She saw him chuckling to himself whenever she slipped back into her cubicle after a break, tugging a shopping bag filled with designer shoes she had snagged at yet another sample sale.

But today was the last day that Marcy would be answering phones for anyone—even someone as professional as Evan. This afternoon she and Evan were traveling an hour outside the city to inspect a conference center where they were considering holding the next executive retreat. Marcy had been given the responsibility for finding the location, booking the caterer, and setting up the meeting space for the seventy-five executives to use in plotting their strategy for the coming year.

She had pursed her lips during her weekly reports with him, the first few times Evan began questioning the choices she had made for the retreat—asking about the type of food, how many people the various meeting rooms would hold, and even whether or not the company would be charged for local calls.

"Maybe you should just see it for yourself," she had finally said to him yesterday after he asked an endless series of questions about the conference center's copy room.

"Maybe I should. Book a car service for tomorrow after lunch. I want to see whether or not you've set this up properly."

She had fumed for exactly the half hour it had taken her to realize that this afternoon away from the office was exactly the time she needed to make her move. She had seen the way Evan's eyes lingered on the seams of her stockings; she knew that if night classes weren't going to get her where she wanted to go, she was more than willing to use those seams to get a promotion out of her executive assistant's position and into a new spot opening up in the marketing and event-planning department, which Evan had casually mentioned during one of their meetings.

The fact that Evan's voice made her squirm in her swivel chair whenever he called her into his office certainly didn't hurt. Powerful people had always been a weak spot of Marcy's, but Evan's slender build, dark good looks and moody eyes made her nervously run her hands up and down the tops of her bare arms whenever she undressed for bed at night.

They rode in near silence to the conference center. Each time Evan asked a perfunctory question to confirm the directions or inquire about the number of people who would be attending the retreat, Marcy would nervously cross and uncross her legs to keep them from sticking to the fake leather seats of the car. After navigating the tollbooths at the George Washington Bridge, he eventually stopped asking questions, and Marcy eventually stopped squirming. They kept up the silence once they reached the center, letting the site manager lead them around each of the meeting rooms.

When they had looked into the third type of suite available for overnight guests, Evan abruptly turned to their tour guide and said, "Would you mind leaving us alone for an hour or so? We'd like to inspect the space on our own."

Marcy pushed a strand of hair behind her ear. Her plan was working, but she wasn't the one leading it. She ran a sweaty palm down the curve of her bottom and wondered if she should have just studied harder, or tried to get a scholarship to someplace like NYU or Columbia instead of taking out student loans for community college.

As the door closed, the silence stretched out across the length of the room.

"Just how badly do you want that promotion?"

Marcy was too shocked to respond.

This was supposed to go more smoothly. More gracefully. It was supposed to be Marcy asking the questions. She nervously slid a finger down her leg along one of her seams before turning around. She needed a moment to collect herself. A moment before the scent between her legs filled the room with her answer.

Opening her eyes, she turned to face him.

"How badly do you want to give it to me?"

Evan brought both of his hands up to cup her face. His lips met hers, crushing, filling her mouth with his unrelenting tongue. His hands reached under her pink sweater and cupped her breasts, twisting her nipples until they turned red through the thin silky T she wore. She felt her knees go limp as he lifted the sweater over her head. Not letting her shrug it off her arms, he held the cashmere tight in a knotted bunch at the small of her back trapping her arms in a vise.

This wasn't it. This wasn't the way she had planned it at all.

Evan had other plans.

Too shocked to figure out a way to pull her arms free, she could do nothing as Evan's hands wrapped around and formed themselves into fists at her scalp; her dark curls screamed before she could, and he forced her onto her knees at his feet. He pulled her head back so that Marcy was looking up, over the broad expanse of his suit jacket, up his Armani tie, and into his eyes.

"I'm not going to give you anything that you don't deserve. There aren't any free lunches in this world. You know that as much as do."

Evan pulled down his zipper.

"You've been asking for this for months."

Marcy's eyes watered as the grip on her scalp loosened just a bit.

"Now are you going to work for it?"

Marcy looked straight into Evan's eyes and nodded.

Her mouth filled with his cock. It took her a moment to realize that what she was tasting wasn't a condom. The dick in her mouth, ramming the back of her throat, filling her airways so that she had to time her breaths through her own passion and breathe through her nose, was pure silicone held in place with a leather harness.

The taste confirmed what she had known for some time. She had seen the slight bulges around his chest at the end of the day when the straps had loosened. She had seen his alumni magazine arrive in the office bearing a woman's name that he claimed was his sister's.

Marcy adjusted her mouth to take in more.

She wondered how long their understanding would last. How long until he turned on her and showed her up at some committee meeting. Stole an idea that she had whispered to him in a late-night dream and forced her back down to the temp pool to start all over again. Evan went limp and fell back on the bed.

Sprawled on the floor, staring at Evan's knees hanging over the bed, Marcy untwisted the cashmere sweater that had kept her arms trapped and tugged it off. In one quick, fluid, agile move, she stood upright. She kept her back to Evan, giving him an appetizing view of that bit of her flesh between the tops of her leather boots and the bottom edge of her black wool skirt. She leaned backward at a practiced angle and raised the edge of her skirt slightly with the back of her right hand. She pulled up the dark edge of her stocking and with just her thumb and index finger, hooked the metal end of the garter strap that had popped off while she had been on her knees back onto her stocking. She took the edge of her fingernail, painted in a pale ballet-slipper pink, and ran it down the seam lying flat against the back of her thigh until she found the unruly spot. She carefully squeezed the sheer silk fabric with the tips of her fingers and drew the seam of the right leg's stocking back into place.

She heard Evan take a sharp intake of breath in the bed behind her. It was the same sound she had heard the two men standing on the corner or Fifth Avenue and Forty-seventh Street make.

Marcy smiled softly to herself before turning back to face Evan on the bed.

"Practice makes perfect."

BRIEF ENCOUNTERS
WILLIAM HOLDEN

I sat at my usual spot, drinking my usual drink and anxiously waiting for the show to start. I only get down to New Orleans once a year, but I never pass up a chance to watch men dancing on the bar. I had arrived about an hour before the show to get the number one seat at the end of the bar that faces the dancers' entrance. This seat gives the best view of the guys as they come out, and also gives the dancer the best view of the person sitting there. Prime location means prime money. But I never come unprepared to pay these guys what they're worth. As I lit another cigarette, I looked around at the crowd. It's strange how you can be gone from a place for an entire year, yet the people never change. It's the same faces, sitting at the same bar, waiting for the same entertainment.

The bright overhead lights dimmed, giving way to small halogen lights that lit only the top of the bar. Smoke drifted through the beams, shifting and swirling before blending into the background. I motioned to the bartender for another drink. She was a large woman, but not fat. Her beautiful Jamaican accent complemented her features and long dreadlocks. I say woman, because that's what she hopes to be some day. She told me once that she was saving her tips to purchase herself a pussy. I often wondered how much one of those cost, but never had the nerve to ask her.

As the music started, the first of the dancers hopped up on the bar. I looked him over carefully, wondering what he was wearing underneath his torn blue jeans. He slid across the length of the bar in his white socks and stopped in front of me, landing on his knees. He spread his legs, as if inviting me in. His slim body moved gracefully with the beat of the music. His body toyed with my eyes as he pulled his black T-shirt up and over his head. His body was smooth. The only sign of hair was a thin trail on his belly leading down into his pants and a few short strands surrounding his small, erect nipples. I pulled out a dollar bill and brushed my hand down his chest. My fingers entered the waistband of his jeans, trying to determine what type of underwear he was wearing. The elastic band felt tight against his skin. I tugged on the band, and then looked up at him. He cocked his head to one side and smiled. His hips moved up and down, as I slowly unbuttoned his pants. The other men were watching me. I could see the shape of his cock pressing against his tight briefs. They were white and ribbed, my favorite kind. He stood on his knees. I pulled his jeans down and ran my hand across the softness of the cotton and the firmness of his cock. I slipped a ten dollar bill into the fly. I could feel the heat of his crotch surrounding my fingers. He stood up, tossed his jeans to the floor and moved on to the next customer. As he walked away, I noticed how well his tight briefs showed off his backside. I sat waiting for a reaction from my cock. It stiffened slightly, but nothing else. He wasn't the one.

The second guy appeared almost out of nowhere. He saw my attention turn to him, and began making his way in my direction. By the time he reached me, his shirt had already been removed. He was wearing dark green Bermuda shorts. Several dollars were tucked into his socks. He stood over me. His long, black hair hung down over his face. His torso, dusted with short hair, moved seductively, enticing me to give a little. I pulled a five-dollar bill out of my pocket. His smile grew into a sensual grin, causing my cock to lengthen in my pants. I sat anxiously awaiting the removal of his shorts. He had a beautiful body, one I could really get into and I couldn't wait to see his underwear and how it complemented his features. I began to imagine how it was gripping his cock and balls tightly within its material, how the soft cotton fabric was caressing and cuddling his damp skin, absorbing his smell into its fibers. My heart raced with anticipation. I could feel my pulse deep in my pants as he unbuttoned his shorts. The sound of the zipper sent chills down my spine.

I lost everything as he stepped out of his shorts. He stood in front of me in a pair of SpongeBob SquarePants boxers. Its silly yellow head and big eyes stared at me, mocking my disapproval. His hips moved back and forth inches from my face. I could see the outline of his cock, bouncing inside the thin material. It appeared long and slender. I handed the poor guy the money and turned to order another drink. He looked at me, bewildered, as if anyone would be turned off by his choice of attire. He got my money, and that was all he was going to get from me. I watched him move along to the next group of men. They were all over him, their hands running up his hairy legs, reaching up inside his boxers. He looked over at me as if I was supposed to be jealous. As I saw it, there was nothing to be jealous of. He had found some men with the same poor taste in underwear as he had. I had higher expectations for the night then spending it with SpongeBob SquarePants.

I turned my attention back to the entrance of the stage and waited for the next guy. I began to think the evening was going to be a bust. I was aggravated at the letdown from the previous two dancers. My hope for the evening reappeared as the next dancer came out on stage.

He was dressed in black slacks with a silver studded belt. His white tank-top appeared a size too small, highlighting his firm tight torso. Over his shirt he wore a red leather jacket. A red fedora sat firmly on his head.

His short black hair and deep brown eyes set off his olive complexion. A thin line of facial hair ran down each side of his face, tracing his strong jaw line. A small soul patch fit nicely just below his lower lip.

He danced slowly to the beat of the music for the few men sitting closest to the entrance. He turned his head. Our eyes met. He smiled at me as he removed his jacket. With each step closer to me, he removed another article of clothing. By the time he reached me he stood in his white tank-top and black slacks. His clothes littered the top of the bar.

He squatted in front of me. I could smell the heat from his body. My cock came alive. On his right arm was a tattoo of the head of Jesus, crowned with thorns. He saw me looking at it and flexed his biceps. He crossed his arms back behind his head. His armpits were covered in a dark patch of hair; sweat had already formed, matting the hair to his skin.

I pulled a twenty out of my pants. The bill felt damp from my own excitement. He looked at what I was holding and removed his shirt. His skin was smooth except for a trail of dark hair leading from his stomach down into his pants. I moved my hand up to his chest. His skin felt hot. He took my hand in his and led it down to his crotch. I could feel his hardness beneath his slacks. I unzipped his pants and slid the bill into his fly. The temperature rose between us as my finger grazed his stiffening shaft.

His underwear was damp, but I could tell it was of the ribbed variety. He leaned down to me, my fingers still hanging on to his fly.

"What's your name?" He whispered in my ear.

"Dean."

"I'm Miguel. Thanks for the money." He stood to leave.

I pulled him back down. "Would you like another twenty?" He remained silent. "Take off your pants and let me see your underwear." I pulled out another bill to show my sincerity.

He stood up and removed his belt. His pants slid down around his hips. I could see the silver waistband of his underwear. My pulse began to race as he stepped out of his pants exposing his white ribbed Unico underwear. He knelt down in front of me. His legs spread out on each side of me. The bulge in his underwear continued to increase. Black strands of pubic hair poked out and curled around the material.

I was lost in the sight of his beauty. My hand reached up and stroked his long shaft. A soft moan escaped his mouth as my hand slid under the edge of his underwear.

My fingers traced the large veins of his cock. I moved my hand farther, until I found the folds of his wet foreskin. My fingers played with the head hidden behind the skin. I slipped the twenty down below his hairless balls before removing my hand. He leaned closer and kissed me. His lips were soft and moist. His breath was sweet.

I looked around the bar for the first time since Miguel had appeared. The men farther down the bar were watching us. They appeared irritated that I was getting all the attention. He looked around as well and slowly stood up. I knew I couldn't keep him there any longer. As he moved away, I couldn't take my eyes off his firm round ass, hidden behind the whiteness of his underwear. The pressure in my pants was almost unbearable. The more I watched him dancing in his whites, the more I wanted him.

The two previous dancers had made their way back around to me. Each of them dancing for me, begging me to give him the attention he thought he deserved. I pretended I didn't notice as I kept my eyes glued to Miguel. As he approached the back of the dimly lit bar, his dark complexion blended into the background. All I could see was the outline of his white briefs still moving seductively to the music. I waited patiently for his return. As he made his way around the back of the bar, the music stopped. Instinctively each of the dancers picked up what clothes he could find and left the bar top. Miguel was the last to leave. As he left he looked back in my direction, then disappeared behind a curtain.

I knew the bartender would never let me go behind the curtain to see Miguel. She was very protective of her boys, but I had to find a way. I stood up and walked to the back of the bar and ducked into the bathroom. I walked over to the trough and unzipped my pants, hoping to release some of the pressure. After a bit of maneuvering I finally pulled my swollen cock out. As I stood there, waiting for release, Miguel sauntered into the bathroom still wearing his Unico's. He didn't stop when he saw me. He just made his way back to one of the stalls and shut the door. Release for me never came. All that escaped my cock was more precome as I thought of Miguel sitting just behind the thin metal wall. I zipped myself up and walked quietly to the door of the stall. I could feel his presence behind the door, hear his breathing from within. I leaned closer, pressing my ear to the cool metal, trying to get closer to him. My heart raced. I could hear it pulsing in my ears, feel the vibrations deep inside me. I pushed on the door. It wasn't locked, and swung open.

Miguel was standing in the stall, waiting. His body, damp with sweat, glistened in the dim light. I could feel the heat radiating from him. His scent surrounded me. His hand reached out and grabbed mine. He pulled me toward him. My hands immediately cupped his ass. My fingers traced the ribbed material of his underwear, feeling the dampness in the crack of his ass. His breath was on my neck as he unbuttoned my shirt. As each button was released, his mouth moved farther down my chest until his tongue was buried in the hair that surrounded my stomach.

I pulled him back up to face me. His brown eyes stared back at me as I pushed his arms above his head. My mouth moved along his upturned arm and found the damp saltiness of his armpit. He moaned as I nibbled the tender flesh that lay below. His body trembled. My hand caressed his stiff cock through his briefs. Without warning he pushed me down onto the toilet and began to remove my pants.

He got on his knees and began to rub his face in my crotch. He took deep breaths of my scent and then blew warm air through my underwear, warming my already overheated cock. He pulled my underwear down to my ankles. He looked up at me and grinned as he saw the length of my cock.

He stood up and straddled my body. He pushed his crotch into my face. I nibbled and bit the tender flesh of his foreskin through the material. His precome soaked through the fabric. I covered the wetness with my mouth and sucked the material dry. His precome was sweet and lightly scented with fabric softener.

"I want you inside of me," Miguel said slowly, but with urgency in his tone. He moved my hands to his ass. My fingers dug deeply into the material pushing the cloth deep into the crack of his ass. I felt the material give slightly; then my finger touched the hot flesh of his ass.

"Yeah, that's it. Make yourself a hole to fuck me."

Without hesitation, I tore into his underwear, making an opening large enough for my cock to fit through. The sound of the threads tearing sent an electric charge through my groin. Precome leaked out of my cock.

Miguel gripped my cock and began to stroke it. Precome poured over his hand. He rubbed it up and down my shaft, using it as lubricant. He lowered himself down onto me and smeared more of my precome over his tight hole. His body moved slowly and gracefully as if giving me a private dance. He let the head of my cock enter him. His warmth surrounded my shaft and he moved farther down my cock.

I looked down and noticed the head of his cock poking out of the waistband of his underwear. He leaned into me and kissed me as the final inch of my cock slid in. He continued to ride my cock, up and down, using the muscles in his ass to squeeze every inch of my shaft. His hips moved back and forth as he rubbed his exposed cock between our stomachs, its head slipping in and out of the foreskin as my cock slipped in and out of his ass.

Our breathing grew heavy. His cock swelled with pressure as it continued to be sandwiched between our sweat-dampened bodies. I reached down and rubbed my hands over the worn underwear. The opening I had made was damp and sticky. Threads from the ripped material stuck to my shaft as it moved back and forth.

Miguel began to pant. His chest heaved with each thrust of my cock inside of him. He leaned closer into me, tightening the muscles in his groin. His strong arms encircled me, holding me tight. I could feel the pressure of his orgasm building against my skin. I covered his mouth with mine to quiet his moans. I could feel the vibrations of his voice deep in my throat. His breathing was becoming shallow. Short, hot puffs of air pushed into my mouth as the first wave of his orgasm covered our stomachs. His hot come mixed with our sweat. He continued to rub his cock between us. The wet sticky sounds of our sex grew louder as he shot another hot, thick load of come across our bodies. His ass muscles tightened one final time, as he continued to ride my cock. I held his mouth against mine and groaned as I filled his ass.

Our bodies were sore from the workout and from the cramped space we were in. He stood up slowly and looked down at my body covered in his come. Then he realized the mess we had made of his underwear. Without saying a word, he slipped out of his underwear and slipped mine on. I nodded my head in approval as he stood there in my white Basket boxer-brief underwear. The orange stripe of the waistband blended well against his dark skin. He looked at his watch.

"I have to go. I'm due on the stage in a few minutes." He leaned down and kissed me. Then he turned and slipped quietly out of the stall.

I stood up and buttoned my shirt, then noticed his underwear lying on the floor near my jeans. I picked them up and felt the warmth of our sex, still lingering in the material. I brought them to my face and took a deep breath. Miguel's scent invaded my senses, a mixture of his muskiness, sweat, and come. I slipped them on. Miguel's dampness felt cool against my skin. I could feel Miguel next to me, his heat and scent comforting me.

I stepped out of the stall and walked into the bar. Miguel was up on the stage doing his thing. As I approached the door I turned to get a final look at Miguel. He saw me looking at him and winked. I lifted my shirt and showed him the Unico underwear that I was wearing. He was smiling and shaking his head at me as I walked out into the night.

THINGS BETWEEN
TENILLE BROWN

Ivy and I were the talk of this town, many years ago when things like this were frowned upon and only whispered about. We were young back then. I was a seamstress seeing clients in my home, and she was the young bride of John Thomas Anderson.

The talk was of what was between us, what business that young woman could possibly have with me. And, yes, there *were* things between us, things spoken in whispers and kisses behind the closed doors of my little house. But those things were between *us*, and no one else.

See, it didn't matter to me that people were talking. I just carried on as if nothing was going on at all. I wasn't one to show off. I never had been and Ivy knew that. I liked to remain subtle, mysterious, if you will, while I left the showing off for her.

Ivy liked that sort of thing. But it wasn't so much that Ivy was a show-off as she was a rebel, or an exhibitionist of sorts. She was a beautiful woman and she knew it, but not in that cocky, sickening sort of way. She was simply confident, the way she stretched those big brown eyes when you were mad at her, making you forget what it was you were mad about in the first place, the way she always smelled so good, even without the oils and perfumes.

She didn't care that people talked. "Let them talk," she would always say.

And it was that blatant confidence that had attracted me to her in the first place. She didn't see a need to cover up what she thought was beautiful and right. This was clear to me from the time I started dressing her. She never did need a stitch of clothes on her. That was one thing that never changed about her over the years and I didn't want it to.

It didn't matter if we were in bed or if we weren't. We could be at the table having dinner or be stretched out on the rug watching television. One thing was for certain: Ivy would rather be doing it without the inconvenience of clothes. She was more comfortable that way, she always insisted, but I was certain she just wanted to tease me.

Sometimes I wanted to ask her if she was that way with her husband, if she liked prancing around for him in her underwear. I wanted to ask if he liked it, if maybe he even asked her to do it. Except, we didn't talk much about John Thomas. When Ivy and I were together, we pretended her marriage to him didn't exist at all.

On a particular Saturday afternoon when John Thomas was out of town, Ivy stood before me topless. The sun beamed through the window and flashed on her ring. I turned my eyes away from it. She and John Thomas had been married three years then, and for three years Ivy had also been coming to me.

I knelt in front of her, my fingers working at the black pants hanging loosely around her hips.

"How do you like these?" Ivy moved so that the pants dipped below the waist of her panties. She pulled at the pink lace. "I picked them up from Arlington last month." She gave her hips a little twist.

I nodded and gave a quick glance, trying not to look any longer than I needed to. I tugged at the seam of her pants, pulled it until the pants rested comfortably around her buttocks and against her hips.

She exhaled. "I got them from the same place I got that set for you, the lavender set. You know which ones I'm talking about, the ones you never wear?"

I knew good and well which ones Ivy was talking about. I knew because every time I put the damned things on, I felt as though my tits were going to fall right out, and I always had to pull at those panties because they were cut so small and sometimes they get lost ... back there.

So I said, "I wear them all the time, Ivy."

Ivy put her hands on her slender hips then. "When? When do you wear them? I know *I* never get to see them."

"I wear them *underneath* my clothes. That is the purpose, isn't it?"

"That may be the purpose, but that certainly doesn't make it any fun. I don't care if you see me in mine, you know," Ivy explained. "How many times have I walked all around this house in nothing but my undies?"

I shrugged. "Well, you're different from me, Ivy," I said. She was different all right. Yin and yang, we were.

Most times Ivy didn't even bother with a bra. She only had a handful of tits to begin with, and she was still young and perky enough not to have to worry about them sagging or flapping all over the place. See, I could never do that. Even if mine were small enough to go without something holding them up, I'd feel all insecure about it.

I pulled the baggy black pants tighter against her thighs and studied them.

Ivy reached down and stroked my hair. "We're not that different, you know."

I smiled because I couldn't help it. She brought it out in me. She would talk to me that way, and it was as if I *was* the same as her.

But the difference between Ivy and me was that she could do things like call me into the bathroom while she was soaking in the tub, or barge in with news that just couldn't wait until I was off the toilet. It would have been annoying if she weren't so damned cute about it and if I didn't love her so much.

Ivy looked down at the stitch I had made in the waist of her pants. "That looks good. That should do fine," she said.

"Okay," I said and stood up. I brushed the lint off my pants and stuck the needle back in its cushion. "You want me to take a look at that jacket?"

"No. The jacket fits fine. And I have this pretty yellow blouse to wear underneath. I'll have to stop by in the morning so you could see how it all looks together." Ivy studied my work in the full-length mirror.

"Do, that," I said. "I'd be glad to see it."

Ivy cocked her head then and began stepping back out of her pants. She was never one for bothering with going into the bathroom or standing behind a dressing shade. She folded the pants and laid them across the chair.

Her voice startled me. "When did you first start to look at me, you know, that way?" she asked.

She was looking at me and I cocked my head, twisting my mouth in thought. I knew exactly when it was and thinking about it made me want to smile.

"Well," I said. "It was during the time I was doing your dress. I remember you were so nervous with the wedding, and one day I was taking your measurements for some alterations and you just stood there in front of me with no bra on." I paused, reflecting. "You didn't cover yourself with your hands or anything. You just stood there half naked like no one was in the room but you. It made me look at you, really *look* at you. You had the nicest body and prettiest brown skin I had ever seen. You still do, you know."

Ivy batted the eyelashes of her big brown eyes. "You know when I first noticed you?" She didn't wait for me to answer. "It was one night after I left here. You had worn a sundress that night, and I remember it well because it was the flimsiest thing I had ever seen you in. Before that, it had always been pants and blouses or dresses that came down to your ankles. I had begun to think you were a bit of a prude. I remember I went home that night and I couldn't stop thinking about the way you looked in that dress. And all of a sudden I was sad because I had my dress already and I knew I wouldn't see you anymore. And I kept wondering what you would look like later that night after the dress came off."

She reached out and touched my hand. "And it wasn't just that I was thinking about you without anything on. It was that I saw that strap of your bra from beneath the shoulder of your dress. It was blue. It was pretty. And I wondered if your panties matched. I wondered how they fit you, if they were bikini or brief, if they were cotton or maybe lace or satin."

I hoped Ivy didn't see me grinning. "Was that when you decided to rip your wedding dress?" I asked.

She chuckled. "Desperate times called for desperate measures."

I looked at her, touched her on her waist and smiled. "I'm glad you did it, Ivy."

"I know," she said and touched me back.

•

I stood over a bed covered with delicates. There were strapless bras, high-waist panties with pretty little bows in the center, satin swatches of material held together by strings.

I scanned the gifts of the last three years carefully, recalling when I had worn a certain garment, how it had looked, how it had made me feel.

It wasn't that the things Ivy bought for me weren't pretty. She had wonderful taste and she was always great about getting my size. She could pick better things than I could pick for myself most of the time, but they were always the tiniest little things, always something with strings for sides or a non-existent crotch. And the ones that did cover everything were made of lace or something that you could see clear through anyway.

I figured Ivy could see me any day in the buff if that was what she wanted. We can just cut out the middleman and bypass the underwear all together, but Ivy didn't see it that way at all.

I lifted a bra-and-panties set off the bed. I ran my fingers over the delicate fabric and wondered briefly what it would be like to stand before her wearing only that. I held them against my body, twisted and turned in the mirror and then, I smiled.

•

Ivy sat on the bed flipping through channels. Her
back to me, she chuckled at something funny she'd found
on television. I imagined her wide, toothy smile and her
sparkling eyes.

I cleared my throat.

She turned.

"I wanted to show you this dress, I said. "I made it from a
pattern I found in my mother's things years ago."

I pulled at the sides of the white sundress to show the
full skirt. The top hugged my long, slender torso. It cinched
my waist. It lifted my breasts. A wide patch of dark brown
skin showed at the plunging neckline.

Ivy nodded. "It's pretty." She turned around so that her
knee and thigh rested on the bed. "And it looks good on you.
You have such a lovely figure. I've always told you that."

My eyes fell and I folded my lips. Ivy always managed to
make me feel like a bashful teenager. "Thank you," I said
softly.

"Well, are you going to turn around so I can see the back?"
Ivy looked interested, anxious even.

I turned slowly. The hem of the dress swayed back and
forth across my calves. I looked over my shoulder once I was
finished. I wanted to see her immediate reaction, that first
look on her face when she saw the things between.

"Thing is," I said while she drank me in, "I couldn't
reach around there to zip it up. Think you could do it for
me?"

"Of course." Ivy reached for me as if afraid. She tugged
at the soft fabric of the dress. She pulled at the zipper. Then
she stopped.

"Something wrong? Is the zipper caught?" I turned my
head only slightly.

"No, nothing's wrong. Well, maybe it is," Ivy said.

She began to pull the zipper farther down. The dress
hung loose against my back and shoulders. I moved so that

the dress fell off my shoulders.

"Is this better?" I asked.

I straightened my back as the dress came down, skimming my skin, floating down to my feet. I stood before Ivy in nothing but the sheer lavender bra and panties she had bought me, wearing them like a second skin. They felt good on me, soft and warm, better than they ever had before, better than when they were covered by a dress or a suit.

Her eyes brightened when she saw me, all of me in those things. She walked around me, studied every fiber that clung to me, from the straps that lay tightly against my shoulders to the sheer band across my back, then lower, where the panties hugged my hips and ass.

And then, having mercy, as if she could feel the heat of my skin, hear the rapid beating of my heart, Ivy reached for me. She touched me as if it were the very first touch. I shuddered and exhaled as if it were the very last. Her touch was gentle, cautious. She touched me as if nothing was there, as if nothing lay between her fingers and my skin.

Ivy came to me and gave me her lips. Her lips remained on mine only a moment before they traveled down my neck, paused at my shoulders, and then fell down to my breasts.

I felt her lips through the sheer fabric of the bra. Gently, she licked, nibbled, and kissed. She fell to her knees, planting wet kisses on my belly and waist. She gave her lips to the sheer fabric that covered my hips and pussy.

My legs trembled. It was as if it had all vanished and all that was left was my bare skin and Ivy's warm, soft lips on me. Suddenly I felt deviant, defiant, not at all myself. She knew how to make me forget it all.

Ivy took her lips away only long enough to come to her feet and relieve herself of her own clothes. She quickly unhooked the buttons that clasped the yellow sleeveless dress in the front and shimmied out of the frock, kicking it aside. She stood in front of me in her red lace bra and panties.

Ivy resumed the touching, resumed the kissing. She brought her body close to mine. And then, when I could take no more, when I felt as though my knees would buckle and I would fall to the floor, Ivy placed her hands on my waist and walked with me to the bed.

She laid me down, stretched me out on the soft, flowery comforter. She climbed up my body and crouched above me, her knees on either side of my hips. I began to tug at my underwear, dying for the sweet freedom of lying beneath her naked.

"No," Ivy begged, "Leave them on. Please, leave them on."

I touched her hand and kept it in its place on my breast. She smiled and continued to brush lightly against the bra and panties, against this new skin of mine. It was a sensation I had never known, one that I welcomed in gasps and moans.

Ivy lay on top of me and we moved against each other, the lace of her bra brushing against the thin net of mine, her breasts pressing against my belly, her belly resting between my thighs.

"See what we can do?" Ivy's voice was raspy. "We can lie just the way we are, do just what we're doing and it can feel so good."

"Ivy ..." It was all I could manage.

And when I was sure I would rip the sheets clear off the bed, when I was certain I would jump right out of my skin, Ivy planted a kiss on my lips and pressed her crotch against mine before finally, beautifully, I came. Ivy arrived soon after, relaxing on top of me, her breath heavy against my cheek.

I stroked her hair, played with the lace that framed her ass. Yes, there were things between us, things unspoken, things that screamed from inside, things that scratched and begged to be free. But these things, they were ours. They were between *us*. These things belonged to Ivy and me, and no one else.

BURLESQUE AND ANSWERED PRAYERS

TERESA NOELLE ROBERTS

Some of my friends occasionally like going to strip clubs, but strippers have never thrilled me. Their goal is to get past what I think is the most interesting point, when a woman is decorated with bits of satin and lace, but not quite naked. I can't help the way I'm wired. For me, pretty lingerie makes an attractive woman look gorgeous and a gorgeous woman look completely, mind-bogglingly, panty-meltingly irresistible.

Stripping is all about making the silky, frilly bits go away. What, I ask you, is the fun in that?

So when my friend Stephanie dragged me to a charity burlesque night, "Pussycat Dolls for Pussycats," at the local community theater, I figured burlesque was pretty much like stripping to retro music; what I had to look forward to was a fairly painless way to support the local animal shelter.

And, of course, an evening in the company of Stephanie. Stephanie was quite the tempting pussycat doll herself, with blonde Veronica Lake hair, a tiny waist, and the kind of round, heart-shaped ass I'd follow across the Sahara or to a church social, let alone to a burlesque show, which would at least involve good-looking women in varying states of undress. Unfortunately, I could never get a clear reading on whether she was interested in me.

And I didn't have the nerve to ask.

Oh, I talk a good game where sex is concerned. All my friends, for instance, had heard my rant about why the

s Secret fashion show is better than a strip club, and
my opinions about the best vibrators. But confront me
ι an actual hot babe and I resort to prayers to Aphrodite
ιat she'll make the first move. Too afraid of making a fool
of myself, I guess; for a grown woman I seem to have a lot
of inner teenage boy.

Unattainable women onstage and one next to me who
might as well be onstage unless she made it clear she was
interested: my right hand and I would be having a hot date
when I got home. Between potential sexual frustration and
uncomfortable seats, I was wondering if this evening out
was maybe not such a grand idea.

But once the swing music started and the first act strutted
onto the stage, a small woman with short brown hair and
an Amazonian redhead who had to have a foot on the other
one, I knew everything was going to be all right. Both the
dancers had glorious figures; in my opinion, this probably
meant that they were about twenty pounds heavier than the
"ideal" weight they had fixed in their heads. Better than a
strip club *or* Victoria's Secret right there! Real curves in all
the right places, that's what I like, and I was willing to bet
their boobs were real because the nicely rounded hips that
balanced them certainly were. They wore red velvet halter-
top dresses with full skirts—picture the white dress from
Marilyn Monroe's subway-vent scene, but in a different
fabric—elbow-length black gloves, and high heels. The
overall effect was retro without looking like any particular
decade, and very, very tasty. Just that visual was worth the
price of admission.

And then they started to dance.

I don't mean they gyrated vaguely in time to the music.
I mean crisp but flowing movements, obviously well
rehearsed and in sync. I mean cute as could be, but as
suggestive as ... well, as Marilyn Monroe on that famous
subway grating. So far they hadn't done anything that
would disturb my church-lady grandmother—make her
blush and giggle, sure, but not actually bother her—and I

was already squirming happily in my uncomfortable chair, along with most of the rest of the audience. The dancers were smiling as if they were having the time of their lives, and I was grinning right along with them. When they peeled off first one glove, then the other, the audience let out a collective sigh.

Stephanie leaned over and whispered in my ear, "Aren't they great?"

As if her hot breath on my skin wasn't distraction enough, she added, "I've been taking burlesque classes with Amie Amour, the tall one."

Naturally I pictured Stephanie up there too in that same sexy outfit, a blonde sandwiched between the brunette and the redhead, and if my blood hadn't already been heated, that image would have done it.

I thought her lips brushed against my ear as she pulled away, but maybe that was just my overheated imagination.

The performers distracted me from the distraction. First, as they made snaky and sensual movements with their hips, they unfastened the halter necks of their dresses. Naturally, that got my attention. Then they turned their backs to the audience with a little kick that lifted their skirts to show off—be strong my heart—Cuban-heel stockings and black half-slips trimmed with red lace. With practiced grace they slithered their dresses down, which left them dressed in just the black petticoats and black lace strapless bras, then spun back around, making the full-skirted petticoats flare.

Why had petticoats ever gone out of fashion?

And why weren't all bras embellished with red fringe like these?

Facing the audience again, they shimmied their shoulders, making their fringe sway fascinatingly.

Stephanie leaned over again. "I've learned that move," she whispered, "and tonight I'm wearing the right bra to do it." This time, I didn't just imagine her lips brushing against me.

Or the little nip at the earlobe, the light kisses on my

throat, the small hand that found its way onto my thigh and made me wish I'd worn a skirt for a change instead of my favorite black velvet jeans.

It would seem that this time Aphrodite had answered my prayers and sent me a woman bolder than I. And her boldness let me be bold in return.

Stephanie had worn a skirt—and a garter belt, which I was able to deduce through its silky fabric as soon as I touched her.

If this had been at a nightclub—which is where you'd think they would hold such a steamy show—there would have been dark corners and lighting that was conducive to making out. Instead, the seats were all in a row, so we were in full view of our neighbors.

I didn't want to detract from the show onstage, so I gritted my teeth and kept it to a light tease despite the serious temptation to push her skirt up and see what she was or wasn't wearing underneath.

The dancers were doing a bit of jitterbug now, showing off some pretty amazing moves along with their pretty amazing underwear. Lacy petticoats flipped up, showing glimpses of stocking top and pale thigh. Breasts barely confined by bras swayed and shook hypnotically, making me want to reach out and touch them.

It just got better when they slithered out of the half-slips, leaving them in bras, Cuban-heeled thigh-highs and the most adorable panties I'd ever seen. I'd expected thongs, but they were hip-huggers, black with rows of red lace ruffles on the bottom, the naughty version of something a spoiled little girl might wear, and they accented those round, delicious asses better than thongs ever could.

The girls knew it, too. They turned around, stuck their bums out, and wiggled them, looking back over their shoulders at the audience and grinning saucily.

With a movement I couldn't quite catch, bras went flying.

They teased us for a couple of measures, wiggling their

bottoms, then turned to reveal black pasties trimmed with more red fringe.

Better than bare, at least as far as I was concerned.

When they started to twirl the tassels like Vegas showgirls, I figured I'd died and gone to heaven.

But my night kept getting better and better.

While the audience was busy staring at the hypnotic twirling, Stephanie's hand crept to the damp velvet at my crotch. "I'm still working on that move," she whispered. "But I have the pasties on. And the panties."

We only made it as long as intermission out of politeness to Stephanie's dance teacher. The "French maid" with a heavenly ruffled crinoline, matching ruffled pasties and strategic teasing use of a feather duster, along with the contortionist in the tiger-striped catsuit with the intriguingly placed cutouts, didn't do much to cool us down.

At that point, we couldn't be bothered with public transit. We hailed a cab outside the Y and made out like a couple of teenagers all the way back to Stephanie's apartment. I got to slide my hands under her skirt, feel the garter belt (and the soft, sensitive flesh underneath), the ruffled panties (and the moist heat they barely contained). More clothed than she, I must have been a frustrating target, but she managed to work my nipples into a good state right through my shirt. I was straining against my velvet jeans, my underwear (a blue satin thong that matched my bra, and for that matter, my eyes) soaked with my juices.

We poured out of the cab and staggered up three flights of stairs to her place, stopping every few feet to kiss. By the time we made it into her front door, I was ready to tackle her on the futon couch.

But she waggled her finger at me, raising her eyebrow as she did so—a ridiculously cute move that had to be something she'd learned from Amie Amour. Then she shoved me down on the couch, switched on the stereo so "Shake Your Lovemaker" by the Cherry Popping Daddies filled the room, and began to dance.

It was obvious she had a lot less practice than the members of the Pussycat Dolls. Her movements weren't polished, and sometimes she was clearly making it up as she went along. Her sweater got stuck when she pulled it over her head, making us both dissolve into giggles. She shimmied out of the skirt easily enough, but then hopped around a little trying to escape its grip on her ankles.

But by then she was in the red-fringed bra, the ruffled panties, stockings, and a red garter belt. Even if she'd fallen down, she'd have looked pretty damn fine to me.

She did know how to do the shoulder shimmy.

It all looked especially good right under my nose, so I could smell her perfume, cup her breasts long enough to interfere with the motion, plant a kiss in the creamy valley between them, then let her go to dance some more.

When the time came, the bra didn't come off quite as gracefully as the professionals' had, so I stood up, put my arms around her and helped, grinding against her in time to the music as I did, then swept my arms around to caress her breasts.

Their weight filled my hands. She hadn't been kidding when she said she was wearing pasties underneath, plain red ones without tassels, but decorated with sequins. It meant I couldn't really play with her nipples, but I worked my hands and my lips over every square inch of flesh I could. She tasted delicious, faintly seasoned with sweat and jasmine-scented powder, and she made adorable little noises.

The song was on endless repeat, so the stereo was singing about "Shake Your Lovemaker" for the fifth time or so when she actually started doing so, letting me enjoy the red ruffles. I sat back down and tried to be a good audience member, but a woman could only resist that fine ass in those fine panties for so long. Soon I was up dancing with her, feeling her almost bare breasts against my still-clothed chest, cupping her ruffled butt in my hands.

We ground against each other for a while. Then I couldn't

stand it anymore. I dropped to my knees and pressed my mouth to the black crotch of the panties. Stephanie's juices had a particularly delicious tang.

The easy thing to do would have been to move the panties out of the way, but I didn't want to. Not yet. Instead, I clutched her ruffled butt and pulled her closer to me; licked and nibbled through the fabric; and reveled in wet satin under my tongue and crisp lace and smooth satin under my hands as warm, soft girl-butt, jasmine, and ocean filled my nostrils.

One of her hands fell to the back of my head. At first she just toyed with my hair, but about the time she started to twitch, it turned into a directing grip, guiding me to applying the right pressure in the right places.

The twitching turned to bucking, fucking my eager mouth. Then I got a delightful surprise: Stephanie cried out something deep along the lines of "Oh my God" and squirted, filling her panties and my mouth with tangy juices.

After that, of course, the panties had to go, as did my clothes.

The panties didn't go far, though.

They ended up in my mouth as Stephanie, clad in a garter belt, black stockings, and red pasties, worked her fingers into me. First one finger, teasing and stroking, then two, working in and out, quickly, until I was trying to beg for more around my lacy gag.

I couldn't actually beg, just make muffled, incoherent noises. I kept trying, though, because each time I moved my mouth it unleashed a little more of Stephanie's juice and fragrance.

She pushed more of the panties into my mouth just before slipping a third finger into me—and I was so wet it really did just slip in. Lace and satin and her seagoing-jasmine taste filled my mouth as her fingers filled my pussy. I could hardly breathe, not because the panties were choking me, but because I was so excited I had trouble remembering how.

So delicious. So full. And my eyes were full, too, of Stephanie looking fiercely hot, her ornamented breasts swaying above me.

Then somehow she worked another finger into my already stuffed pussy and I exploded, seeing not stars, but sequins, screaming into soaked lace.

It seemed (I learned over breakfast the next morning, wearing a borrowed dragon-print silk kimono that tickled my still-sensitized nipples) that Stephanie had been making evil plans for me ever since she heard my strippers-versus-Victoria's-Secret speech. Even taking the burlesque class had been part of her trap. It seems my lovely Veronica Lake look-alike also has a thing for the racy and lacy. Only she likes wearing it, and showing it off, and sometimes, as I'd discovered last night (my jaw ached a bit, but it was so worth it!) making creative and slightly kinky use of it. She figured that at worst we'd have one fun night and at best we'd be a match made in heaven.

It's been six months since the night of the Pussycat Dolls benefit and I think we may be working on the match made in heaven. This weekend we're going to New York to go lingerie-shopping.

Yes, this time Aphrodite definitely answered my prayers.

NINE TO FIVE
STAN KENT

I always arrive early at the office to make sure that I serve my boss her first cup of coffee by nine. She likes her java strong, with dollops of thick condensed milk to sweeten the espresso's eye-popping bite. It takes me no more than ten minutes to prepare, taste, and adjust the tanned elixir, but I allow myself at least a quarter of an hour in the event something goes wrong. Once I'm certain the brew is exactly the way she likes it, I place the steaming mug on her Gucci coaster and scoot under her desk.

I sit on my haunches, eager to know whether I've passed the first test, but my boss keeps me on tenterhooks with the tapping of her plectrum nails on the coffee cup. The high-pitched drumming rises above the swirl of distant voices heard over the static of her speakerphone. She's discussing yet another gargantuan buy of her world famous designer fashions, but I'm only interested in her private attire. I stare at her voluptuous outline as she metronomes her body slowly from buttock to buttock. Her executive chair creaks under the hypnotic motion. The leather slips and crackles as it resists the intimate tug-of-war with her clothes. The telephone babble fades. I focus my dark-adapting eyes on the twin columns of her legs, her calf muscles sculpted tense by Via Spiga ankle-strap high heels. In the murk of the desk's walnut underworld, the whiteness of her pressed tight knees twinkles through the charcoal mesh of her expensive pantyhose. Her patellae are such tempting morsels.

She stills her teasing undulations, pausing in mid-sentence. Across the oceans, oblivious to my predicament, powerful men hang on her words. I hold my breath, a frisson of sexual anticipation gnawing at my desire. *Please, please, please let the coffee be to her taste.*

A sip. A swallow. A sigh. Her words flow steely into the speakerphone, but I sense her satisfaction. Her legs inch apart. I breathe. She approves of the coffee. I smile, knowing I have given her the first of today's many satisfactions. I kneel on my strategically positioned cushion. My head bows. She inches forward to the edge of the chair. Her hand cradles my head, toying with the short hairs on my neck as she pulls my face deep into the warmth of her thighs.

Above the muffle of her limbs, I hear her antique clock chime nine.

My workday has begun.

Through demanding sentences punctuated by sips of my lovingly made coffee she dictates terms and conditions to her telephonic audience. She pulls my head under her Versace skirt and washes my face against the taut Wolford nylon cloaking her mound. She makes unflinching financial demands of her buyers as static charges prick my skin. I inhale the damp of her pussy. An amorous cocktail of sex juice and perfume wafts into my brain, firing all the right synapses. I am delirious. There is nothing like the penetrating odor of feminine lust through pantyhose early in the morning. It speaks of licentious nights and crack-of-dawn sex raining down a sweet deluge of sticky juices. She is all pantyhose, pussy, perfume, and power.

She pushes my head from her lap and presses my face to her knees with a brusqueness I find addictive. She does not deny my craving. Her firm hand grips my neck, guiding my lips from one knee to another in dizzying circular motions of my head. I plant kisses, lingering long enough to soak her skin through the tightly woven fibers of her Wolford pantyhose. The dampened Lycra sticks to my face as she turns my head to a fresh, dry patch of stocking. She pulls me higher, her hand and thighs funneling my tongue back to her sex. Like a cat cleaning its fur, I drag my tongue across the shining nylons, relishing the luxurious texture.

She lifts her skirt above my head, bunching the Versace around her waist. My eyes flood with stark, fluorescent light, revealing a vision commanding worship. My boss is loveliness incarnate. White skin, red lips, jet black hair piled high above her head, curled wisps cascading down to caress her cheek bones over which the darkest of eyes peers down at me. Averting my gaze, I see the mirroring blackness of her sex hair, pressed flat against her slight pubic curve by the charcoal stricture of the pantyhose. She's not wearing panties, as is her want with sheer tights. She hates panty lines. Thanks to her fashion sense, I have a splendid view of her hairy sex. Contrasting the whiteness of her skin, her pubic hair is like a pool of ink begging to be blotted by my tongue.

I lap at her darkness. Her sex lips hide underneath the tights' reinforced crotch, but my tongue discovers the telltale swell of her labia and their sticky parting. I lick along the Wolfords' vertical seam, increasing my pressure with every stroke, burrowing the silky material's ridge into my boss's heated flesh. Through the fine Lycra mesh my saliva merges with her juices, swamping her thighs. She edges forward, pressing her marshy cunt into my face, squeezing her thighs against my ears, burrowing my nose into her pussy as far as the Lycra hymen will allow. The Wolfords stretch and strain, but the pantyhose are resilient. I can hardly breathe.

She continues her business call. The words are an indistinct blur to me as I gasp for cunt-tinged air, but her tone suggests an agreement has been reached. Her body confirms my suspicions. She softens her arched back. Her fist grips my hair. She pulls my head out of her crotch. My mouth drags over the sodden pantyhose. I hook a tooth on the mesh, tugging the nylon away from her flesh. I grind into the tensing fibers, renting the weave.

"Ciao," she says as she clicks off the call.

"Eat," she says, looking down at me.

I do. I am a ravenous creature. I tear through the pantyhose with my teeth, splitting the luxury hose along its seam. I refuse to use my hands to enlarge the opening, making wider gashes with pit bull shakes of my head. The nylon resists tearing, but ultimately my animal gnashing wins. The swell of her sex bursts through my incisions like an overripe fruit splitting its skin. Unhindered by the Wolfords, I bury my face into her naked cunt, feeling the damp tickle of her pubic thatch envelope me. I suck her unfettered scents into my lungs, but she gives me no time for a cunt connoisseur's lingering as she rocks in her chair, smacking her clitoris against my tongue. Each throbbing impact feeds the next as she batters my mouth with her mound. She is a nuclear bomb built of sexual energy. Clitoral mass has been reached. Frisson is underway. Her legs flail, her high heels prick my back, but I am resolute in my attention. I keep my tongue outstretched for her to find the release she craves. She shudders. She stiffens. Meltdown. I pass another of my work day's tests.

As quickly as it began, the frenzy subsides, and my boss regains control of her body. She anchors her legs over the chair's arms, using her hands to open wide a psychedelic cunt-melt of glistening pinks, carmine reds, and earthy browns amid the dripping canvas of her white skin and black bush. Now I can dally.

I spiral the tip of my tongue around her sensitized clitoris, coaxing the beating heart from its protective shroud. When her squirming hips tell me she can't take much more, I punctuate my clitoral attentions with sedate tongue baths of her labia, minor and major. I begin at the puckered darkness of her anus, probing the tightness with my tongue, clamping my lips French-kiss-like around her sphincter. After a thoroughly mushy ass-hole tonguing, I place my tongue flat against her perineum, lapping gently over the sensitive boundary between anus and cunt. I continue my cunnilingual odyssey by peeling apart her fleshy labial folds as I slide toward her belly. I skirt her vagina with a swirl, folding my tongue upward to once again attach to her clitoris. There I dawdle, dripping my cunt-tinged saliva down her mound, trickling the elixir between the pressed tight curve of her ass, soaking her expensive dress.

I glance at my boss as often as I can without being obvious. She is rapturous, her head sometimes bobbing forward to stare at my tongue having sex with her. At other times she's a lolling rag doll, her head hanging over the rear of the chair, her neck stretched tight, her Adam's apple bobbing as she moans rude words of encouragement. Flailing her hooked legs over the padded arms of her chair she swings to and fro, rocking her body on my tongue. I have no illusions as to my role. I am her dildo, and she's masturbating on my face, taking aggressive control of my ministrations. My nagging pleasure is of no concern to her, and truly, it matters little to me. I only want to please her, and in my enthusiasm I probe too hard. She reacts as if I'd shocked her with a stun gun. Her back arches, her legs stiffen. She grabs her ankles and stretches her pussy wide, as if she wants to split another orgasm from deep within herself.

I back away, offering temporary relief, but the thrust of her hips and the slap of her hand against the back of my head tells me not to relent. I resume licking her inner thighs, pulling farther asunder the torn Wolfords with my teeth. The more accessible her sex becomes, the more I play, making wavy designs in her sodden pubic hair. I travel from thigh to thigh, crossing over her erupting cunt with a swipe of my trawling tongue. Each traverse results in an increasingly violent pussy spasm, and soon the paroxysms are happening on their own, faster and faster, harder and harder, wetter and wetter. She's shaking, the tendons in her agape legs knotting as her body fights to hold itself together. I plunge my wide open mouth over her convulsing sex, clamping my lips over her labia. I suck her mound into my mouth, collapsing her pussy into a bubbling hotness that reminds me of a hot fudge sundae topped with a sweet, hard cherry. I try to tie the cherry's stem into a knot.

She explodes.

I sputter amid her juices. Her thrusting pelvis batters my face, but I hold on to her bucking body, grabbing her clenching bottom with my hands. Her legs clamp shut around my head, and I wonder if I should retreat, but I feel her hands on the back of my head grinding me into the vortex of her sex. My face is soaked, my lips bruised, my tongue sore. Her come washes over my face, the excess bubbling from my mouth, fountaining into my nose, dripping down my chin. I feel like I'm drowning in a vat of womanly juices.

Her gyrating subsides. Instead of pulling my face into her sex, she pushes, squeezing her thighs tight together. My head pops out from between her legs like a cork from a bottle of champagne. I collapse to the floor. Her high heels land next to my head. I kiss the pointed toes, conscious that I'm smearing the high-gloss polish with streaks of her come. I look up her towering legs, past her riven pantyhose, over her dripping cunt, skirting her rain forest of pubic hair to rest upon her eyes. She smiles.

"Get me a new dress. The short sleeveless Dolce and Gabbana black number will do. I have a meeting in fifteen minutes, then lunch with that brat from *Vogue*. During my meeting you can polish my shoes. Use the Versace. That's all it's good for now."

I search through her closet, through the bank of fine garments, presents from other envious designers. The velvet D&G feels like liquid. I hold it open for her and she steps into it.

"Zip me up," she commands, bending her head forward, holding the wispy curls of hair from her neck. I slowly snake the metal teeth together along the length of her spine, reluctant to hide her naked skin, but as she steps away from my touch I see that her beauty cannot be obscured, only amplified. She is spellbinding in the Dolce and Gabbana. It swirls out from her shoulders like a flowing cape. The hem hovers at mid-thigh. Mid-charcoal-Wolfords-with-the-crotch-eaten-out-pantyhose-covered-thigh. I'm so glad she didn't sheath her legs in a new pair of hose, but decided to wear my savaged nylons.

I gather the ruined Versace and kneel on my cushion underneath my boss's desk. She greets a peon from advertising and sits down in front of me. She crosses her legs, offering me a shoe. While she talks about the details of her latest media campaign, I polish the leather to a sparkle with the designer garment that cost more than a month of my salary. The peon has no idea that I'm there. My boss shows no sign of distraction from my ministrations as she juggles dollars and strategies. She angles her ankle upwards, presenting me with the high heel's sole. I kneel and kiss the barely scuffed leather, tracing the Via Spiga lettering. She doesn't wait for me to finish my tongue dance, uncrossing her leg to present the other shoe for polishing. I barely have time to plant the tiniest of kisses on the sole before she stands, almost stepping on my tongue as she dispatches the advertising rep to the bowels of the building.

She looks down at my prostrate body, my tongue still dangling across the plush carpeting of her penthouse office.

"I'll be at lunch for several hours. When I return I must dictate several urgent memos. Busy yourself until then."

She spins to leave. The D&G flutters upward and as she strides to the door I see the garden of her bush flowering from the torn pantyhose. I swoon, privy to a vision of perfect imperfection. Her beautifully wet pussy bursts from the devastation of ripped material. I am ecstatic to have created such a priceless work of sensual art, proud that my boss, one of the world's most famous fashion designers, would choose to wear my mouth's work to lunch.

In reverent celebration I dive into her executive chair, smothering my face in the cunt-tinged leather, wallowing in the aftermath of her presence. I spend the rest of lunchtime sniffing her seat, licking her secretions from between the leather grain, drying the wet spot with my hair, masturbating but not orgasming on her come-stained Versace dress that I used to polish her shoes, remembering the day when my life gained purpose.

It was a year ago when I saw the announcement of an opening for her personal assistant. I cried tears of unbelieving joy when I learned I had made it through the vetting process onto the short list. I shook when she ushered me into this penthouse suite for a final interview. I calmed immediately when she asked me her first question.

"Do you eat pussy?"

I had often felt unsure of my administrative skills, but I was a skilled cunnilinguist. I didn't hesitate.

"Yes."

"Show me."

I dropped to my knees, crawled to her chair, and secured the job three hours later. A year has gone by and I am content in my nine-to-five sex-slave role. I'm paid well for my time spent between her thighs, and I never have to worry about sexual harassment. I'm paid to lick my boss's pussy. I do no normal office work like phone calls or filing. The extra little things I do for her like polish her shoes and make her coffee I do out of a delirious desire to satisfy her every whim. I am her devoted fashion slave.

•

Yelled orders about an urgent FedEx package to the people who have to worry about the normal office routine tell me that my boss has returned from lunch. I scurry back under her desk. Skyscraper legs tower in front of me. A toe taps.

"Hungry?"

Yes, I nod.

She drops a bag at my nose.

"Warm this up and bring the contents to me. It's feeding time."

I scoot to the microwave and zap the cartons. "Not too hot," she commands. "I don't want you to burn my pussy."

I terminate the microwaving early, placing the heated containers on her desk. I sit on my cushion. She stands before me, legs planted wide apart. I follow her lean, tensed limbs along the shimmering outline of the Lycra pantyhose. She pulls the Dolce and Gabbana over her head and tosses it skyward. It flutters to the ground. She stands spectacular in the ripped tights, long legs shining, black bush sprouting out of the torn charcoal frame. She sits down, legs apart, bra-less breasts bobbing. She rolls her chair toward me. She reaches for the cartons, pops the lid, and sniffs inside.

"Melted brie smells so much like boy-come. Don't you think?"

She takes a scoop of the molten cheese and slathers it on her pussy, working the strands into her bushy nest. I lean forward, working my nose into the goo. She's right. The smell does resemble a man's orgasm. The lusty bouquet of melted brie and my boss's sex juices fuels an image of me eating a man's oozing come from her cunt. I eagerly nod my agreement with her observation, pulling a dollop of cheese and pubic hairs into my mouth.

"Tortellinis look like little pussies, don't they?"

She places a plump pasta between her labia. She's right again. It looks exactly like a small pussy. She smears melted brie over the tortellini.

"It's filled with salmon. Bite into it. It smells like pussy."

I split the tortellini. She's right again. Its scent blends with her own musk. I'm overcome by a sensual smorgasbord of tastes and smells. She laughs as I gobble at the morsel. She places her legs on the desk, opening wider my feeding trough.

"I had pussy-looking, pussy-tasting pasta in boy-come-sauce for lunch wearing cunt-ripped Wolford pantyhose, and the *Vogue* editor wondered why I didn't pay her any attention. I soaked the chair thinking of you eating your lunch from my platter. Heaven knows what drivel she'll print about me."

I swallow the salmon tortellini pussy soaked in melted brie boy-come, soaked in my boss's juices. She pops another pasta into her vagina, coating her labia in more melted brie.

I bite and slurp, working my tongue into the intricate ridges of the morsel. I lift the impaled pasta upwards, rubbing it over her brie-covered clitoris. The tortellini slips and slides around the reddened object, worked to and fro by my tongue. I curl my lips over my teeth and mush the pasta until it bursts, but I don't swallow, purposefully spilling its strong smelling contents across her sodden sex. She grabs a handful of tortellinis and rubs them onto her tits, anchoring the pasta to her hardened nipples. I reach upward as I eat my lunch from between her thighs, crushing the pasta between my fingers, pinching her nipples as the semolina disintegrates under my touch. But I don't stop. I work the pink salmon around the brownness of her attentive nipples, massaging the mess into her soft breast flesh.

I scoop the mashed tortellini from her breasts, sliding the squashed little pussies down her belly, over her slick mound, and into my open mouth. As I swallow I flick little bits of food from her clitoris, splattering the excess across her belly and onto her thighs. I smack her clitoris with my tongue as I dislodge a stubborn piece of congealed brie. She comes with a maenad violence, blowing a miasma of cheese, pasta, and come into my face as she arches her body from the chair. She pulls my head into her steaming opening and works me into her, grinding her cunt across the features of my face as if I were a food processor and she the contents.

She slumps into her soiled chair, her legs anchored to her desk, bits of food littering her body. I kneel on my cushion, licking my lunch from my lips, sputtering pubic hairs from my throat as she speaks.

"Clean up this mess while I take a shower. Afterward I'm going to dictate those memos, and by then it should be time for afternoon tea."

Ah, afternoon tea, my favorite part of the day. Creamy chai, finger sandwiches, chocolate eclairs, scones with clotted cream and strawberry jam, kiwi tarts, and grapes for palate cleansing. Then it'll be five and time for me to go home. There I'll wait for my wife to get home from her office. She'll fall into the room, tired from a long day, and ask me how my day was. Just fine, I'll say. The usual nine to five. She'll laugh. While I cook dinner, I'll run her a bath and give her an exquisite foot massage between stirring the piquant dishes she favors. After a relaxing meal we'll make slow love. I'll take my time releasing the sexual tension eight hours of subservient foreplay have conjured. Then we'll both fall asleep.

We both need our rest.

She's a famous fashion designer and has her empire to run.

And I have to be there by nine to make her coffee.

STUDENT BODY

KRISTINA WRIGHT

I looked at the door in front of me. It sported three stickers with the names of heavy-metal bands I vaguely recognized and a jockstrap hanging rather forlornly from the doorknob. It was, I decided, the low point in my life to be standing at that door.

The problem with returning to college at the age of forty is that everywhere I look, I see someone who could be my kid. This is not a good thing. I don't know when or how forty snuck up on me, but it did. I don't look forty, but, more important, I don't feel forty. It doesn't matter, though. I'm forty and that means half of the students on campus are young enough to be my children. Okay, maybe even more than half.

Being a graduate student only helps a little. True, a lot of people in graduate programs are older—there are even a few who are older than me—but with the new accelerated programs, there are plenty of kids in my classes. Kids who just started drinking legally and who think "I Love the 80s" is cool because it's so retro. Truth is, I don't usually mind being the oldest chick in the room. I get along better with people who are younger than me, but it's hard to keep up with the slang, never mind the technology, and sometimes I feel my age.

It was a computer project that was kicking my ass. I can write a twenty-page paper, no problem, but tell me to do something with a computer-based presentation and I'm like a deer in the headlights. My son, Charlie, is always after me to take a class at the local library, but I'm getting my M.A. in English, not engineering, so I figured I could muddle through with the basics of word processing. That was until I got an English professor who wanted us to "think outside the box" and create a multimedia presentation.

I got married young, while I was still an undergrad, and had Charlie right away. His dad took off when Charlie was four, so it had always been the two of us and I usually felt pretty young and cool, the ubiquitous single mother doing her thing. Now, facing the complications of computer software, I was definitely feeling my age. Unfortunately, Charlie was several thousand miles away doing a semester abroad in China, leaving me alone to figure things out on my own.

My professor, a woman who was probably five years younger than me, had given me the number of her teaching assistant. Matthew Wheaton apparently was not only an excellent English literature student but also a whiz with computers. He also sounded like he was twelve years old on the phone, which made me feel like an even bigger idiot.

So there I was, nervously knocking on the door of Matthew's off-campus apartment and vowing to take a computer class over the summer, when someone spoke behind me.

"Sorry, I ran out for some stuff and it took longer than I thought."

I jumped and spun, nearly stumbling. I recognized Matthew from around campus. He had the boyish good looks of a college nerd who didn't realize his charm. He wore battered jeans with rips at the knees and a T-shirt of one of the bands whose decals were plastered on the door. He smiled crookedly and my heart started hammering in my chest like that of some adolescent girl with a crush. I pulled myself together and tried to act my age.

"Hey," I said, sounding like a croaking frog.

"You're Andrea, right?"

"Oh, right. Sorry." Sweet, young Matthew had me stumbling over myself and we weren't even in his apartment yet. "Dr. Hanover said you'd be able to help me with this presentation."

He maneuvered past me and opened the door to his

apartment, tossing a wayward jockstrap inside. "My roommate's idea of a joke. Laundry day," he said, by way of an explanation. "Come on in."

I'd raised a teenage boy, so I was expecting the worst, but Matthew wasn't so bad. It was a small apartment, and, judging by the laundry basket by the door with women's underwear folded neatly on top, I assumed his roommate was a girl. The place smelled like pizza and pot and the furniture was old and worn, but for the most part it looked sanitary.

Matthew went into the kitchen, which was little more than an alcove with the basics, while I stood awkwardly by the door, waiting for him to put away his groceries. As with most college-age guys, his groceries consisted mainly of potato chips, sandwich stuff, and beer, with granola bars, a bottle of juice, and some fruit thrown in for good measure. He kept glancing up at me and smiling and I fidgeted nervously, contemplating taking an incomplete in the English class just so I could get out of there.

Matthew wadded up his shopping bags and shoved them into a paper bag by the refrigerator. When he bent over, I could see the white band of his underwear above his low-slung jeans. "Okay. Now we can get to work."

I looked around the apartment, spotting the television, stereo and gaming system, but not seeing a computer. "Um ... where?"

Carrying two beers, Matthew headed down the hall. "My room."

I'm glad he wasn't looking at me, because I was pretty sure my eyes were bugging out of my head. I had no idea what the hell was wrong with me. As I followed Matthew down the short hall, trying not to notice his cute butt, I chastised myself. I was old enough to be his mother, for heaven's sake! Somehow, whatever mechanism controls the libido wasn't buying the old-lady lecture. I felt young—and horny. I did some mental math and figured out it had been nine months since I'd gotten laid, so it was no wonder I was itching to get into Matthew's bedroom for more than just the necessary tutoring. But still, this was definitely the wrong place at the wrong time.

"Crash anywhere you want and I'll boot up my computer," Matthew said, dropping into his desk chair, which happened to be the only chair in the room.

I looked around nervously, but there was only one place for me to sit: the bed, the king-sized bed. I perched on the edge, nearly falling off in the process, more than a little conscious of the rumpled sheets beneath me and Matthew's wide shoulders in front of me. Granted, he was hunched over his computer and not flinging me down on the mattress, but I have a good imagination. Too good, maybe.

I fixated on the way his jeans rode down when he leaned forward, revealing the top of his underwear again. Something about that line of white above the faded blue of his jeans made me squirm in my own jeans. It was, quite possibly, the sexiest thing I'd seen in a very long time.

"So, where do we need to start?"

I was so lost in my fantasy of slowly stripping sweet Matthew and discovering whether his underwear were boxers or briefs that I hadn't really been listening. "Huh?"

He looked at me over his shoulder. "Where do you want me to start?"

I could think of a few places, but I refrained from offering those suggestions. "Well, I know how to use a mouse and I know how to turn on the monitor, but beyond word processing, I'm clueless."

Matthew made a little grunting noise and nodded. "Okay. Don't worry, I'll get you up to speed."

Over the course of the next two hours and four more beers between us, Matthew was true to his word. I not only learned how to put together a computer-based multimedia presentation, I got a pretty good start on my "Frankenstein: Monster or Man?" project. I also had a pretty good buzz. That's another thing about getting older: I couldn't hold my liquor anymore.

I giggled and didn't even care that it didn't sound very adult-like.

Matthew gave me a sidelong glance. "Um, you okay?"

"Sure? Why?" I giggled again.

He smiled. "'Cause you sound a little drunk."

Oops. I'd been caught. I felt warm, but I couldn't tell if I was blushing or if it was just the beer raising my temperature. "I don't usually drink that much."

"You only had three beers."

"Exactly," I said. In truth, I wasn't drunk. I knew exactly where I was and exactly who I was with. And exactly what I wanted to do with him. To him. "C'mere, Matthew."

He stared at me.

I patted the bed. His bed. "C'mon, I'm not drunk and I won't bite." I gave him my best come-hither glance, hoping it wasn't too dusty—from lack of use—to be effective.

Confusion turned to recognition. One minute Matthew was sitting at his desk and the next minute he was sitting next to me. "Okay, I'm here."

I smiled. Matthew smiled. I'd love to say it was the alcohol buzz that made me lean forward for a kiss from a man nearly half my age, but it wasn't. It was lust. His mouth tasted like beer, and mine probably did, too. His lips were warm and firm and however young he was, he definitely knew how to kiss.

At some point, Matthew decided I was wearing too many clothes and I felt him unbuttoning my shirt. I moaned when he fondled my tits, my nipples standing at attention and probably wondering what the hell was going on. He got my shirt off easily enough, but I had to help him with the bra. Apparently, he wasn't used to front clasps. I giggled and fell back on the bed, pulling him down with me.

"This is crazy," he mumbled as he kissed and nibbled his way down my neck and across my collarbone.

At least he hadn't said "weird." "Crazy good or crazy bad?" I whimpered when he latched onto one swollen nipple.

"Good," he said, his mouth full.

I was anxious to get things moving past second base, so I nudged his shoulder. "Hey, Matthew?"

He looked up, his eyes heavy-lidded with his own growing lust. "What? Did I do something wrong?"

Younger men are just so damned adorable. "No, I just wanted to know what kind of underwear you're wearing." To accentuate my point, I ran my finger along the elastic of his underwear.

He looked at me as if I'd asked him who his long-distance provider was. "Huh?"

"Boxers? Briefs? Oh, never mind, I'll find out for myself." I reached for the waistband of his jeans and got them unfastened. The rasp of the zipper made my clit tingle. "Oh," I sighed, tugging his jeans down his legs. "Boxer briefs."

Matthew raised his hips so I could get his jeans off and reached for the waistband of his underwear.

I put my hands over his. "Wait," I whispered.

"Why?"

I spoke to his impressive erection.

"Because I like your underwear."

Matthew's boxer briefs fit him like a second skin, hugging the bulge of his swollen cock. I licked my lips. I was looking forward to seeing him naked, but I was teasing myself—and him.

"You're driving me crazy," he whispered, reaching for me.

I pulled back. "Wait." With a few awkward moves, I got my jeans and panties off and stretched out on top of him. "Mmm, that feels nice." I wiggled on him, feeling the press of his cock between my legs.

"C'mon, baby," he said.

"Not yet." That's the thing about us older chicks, we know there's plenty of time to do everything we want to do. No need to rush. "Not just yet."

I kept rubbing against him. The friction of the cotton against my clit was nearly enough to make me come. I knew I was leaving a wet spot on his underwear, but I didn't care. I kept rubbing. He pressed his hips up to meet my downward movements, anchoring his hands on my hips as I undulated against him.

As if sensing my approaching orgasm, he started thrusting against me harder. I whimpered, burying my face in his neck as my orgasm slammed me. He kept sliding me up and down his crotch as I clung to him. I felt like I'd never stop coming and I ground myself against him, wanting something inside my throbbing cunt. Finally, my orgasm subsided and my breathing returned to normal.

"Wow," I said.

"Hell, yeah." He laughed.

I pulled away and leaned over his body, pressing my lips to his cloth-covered cock. His underwear tasted like me. His cock twitched against my mouth and seemed to swell even more, if that was possible. I traced the outline of his arousal with my tongue. Finally, I zeroed in on the head of his cock, sucking the engorged tip between my lips. He lay there, arms at his sides, eyes closed, content to let me have my way with him. I sucked him through his underwear until the cloth of his boxer briefs was soaked through and the white cotton clung to his cock.

Slowly, ever so slowly, I dragged his underwear down until his cock popped free. It was so hard and beautiful, I ached to feel it inside me. I hesitated.

Reading my mind, he pointed to the table beside the bed. "In the drawer."

I found a box of condoms and fumbled with one until I got it open. I rolled it over the tip of his cock and down the thick shaft. Lying there with his boxer briefs pushed down to just below his ass, his heavy cock resting against his thigh, Matthew looked at me and said one word: "Please."

I straddled his hips, guiding his thick cock inside me, inch by excruciating inch, until we were both panting with need. Finally, I slid all the way down on his erection and felt the slightest twinge of discomfort before raising myself up and sliding back down again. Up and down, I rode Matthew's cock until he couldn't take any more of my slow movements and quickened my pace with his hands on my hips.

"Oh god, fuck me," he groaned. And I did.

I arched my back, reaching behind me to twist my hands in his boxer briefs, which had slid down his thighs. He moved his hands inward across my hipbones, his thumbs settling on my swollen clit. With every downward thrust, he rewarded me by rubbing my clit until I was riding him as hard and fast as I needed to come again.

"Yeah, that's it," he gasped.

I started coming as he thrust up into me, a combination of his cock hitting my G spot just right and his thumbs working their magic on my clit. He threw his head back and moaned, the tendons in his neck bulging with his exertion as I rode his throbbing cock. He tried to hold me still but I kept grinding on him, milking every ounce of sensation from his cock.

Finally, I let him pull me down, my body as limp and damp as his. He stroked my back slowly, soothing me.

I kissed the pulse in his neck and sighed. "Thanks. You're a great tutor."

"You think?"

"Oh yeah," I nodded against his chest. "You can always tell a good teacher by his underwear."

SURPRISE PACKAGE

RADCLYFFE

Happy birthday to me!

Briefs. Boxers. Thongs. Jockstraps. Silk. Pro stretch. Cotton. Button fly. Y-fly. Pouch front. Mesh. Drawstring. Satin stretch. Trunk. Micro rib.

Who knew there would be so many colors and styles and fabric? My five-minute stop in the men's department had morphed into the better part of my lunch hour, and I still hadn't made a decision. I staggered from one rack to the next—fingering, fondling, everything but smelling—my mind filled with possibilities, all of them delicious. I caressed material, eyed flies and pouches, and visualized bulges and butts until my mouth was dry and my pussy was wet.

I imagined the curve of a thick cock tenting out the front of those black silk boxers, me on my knees, my lips wrapped ever so delicately around the fat head, sucking until I'd made a perfect wet O. *Oh, oh, oh … oh baby, come in my mouth.*

I admired the way the white cotton briefs bunched the payload into a tight fistful of promise I could jack off in my palm. I could almost feel the quivering abdomen beneath the wide elastic waistband, the trembling thighs encircled by the snug leg openings, the strangled grunts of pleasure, the hiss of breath before the big bang. *Go ahead, baby, come in my hand.*

Then there were the jockstraps. Could anything be sexier than a slash of white cutting across a firm, tanned thigh, unless it's the hard-on swinging in that arrowhead sheath? Let me *ride, baby, ride* till I burst.

Too bad I was likely to combust before I could make a purchase. My eyes blurred and my stomach did the little jiggly thing it does when I need to come. All the thinking about what I was thinking about was making my clit dance. I glanced at my watch. I was going to have to find a rest room so I could masturbate or I'd never be able to go back to work. No way could I sit for another four hours in court like this. Not and concentrate. Not without squirming.

"May I help you with something?"

I hated to disappoint Mr. Tall, Blond, and Handsome, but what was to help? I mean, I knew how everything worked. It's not like they were complicated enough to require instructions. You put them on, you pull them up, you settled the various and sundry equipment into the little extra spaces so cunningly built into the crotch, and *Presto! Ready for action.*

There was *one* thing though. It might be *my* present, but I didn't want to be entirely selfish about the whole deal. I kept my gaze carefully above shoulder level, not wanting any reason to speculate about just what version *he* was wearing under his casual gray trousers.

"Which ones make you feel the sexiest?"

He blinked, but his smile never faltered. "Well," he said with perfect salesperson cordiality, "I prefer boxers."

"Without getting X-rated, any particular reason why?"

"Freedom of movement and, ah, multiple avenues of easy access."

Oops. There I was on my knees again, only this time I saw myself peeling up the bottom edge of the leg opening so I could get my hand around a thick, stiff shaft. And of course, my mouth followed. I could feel it, hot and hard against the back of my throat.

"Gotcha." Back to the black silk boxers then. Or maybe the blue.

Yes. I smiled and reached for the royal blue. The blue was the exact color of her eyes.

Court ran late, and I never did get a chance to get off a quickie do-it-yourselfer. By the time I got home, barely five minutes before Jordan, and spread out my little birthday surprise on her pillow, I was ready to come just from the feel of the silk sliding between my fingers. *Just another few minutes*, I whispered to my screaming clit. I ran for the shower. Since she worked at home in the converted garage, her schedule never varied. Even when I'm hurrying, it takes me fifteen minutes, so I knew she'd be waiting.

When I came out, she was lounging on the side of the bed, shirtless, shoeless, wearing threadbare jeans, a big grin, and—as I ascertained in one quick glance—a nice fat hard-on. I glanced at the pillow and saw that it was bare. Thank god she knows her woman. "Hi, baby."

"Hey," she said, casually brushing one hand across the bulge in her crotch. "I thought you were the one supposed to be getting presents, seeing it's your birthday."

I smiled. "I'm going to. Starting right now."

She was leaning back just a little, an arm out to either side, her palms flat on the mattress. The position lifted her small, tight-nippled breasts into perfect kissing position, and seeing as how they were there, I dropped the towel I'd loosely tied around my chest and, naked, straddled her legs, my crotch a few millimeters above hers. Then I had only to dip my head in order to clamp my teeth around the taut pink nub. I worked it with my lips, my tongue, and my teeth until she was moaning and making quick jerking motions with her hips. Every time she did, her cock bumped my clit. I was dripping onto an ever-widening wet spot on the front of her jeans. I was already so ready that if I rubbed my clit over that denim-covered cock, I'd come until tomorrow. Oh, Jesus, how I needed to. But it wasn't denim I wanted to soak with my juices when I came, screaming, all over her. I let her tortured nipple pop from my lips and knelt on the floor between her hard, quivering thighs.

"Whatcha got for me in here, baby," I crooned, tugging down the top of her jeans with one hand and exposing the royal blue waistband where it cut across her belly. I slipped my fingertips underneath the edge of her boxers and swept back and forth over her belly, stroking silk above and below. She tensed and hissed, *Oh yeah*. I popped open the first few buttons on her fly and the ridge of her silk-covered cock sprang out. Her clit had to be as stiff as mine under that load. I laid my cheek on her boxers, right over her cock. "Where's my present, huh?"

"Keep digging, sexy," Jordan murmured, twisting a fist in my hair and bumping the corner of my mouth with her hard-on. "There's more than one in the package."

She wanted me to suck her. She likes to come like that, with me jerking her cock and her clit together while I blow her. But making her wait always makes me come harder, and I wanted to come so, so hard. I flicked open two more buttons so I could lick the length of her cock. I took my time, working the slippery material back and forth with my lips over the hard ridge and fat head, sliding the wet fabric up and down like a blue silk foreskin. I licked and sucked and bit until the blue was black with my saliva, her hand all the time clenching and unclenching against the back of my neck, her belly heaving.

"Suck it, honey, Jesus, suck it," Jordan groaned, pushing my head toward her cock. "Get me off, please get me off."

I teased the waistband down until just the head was bare, the rest of her cock still pinned to her stomach by the top of the boxers. Mouth open, eyes glazed, she stared at me as I fisted the shaft through her shorts and delicately tongued the tip. The sound she made, something between a whimper and a plea, shot to my cunt and it convulsed like it does right before I come. Shuddering, I clamped my free hand hard between my legs and squeezed until the orgasm backed off a breath.

"Get your jeans off," I ordered around a mouthful of her dick, "and get up on the bed. Hurry."

I gave her one last tug and leaned back enough for her to push her pants off and shove her body back up the bed. She knew better than to touch her boxers, and now her cock, freed from the tight jeans, sprang up beneath the bright silk. I clawed my way up on top of her and spun around until my cunt was over her face.

"Lick me," I ordered as I chewed on the soaked boxers stretched across her crotch. Her mouth closed around me, and I screamed into her cunt, "Suck it, goddamn it, suck it there, there, oh yeah, fuck ..."

My insides clenched, spurting juice in her face, and I shoved both hands up the leg holes of her shorts. Dimly I remembered Mr. TB and H saying, *easy access.* The harness straps framing her cunt were slick with her come. I fingered her open and mashed on the base of her clit so the tip would protrude, bare nerves crushed under the base of her cock. She pleaded some more, and I smiled and dug her cock out through the opening in her shorts. It stood straight up, with the blue silk gathered in folds around the base. Another series of quick clenches in my cunt and I couldn't hold back any more.

"I'm gonna come all over your cock, baby," I gasped, swiveling around until I crouched over her hips. "Hold it for me."

Groaning, her face glistening with my come, she fisted it, her fingers white against the royal blue ocean. Her eyes closed, and she sucked in a breath.

"Nuh-uh, no jerking off," I snapped as I saw her wrist vibrate.

"I gotta get off," Jordan pleaded, hips twisting. "Ten seconds. Just ten—"

"Not *yet.* Now hold still!" I lowered myself, an inch at a time, onto the length of her cock, my cunt more than wet enough to take her in. When I hit bottom she slid her hand off, but not before she twisted my clit a time or two. *"Bitch."* She laughed.

I was flying, and I knew she was, too. I reached behind me and squeezed a handful of silk and skin and leather and cock and jerked her hard and fast until her eyes went blank and I knew she was on the edge and then I stopped. *"I'll* tell you when you can come, and not before I ... uh ..." I was suddenly dizzy with how full she made me. "Oh *fuck,* I'm gonna come now. Fuck yeah, here I come."

I grabbed a fistful of her boxers on either side of her cock, twisting the waistband around my fingers like a horse's reins, and I rode her like she was my stallion. Head back, staring into her dazed face, I whipped my hips and pounded her cock, in and out, in and out. Her fingers dug into my ass, the muscles in her arms tight as ropes.

When I knew I was there and there was no stopping it, I slid all the way up her cock until the just the head was in, and then I yanked on her boxers so hard her hips jumped off the bed. Her cock slammed into my cunt and I came and came and came all over her cock and what was left of the royal-blue silk.

"Ohhh, man," she yelled, her legs jerking straight out, her belly heaving as she shot her load inside her shorts.

"Unh-hunh," I sighed, collapsing on top of her, sweaty and sticky and totally, wonderfully fucked. "Blue's such a great color on you."

"I think I heard them rip," Jordan muttered, her voice slurring as she dragged a hand lazily over my ass.

"S'okay. There's about a dozen other ones I wanna try."

Briefs, thongs, jockstraps, button fly, Y-fly ... oh yeah.

THE WASH LINE

LEW BULL

I remember as a young boy growing up in a typical suburban area how little there was to amuse ourselves with and how we had to create our own entertainment. Next door to us lived a family, the Fletchers, consisting of a husband and wife with six children of varying ages, which was considered to be large. There were four boys and two girls, who were the "babies," and although the family was not blessed with wealth, they were certainly blessed with beautiful children. There was no doubt the parents had beautiful genes to create such handsome and lovely children.

My bedroom window upstairs overlooked their back garden, which contained mainly a couple of trees, a table and four chairs, and a wash line. The trees obviously offered shade for the table and chairs, but it was the wash line that offered me interest. On washing day I would gaze down from my bedroom window on the line to admire the family's various underwear. Now I know that to most modern-day people this might sound like a very dull and unimaginative exercise, but to me, seeing people's underwear revealed a great deal about them. I saw it as being like their souls— what they wore under their outer clothing afforded an insight into their being.

The Fletchers did not reveal too much to me as a young boy. The men all wore similarly designed underwear, the type that is mass-produced and cheap—all white and cotton—while the females of the family did likewise, wearing all pale pink and silky-looking underthings; the only differences were the sizes. I wasn't much interested in the women's undies, but the men's meant a great deal to me. From the sizes I was able to determine which pairs belonged to which boys, and as I fantasized over Cliff, the second eldest, I was almost certain I knew which was his hanging on the wash line each week. I would watch the boys from my bedroom window playing in their backyard and imagine what Cliff was wearing under his rough fabric shorts and how his flaccid cock might be lying encased in the white cotton, and sit masturbating myself until I came into my own underwear and felt fulfilled.

One evening, I remember creeping through the dividing hedge between the Fletchers' property and our own and going quietly to their wash line and finding what I assumed was a pair of Cliff's underwear, taking them from the line, and stealthily heading home with my trophy. Many a day after that, whenever I saw the boys romping and wrestling with each other in the backyard, my hard-on would be pulled from its safe hideaway in my shorts and I'd fondle myself until I was ready to shoot my load and then come all over Cliff's white cotton briefs.

●

Twenty-five years later I found myself in a similar position, but in a more up-market area. I had moved out of home and had acquired a double-story house of my own. Next door to me lived a very friendly family, the Arnolds. The family consisted of a husband, wife, and three grown sons, whose ages ranged from nineteen to twenty-eight. All four men were what might be considered average-looking, but all had athletic builds. Although my master bedroom did not overlook their backyard, one of my spare bedrooms did, so I turned that room into my study, and from there I could work and watch the neighbors at play in the backyard, while their washing was hung out to dry.

Mike, the father, had once been a professional football player; Grant, his eldest, had the looks of a swimmer or track athlete; Chuck, the middle son, looked as if he might be following in Dad's footsteps as a college football star;

and Danny, the "baby," although physically well built, didn't seem to involve himself in athletic activities like his brothers.

The first occasion after they moved in that was a wash day, I took the liberty to do some "soul-searching" by going to the upstairs study and surveying the wash line to see their underwear. This, I believed, would provide me with some revelations about their characters and personalities. Why would they choose the underwear that they wore? Was it monochromatic or not? Would it be tight-fitting or loose, allowing for more penile freedom? Knowing the physical build of the four men, the apparent size of their underwear might possibly give me some idea as to the size of their packages. Of course, I was very aware that this was all purely theoretical and that in my imagination what might have been regarded as a barge pole might in fact be merely a twig.

From the open window I saw the wife come out into the backyard carrying the laundry basket and proceed to hang the washing on the wash line. I wasn't really interested in the shirts and skirts, but then I saw her take some of the men's underwear from the basket and hang it on the line.

Two pairs of red briefs were the first to make their appearance, and I immediately wondered whether the saying "red car, small dick" might also apply to the owner of the red briefs. These were followed by three pairs of white briefs, which looked ordinary until I noticed that the material was diaphanous. Surely they must belong to the wife, but the more I surveyed them, the more I realized that these belonged to a man. I wondered if perhaps they belonged to Danny, he being the least athletic of the four men, but then I ridiculed myself for adopting such a stereotypical outlook. However, the more I looked at them, the more I began to imagine Danny's cock, cut or uncut, I did not know, lying heavily within the soft material and being able to see its shape and color through the fabric.

I felt a twinge of movement within my own briefs as

I closed my eyes and visualized Danny standing naked, except for his sheer briefs. By the time I reopened my eyes, I had a full hard-on and rubbed my hand across the swollen bulge in my jeans. When I refocused on the wash line, the wife was nowhere to be seen, but the line now had three jockstraps and a couple of pairs of floral-print boxer shorts. I noticed how the sight of the boxer shorts became a turn-off and my rock-hard cock was in the process of deflating. Maybe Dad wore the boxers, I thought, as a sign of having passed his prime and, being in no need to hold that mature cock in place, instead let it hang loose. Common sense told me that Chuck was probably the owner of the jockstraps because of his football prowess, but again, was I thinking in stereotypes? Even if I was, I had decided within my own mind that they belonged to Chuck.

I once more closed my eyes and visualized the muscular Chuck now standing before me only in his bulging jockstrap, which was stretched to its extreme as it fought to retain the massive man-meat that lay inside. Again my cock hardened, but this time I unzipped my jeans, shucked them to the floor, and ran my hand over the extended front of my briefs, feeling a wet patch where my precome had leaked. I squeezed my engorged cock as I imagined Chuck doing it to me. I visualized taking hold of his jocks and pulling them down, releasing his throbbing cock, waiting to receive tender attention. I was deep in wonderland when a noise outside brought my thoughts rushing back to reality. I opened my eyes and looked out of the window to see what had distracted my pleasurable dream. There in the garden, standing next to the wash line was Mike, looking up at me in the window. He stood smiling at me while I stood looking blankly at him, fondling my hard-on. I suddenly realized what I was doing: *Could he, and did he, see me fondling myself?* I wondered.

"Can I come over?" shouted Mike.

I stammered some reply as I fumbled to pull up my jeans, and then fled the room heading downstairs. When I reached downstairs, I heard a slight knock on the back door. I checked myself and tried to rearrange my still swollen cock before opening the door.

"Hi there," came the cheery voice of the visitor. He stretched out a hand to shake mine. "Mike's the name, neighbor."

"Oh, hi, I'm Gary," I stammered.

"I saw you at the window as though in a deep euphoric trance, so I thought I'd come over and introduce myself."

"Oh please, you must think me rude. Please come in."

Mike entered and I closed the door behind him.

"I couldn't help noticing how physically well built you looked at the window, and now that I'm close up I can see that I was right," said Mike with a broad smile, revealing the most perfect set of teeth.

Immediately I looked down and noticed that my hard-on was still evident and wondered whether Mike was referring, albeit subtly, to this.

"You must have quite a view from that room of yours."

"Oh, yes," I said, rather startled. "I mean, not really; it merely overlooks your backyard, but I don't mean that you've got a unsightly backyard."

I knew that Mike could sense my embarrassment.

"I wouldn't mind having a view of my own backyard. Do you mind if we go up and take a look?"

"Of course not," I replied, leading the way upstairs.

When we reached the open window, Mike peered out at the wash line with its collection of clothing.

"Not a very good sight," said Mike leaning out of the window. "Only my underwear."

I moved closer to him in the window and was tempted to ask which was his.

"Oh, I don't mind the view," I replied, making it sound like some lame excuse.

I sensed a warmth emanating from Mike's proximity to me when suddenly I felt a muscular arm wrap around my waist as Mike pulled me closer toward him.

"I didn't think you minded the view considering this," answered Mike, sliding his hand onto my crotch and giving my cock a squeeze.

I didn't know how to respond. The feeling was exciting, yet at the same time I wasn't sure what his intentions were.

"Does seeing those jocks and briefs turn you on?" inquired Mike, whispering closely to my face.

I could feel his warm breath on my face and at the same time could feel my throbbing cock straining to break free. I really had no idea how to respond to his question. My head was saying "Deny it," but my cock was saying "Yes, yes, yes!"

I know he knew the truth because he pushed me away from the window and into the center of the room, pulled a chair from my desk, and commanded me to sit. I did as I was told and could feel my hard-on pushing awkwardly against my jeans.

Mike stood in front of me, his muscular legs astride mine, and slowly, seductively began to pull down the running shorts that he was wearing. As his shorts revealed more of his body, my greatest fantasy was realized. I saw the coarse white material of his bulging jockstrap. My eyes must have revealed my pleasurable sight because Mike smiled at me and said, "Do you like what you see?"

For the first time I was able to speak. "Yes," came the faint reply.

Mike stepped closer to me and thrust his quickly engorging encased crotch in my face. I could smell the sweet mixture of sweat and stale piss. I inhaled deeply, feeling his hardening cock rub up against my lips and nose. By now I couldn't contain myself. My hands took a firm grip on his solid ass and pulled him closer to me while my tongue licked over the coarse material. Mike held my head as he rubbed his hard-on across my mouth. I remember groaning as he did so, then he pushed my head down so that my nose and mouth were between his legs and the strong musky manliness that I smelt forced my tongue to head for his pucker. As I lathered between his legs I could feel my own cock throbbing and dribbling precome.

Heavy sighs and gasps emanated from Mike as he began face-fucking me, the coarse material of his jock rubbing roughly across my face, the front of it now soaked in spit and precome as my tongue and mouth traveled along the length of his now fully enlarged cock. So distended was his cock that the tip of a cleanly clipped mushroom-shaped head appeared above his jock waistband. The tip of my tongue found the slit opening at the tip of his cock and I gently inserted the tip of my tongue and flicked it. His groans became more incessant the farther I tried to insert my tongue into his piss slit, and his thrusts became more frenetic as his buildup to his climax neared.

"I'm gonna come," he gasped, firing a heavy load that seemed to shoot from the base of his balls up over my face and fall over the waistband of his jock, soaking into the coarse material. He continued to thrust against my face, smearing his warm come over my cheeks, nose, and mouth. When he had depleted himself, he leaned forward and kissed the top of my head. "Thanks, neighbor," he whispered, then he lifted my head so that I looked into his sweating, smiling face; only then did I release my grip on his firm ass and run a finger along the length of his still throbbing cock.

"But what about you, Gary?" asked Mike. "Don't you want to come?"

I smiled back at him and replied, "Feel between my legs and you'll see how wet I am."

He did as I said and smiled, realizing that I, too, had shot my load into my briefs. Before he had a chance to pull on his running shorts, I stood up from the chair and said, "I think those jocks will need a good washing now, don't you?"

He laughed and said he'd throw them in the wash basket for the next wash day.

"But then your wife will see the evidence," I remarked. "I think it would be better if you took them off and I'll wash them, then when they're clean you can pop around and get them."

"I think I like that idea," he replied with a knowing glint in his eye. Mike handed his sweaty jocks to me and pulled on his running shorts. I held the rough material to my nose and inhaled deeply, taking in as much of Mike's muskiness as I could gather from the wet jocks.

As Mike made his way to the front door, I stopped him and said, "I have to know whose white translucent briefs those are hanging on the line."

Mike smiled broadly at Gary and asked, "Why?"

"I think they're sexy and I could just visualize its owner's well-hung crotch being supported in that see-through material and me getting hard just from looking at it."

"Well maybe I'll bring him round next time I visit."

"Who?"

"Let's just say that Chuck and I share a lot of things, and I don't mean just underwear!"

DESIGNER FANTASIES

MINAROSE

"I had some major inspiration today, Baby!"

Charlie had barely set her keys on the entryway table when her lover made this announcement. She bent to take off her shoes, leaning against the wall. "Oh, yeah?" she shouted, to be heard over the thrum of the sewing machine. One boot unlaced, and the sewing stopped. "Should I be excited?"

"You should be on the edge of your seat." Lacey's voice was muffled as she closed a door. Charlie finished the other shoe and set them both on the rack. She walked around the corner into the living room, taking in the closed sewing-room door and smiling to herself. She loved Lacey's little fashion shows. Her lover worked in fits and starts, some days designing a whole line of lingerie, some days sitting on the couch watching cheesy soap operas and munching rice cakes. These days were her favorites—the inspired ones. The ones that ended with her coming home to the fruits of Lacey's labor barely covering her body as she proudly displayed her work.

Charlie plunked down on the couch facing the TV, her back to the sewing room, and waited. The anticipation was part of the fun. All day she thought of Lacey at home, a pencil between her luscious lips, working on her designs. All day she writhed in her seat, turned on by the thought of Lacey piecing together tiny bits of satin and silk with the same nimble fingers she used to caress Charlie's body.

Charlie was brushing her nipples lightly through the gossamer material of her shirt when she heard the door open behind her. She didn't turn around. She knew that would cheapen the thrill she always got when Lacey strutted into her peripheral view. The wait was always worth it.

This time was no exception.

Lacey eased around the side of the couch like something liquid. The teddy she wore looked like a breathtaking waterfall that had suddenly turned into fabric. A shimmery sheer fabric was all that stood between Charlie and the sweet curves of Lacey's body. The rippling spaghetti straps crisscrossed over her cleavage and wound around to elaborately decorate her otherwise bare back. The body of the teddy was sparse and placed just-so in order to draw the eye around the wearer's body in undulating waves. As Lacey did that sexy catwalk turn in front of her she was astonished by the pure ingenuity of the little teddy. It really did look as if her lover's body were being clothed by a stream that lived and breathed just to be near her skin. To top it all off the outfit was completed by a piece Lacey had made for her hair. The same twisting shimmer of water incarnate fell through her curls and cascaded over her shoulders.

Charlie gazed at Lacey, jealous of the girl's talent, but even more jealous of the fabric that lightly caressed her skin. She envisioned herself as that little teddy, gliding bodily along the length of Lacey, touching her in places that would make her shiver. Charlie realized that she had closed her eyes to enjoy the thought rolling around in her head. When she opened them Lacey was inches from her face. "I hope you're thinking wicked little thoughts in there," she whispered. "There is more yet to come." And with that she turned around and flowed from the room.

Charlie laid her head back on the sofa cushions and got herself a little more comfortable. She sighed as she let that little teddy fantasy roll around in her head. She slipped a hand between her legs and began to run one finger along the moist crotch of her panties. She relished the image of being a piece of gossamer fabric twisting her way along the length of her lover and finally coming to rest in the warm center of her body. She would be a naughty little piece of fabric that would slip and slide along Lacey's sweet nether lips all day, making her so horny she would finger herself wildly while still sitting at the sewing machine. The thought made her even wetter as she continued to rub her fingers along her own pussy.

The door opened behind her and she sat up a little straighter. She didn't hide the fact that she had been playing with herself; Lacey knew these little shows made her hot, but she did move her hand to her thigh, giving the next piece the attention it deserved.

Completely the opposite of her first creation, the red patent leather that now adorned Lacey's body took her breath away. An intricate corset took in her already slim waist by at least three extra inches, making the offering of her breasts that much more impressive. The leather cupped her to just above her nipples, hiding those sensitive buttons rather deviously from sight. Little glimpses of her pale flesh showed the length of her torso where the corset had been laced up the front and back with wide black ribbons. A closer look at the leather revealed that it had been painstakingly topstitched with black thread. The black touches were obviously meant to help the corset go with the other pieces in the set: the black patent leather thong panties and the matching choker that laced up along the back of her neck. She looked like a submissive's wet dream come to life. Without a word Lacey turned on her red patent leather stiletto heels and sashayed back to the sewing room.

Charlie sat on the sofa blinking. Her teddy fantasy had quickly turned into a leather one, as she saw herself gleaming and red, hugging Lacey's body fiercely with her own. She would be a harsh corset, one that would not tolerate even an inch of give. She would bind Lacey's waist to its smallest measure and force her back ramrod straight. She would pinch Lacey's nipples relentlessly as she lifted her breasts, showing them off as they deserved. Lacey would squirm as her black Charlie thong put irresistible pressure on her clit, making her moist and ready for the games she had dressed for.

Charlie tugged her panties to the side and inserted a single finger into her vagina. The thought of being Lacey's underwear always got her so hot and bothered. Underwear is able to touch women in ways that even lovers can't. To be able to place her whole being against her lover in that intimate a fashion had always been one of Charlie's deepest desires. She worked another finger into herself as her fantasy played inside her head. She brought her other hand slowly up beneath her blouse to tease her nipples through the thin material of her bra. She was moaning softly as the sewing room door opened a third time.

"I see you've been waiting for me," Lacey purred as she came into view. This was definitely one of the most unique sets of lingerie she had ever designed. Charlie didn't even pause in her masturbation as she looked her lover up and down. Lacey looked as though she had stepped out of a pornographic video game.

Her hair was combed into a high, tight ponytail, the kind usually reserved for strippers. She wore a very tight white tank top made of material so thin Charlie could see the stiff dark points of her nipples. The neck and waistlines were adorned with the tiniest lace she had ever seen, just enough to make it look tantalizingly feminine. Below that, a pair of black stretch velvet boy shorts played along Lacey's hips, covering her just barely in the front and creeping up the crack of her ass in the back. What was possibly the greatest element of the set were two matching black velvet gun holsters that strapped to each thigh. A bottle of flavored lubricant rested in the left holster, and the head of a frosted white glass dildo peeked from the top of the right holster. A pair of white combat boots was the icing on this particular cake.

"You've outdone yourself, my darling," Charlie whispered hoarsely, watching Lacey turn before her. She spread her legs and moved her fingers to her clit, rubbing the aching little button furiously. Lacey knelt between her knees.

"You ain't seen nothin' yet." Lacey grinned as she took the dildo from its holster and twirled it in her fingers like a Wild West gunslinger. She managed to continue twirling the dildo obscenely as she pulled the lube from its holster and flipped the cap. She spread the thick, strawberry-scented liquid along the length of the glass penis with slow teasing strokes of her hand.

Without preamble, she plunged the dildo into Charlie's dripping pussy, shoving it in to its base. With a practiced and excruciating slowness, Lacey began to slip the dildo out of her lover's vagina, never taking her eyes from Charlie's. She loved the way Charlie arched herself toward the dildo, trying to keep it inside her as long as possible. When it was free she brought the rod to her lips and began to lick her lover's juices from it. "Mmmmmm ...you taste good. Like strawberry wine," she purred, lowering her head. "I want some more."

Lacey placed her tongue at the base of Charlie's vagina and licked upward along her slit, barely brushing her. Charlie moaned and pressed her hips forward. She reached out and teased Lacey's nipple through the thin material of her camisole, loving the feeling of the soft cloth covering her lover.

As Lacey's tongue neared Charlie's fingers on her clit, she started over, this time pressing only slightly harder, barely pushing the tip of her tongue between Charlie's pussy lips. Each time she started over she pushed her tongue only a little farther, drawing the pleasure out maddeningly. Finally Charlie grabbed her by that high, tight ponytail and pulled her head back to face her.

"You are driving me crazy!" She gasped. "Get up here."

Lacey climbed onto the couch and assumed an all-fours position off to Charlie's side with her knees close to her hands. This time when she lowered her head, she took her lover's clit into her mouth and sucked on it until a scream came from Charlie's throat. She re-placed the dildo deeply inside Charlie, working it in and out as she continued to suck her off.

Charlie's hand finally found its way to the crotch of Lacey's boy shorts. The velvet was soaked as she stroked her fingers along it. She got impossibly wetter as she manipulated Lacey's clit through the panties. She twirled her fingers through the crushed material and worked her hand back and forth cupping Lacey like a second pair of underwear. She began to apply a firm pressure against Lacey's whole vagina, working her hand so she pushed her lips together in a pulsing rhythm, squeezing even more moisture into the velvet.

The dildo between her legs, the steady sucking on her clit, and the spill of Lacey's own orgasm drove her over the edge. She bucked on the couch, moaning and writhing as Lacey continued to lick her pussy. When the first orgasm had almost ended she was thrown into another one as her lover pushed the dildo even deeper inside her.

Lacey's second orgasm came when Charlie finally pushed aside the material of her boy shorts and plunged three fingers into her. They rode wave after wave of ecstasy together until they both lay spent, tangled in each other's underwear in a sixty-nine position.

Charlie sighed as Lacey moved off her and onto the floor by her head. They kissed fervently, tasting their own passion on each other's lips. Lacey pulled back from the kiss and wiggled her eyebrows, grinning. "You wanna see the fourth piece of lingerie I designed today?"

THONG APPEAL

PAUL CHAMBERS

I never imagined that I'd have much of anything in common with Bill Clinton, aside from our both being Democrats, until a girl snapped her thong at me and had my cock rock-hard within seconds. But before I tell you about the thong, let me tell you about the girl—and about me. I'm thirty-nine, though I like to say I'm thirty-five, and I usually get away with it. I'm a high-level studio executive, reading and greenlighting scripts, dealing with directors and producers, and generally ensuring that my films get made without a hitch. Needless to say, hot girls are a dime a dozen around here; whether bottled or natural, I've got blondes in and out all day, every day, with the occasional stunning brunette thrown in. Almost all look like they came from some sort of model factory—thin, stick-straight hair to match their bodies, gleaming white teeth and smiles that don't quite reach their eyes. I've learned through experience that most of them look at me as a rung on their ladder up toward the top, and aren't that interested in the details. They wear either raised platforms or imposing heels, jeans, and tank tops that look casually simple, yet run several times a day's pay.

But back to this girl. Like Monica Lewinsky, nobody was going to mistake her for a model—and that's a compliment. She did, however, stand out, not just with her looks, but with her smile. I could tell as soon as she came in to read for the role of the slutty teenage daughter that there was something different about her—either she'd just arrived in L.A. or possessed some kind of special resistance, like immunity, to the pressures of the job. Not only didn't she look like all the others, she didn't act like them. She had tumbling curls of red hair that spilled down her back. She tried to keep them back with a barrette, but they weren't having it. They were wild and unruly, just like her. She was chewing gum, loudly, smacking it as if to say, "I don't need you or your puny job," even though gum wasn't mentioned anywhere in the script. And her outfit—she was wearing a tight, cheap tank top, white, and I could clearly see her sheer white bra, and therefore, her big, round nipples, beneath it. Her jeans were made of dark denim and cut very low on her small hips. She had high platform flip-flops, the kind with flowers on them, the kind trying to distance themselves from their origins as things to be worn to the beach and then tossed aside. Her platforms made her tower over most of the other girls, and that, along with the half snarl on her face, made her imposing yet enticing. But the real pièce de résistance was her thong. It was fluorescent pink, not just hot pink, but that special Day-Glo color that peaked around 1984. She had the bratty teen look and act down pat, but there was something more going on; I could tell she wasn't just playing a role. She really was bratty and just waiting for the right guy to snap her thong and put her in her place. We had to keep seeing people about the part, but I offered her a job helping out as an assistant, a job we'd been looking to fill, but mostly because I wanted to continue checking her out. With her same blasé attitude, she accepted. "I guess I could come in tomorrow, but don't expect me to be on time." From anyone else, that attitude would've gotten their offer rescinded, but from her, it made me want to bend her over my desk and spank her silly. She seemed to know it, too, winking at me on her way out.

She wore the thong strategically, so that even if she wasn't bending over I could still see it peeking over the edges of her pants. Even just the teeniest glimpse of its piercingly bright fabric made me think about the rest of it— the way it nestled snugly in her ass crack, the tiny triangle covering and clinging to her pussy lips, the straps expertly curving around her hips. Somehow, the thong is the perfect embodiment of the phrase "less is more." It shows that the girl wears underwear, but suggests that she longs to take it off. Certainly, from the minute I saw this girl, before I even knew her name or anything about her, I wanted to see her ass bared in only that thong. I wanted to bring her thongs to try on, I wanted to watch her work a stripper pole, thumbs snagged around the edges of that thong. I wanted to watch her put it on and take it off, wanted to trace my tongue along the skinny line as it wedged itself into her ass crack. Mostly, I wanted to get to know a girl who flaunted her thong so boldly, who dared everyone in the office to look at her and get a hard-on before she walked away with her nose in the air.

Finally, one day I summoned her into my office. "I think it's time I laid down the rules for you. I'm Jack, if you didn't know, and I'm in charge around here."

Not exactly the smoothest opening line, but it was something. "I'm Jill, isn't that funny?" she said, her laugh more knowing than amused. I already knew that, and had thought of the joke myself, but I smirked nonetheless. Once again, she was wearing a hot-pink thong that peeked out of her camouflage-green cargo pants and tiny white tank top, no bra. A thong but no bra? Interesting. She thrust her hip out at me, as if offering me the tiny piece of string. I tried not to look as I pointed to the chair.

"Would you please take a seat?" She stared back at me for a moment, as if contemplating my question, debating, deciding first whether she would sit or not, and then, as she eased that perfectly pert ass into the chair I indicated, whether she might not try to sit in mine instead. "Now, you may or may not be aware of it, but we do have a dress code in this office," I said, trying to sound serious even as my cock throbbed in my lap. That was true enough, but we usually waited until a complaint was voiced before giving an employee a verbal warning. I rustled some papers, reading from the skimpy legalese: "Employees may not wear any clothing that reveals anything of a revealing, sexually provocative nature."

She opened her mouth to protest, but I kept right on going. "I realize this standard is different for everyone, but I must tell you, to put it bluntly, we've all noticed your thongs." I paused, not sure how far I could actually go with her. "Some of us more than others."

She stared back at me, and this is when I really knew she was different from the other girls. "But what if I wanted you to notice? Well, not all of you, necessarily, but some of you?"

"Well, I can't say I'd be surprised," I replied, my cock stiffening even more as I wondered just what I'd have to do to see her in a thong and nothing else. Jill leaned forward across my desk, her blue eyes intent on mine, her pushed-together breasts bulging forward from her top. "Can we make a deal? I won't let anyone here see my thong, if you let me show it to you tonight. At your place. Just the two of us. I promise, you'll like it," she said, moving back to her seat and slyly reaching behind her to pull up her pants. I pictured the thong covering only the tiniest parts of her, leaving the rest of her luscious ass to press against her pants, pictured easing them over her hips and unveiling what had to be the most gorgeous set of butt cheeks in this city. I was fixated on seeing her ass, on tasting and touching and cupping her globes.

I didn't want to come across as that easy, knowing she'd just played me like a fiddle, but I couldn't have said no if my job depended on it. All that seemed to matter anymore were Jill and her thong. I agreed and gave her my address.

That night, like the girliest of girls, I agonized over what to wear. Maybe I'd imagined the entire innuendo, and she was going to bring an extra thong, hold it up for me, and leave. Maybe she was just a flirt, a con artist, a daredevil. But then I remembered the way she'd swung her hips on her way out the door, her hand idly reaching behind her to toy with the blue strap that worked its way over her hip. I chose a white button-down shirt, a blue sweater on top, and dark jeans. When she arrived, I realized it wouldn't have mattered what I wore—she wanted me. She sashayed out of her car and the first thing I saw, before the cascades of red hair and curvy breasts, was indeed a thong, this time in electric green, practically glowing as she scampered toward me on tall silver heels, the kind that were impractical for anything besides drawing the eye toward her perfect arches and calves, encased in delicately designed fishnets. Her skirt fell low on her hips, as if just there as a prop for her thong. In fact, her whole body seemed like little more than a prop for her thong, for her perfect, devilish ass, which I couldn't wait to get my hands—and cock—on. I opened the door and ushered her inside without a hug, even though I wanted to slam her back against it and pin her there—make her writhe.

Instead, I settled onto the couch with her with drinks—a Manhattan for me, a vodka tonic for her—while she told me about how she'd moved to L.A. last year and worked lots of odd jobs. "I even worked at a strip club for a while, which is where I really learned the power of a good thong. My favorite trick would be to wear two, black on top and some bright color underneath, then tease the guys by tugging down on one to reveal a glimpse of the other. I loved bending over so they could see my ass, with just that little piece of fabric separating me from them." As she talked, her hand slid down the expanse of bare skin along her hip, gently pushing downward. My gaze followed her movement, and she noticed me looking at her. "I could show you if you want," she said, before taking my glass from my hand and setting it down on the table behind her. Then she pushed me back into place, my arms at my sides, my legs slightly spread, as she began to dance. There wasn't any music playing, but Jill didn't need it; she was dancing to her own beat as she slithered between my legs, her body pressing up against me one moment, then stepping away the next. My cock was pressing forward urgently against my jeans, and she ran her knee lightly between my legs, letting me know she could feel it. My eyes gobbled up her every practiced move, my mouth salivating over being so near and yet so far.

She straddled my thigh, grinding down against me so I could feel the heat from between her legs as she leaned backward, clutching onto me as her sheath of red hair dangled behind her, her neck upturned. She took my hands and put them on her hips, and my thumbs automatically hooked into her thong, tugging upward, knowing she could feel the press of fabric against her pussy lips.

"Yes," she hissed, ceding control as I pushed her pants down enough to see the thong as it covered her precious lips. But I'd fantasized about her ass so much that I needed to see that, too. I turned her over, and her behind looked just like I'd expected, two taut, tight, firm cheeks bisected by a tiny string of green. What I couldn't see was more alluring than what I could, and I pulled apart her cheeks, holding her open as the thong slid in deeper.

"Where do you want my hard cock, Jill? In your ass or your pussy?" I asked, my voice low and husky. As I spoke, I let go of her ass and undid my pants, pushing my own underwear down to let my stiffness brush against her. I held my cock in my hand, rubbing the head along her cheeks, lightly brushing her with my precome. I held my shaft in her ass crack, letting her feel my firmness, while my fingers continued to stroke her thong-covered slit. I played with her clit beneath the green fabric until she unraveled beneath me.

"There, there, fuck my pussy," she said, her breath practically gone as I finally, at last, peeled her thong down, leaving it clinging to her thighs as I slid a condom out of my pants pocket, hurriedly rolled it on, and then shoved my cock deep inside her. I lay down on top of Jill, pinning her to the couch with my weight, as I finally did what I'd wanted to do every time I saw her. I realized at that moment it didn't matter what she wore or didn't wear, it was the promise her outfits offered, the tease, and her thong was just the bait.

"You're so tight, Jill," I said as I reveled in her vise-like grip as I thrust my hips back and forth. Finally I got impatient and pulled the thong off, keeping it clenched in my hand as her legs spread just enough to let me sink between them. I sat up a little and watched my cock as it entered her, then emerged slick with her juices. Once again, I held apart her ass cheeks, her tiny pink pucker winking back at me. "You knew exactly what you were doing from day one, didn't you? You knew you had my cock at the ready with just that little peek at your panties, didn't you?" I growled as I slammed into her, making her growl in response.

"I know you like to be teased," she said in between gasps. "You like what it seems like you can't have, and I knew that thong was the way to lure you in. I was right, wasn't I? You were the only reason I wanted to stay at that job anyway," she said as she tightened around me, her hand dipping under us to flick at her clit until she came, spasming beneath me. That was all it took for me to spurt my load deep inside her.

We lay there together, recovering, until she finally stood up, rooting around for her clothes. I figured she'd just forgo the thong for the drive home, but instead, she took it from me and slipped it back on. "The better to remember you by," she said, giving me a lusty kiss before heading out the door, leaving me stunned by the intensity of our encounter. I'd expected sex with Jill to be fast and furious, but hadn't known just how wild it would be. In case you're wondering, she got the part, and I had the writers add a line stating that she had to wear a thong in every scene. They didn't ask why, and I didn't care what they thought. Seeing her prance around with just the hint of a thong was enough to make my workday speed by. Jill even managed to incorporate it into her part, toying with the edge or subtly moving her hip to highlight the thong. She wound up stealing the show, and I'm hoping to get to work with her again. In the meantime, she's been giving me private thong viewings every night, and I'm more than happy to keep her supply of G-strings well stocked. She's my one and only thong babe, and I intend to keep her around as long as she'll have me.

THE BANANA DASH

T. HITMAN

The irony of it was, Caffrey had undressed Kevin Lyons and Jason Starkman repeatedly—in his mind, of course, and not only down to their banana holders. A self-confessed crotch watcher for as long as he could remember, Garret Caffrey knew that Kevin, the lead stud at the company, hung to the left in his dress slacks. Jason, Kevin's best buddy and a perfect source of masturbational material in his own right, dangled straight at the center, and often Caffrey fantasized about sucking on his cock, his mouth speared like the center dot on a bull's-eye.

Caffrey narrowed his gaze on the advertisement, a sheet of white paper with a crime-scene burst of blood-red color.

"You in?" asked Kevin. The question was more of a demand, said in that musical growl that, for reasons that made no sense and complete sense, hypnotized Caffrey whenever the late-twenties former college jock with the brush cut spoke to him.

Before he could stop himself, just like that, Caffrey committed. "Yes," he said too quickly.

"Awesome. So's Jason. The more the merrier. It's for a great cause."

Caffrey watched as Kevin released the single sheet of paper. It floated to the top of his desk. Caffrey read: THE BANANA DASH. Caffrey's eyes zeroed in on a cartoon of a man, naked except for sneakers and a pair of Speedos, the upside-down triangle of bright red color covering his cartoon gonads. The man was depicted shivering. The total lack of congruity in that patch of red pretty much summed things up: when you jogged through the Boston Common during the holiday season for charity, good cause or not, what you ended up with was shrinkage of the worst kind.

"This is perfect. Me, you, Jason," said Kevin, his magical voice snapping Caffrey out of the spell of thoughts he'd fallen victim to. "You live right near the finish line, so we can hustle over to your place to warm up. Gotta warn you, dude—it's the worst case of blue balls you'll ever get."

The mention of Kevin's rocks instantly shot a jolt of adrenaline through Caffrey's blood. He tried to swallow, only to nearly gag on the ball of heat that blossomed on his tongue, his mouth completely desiccated by the thought of running in public in a pair of skimpy nut-huggers. That, and Kevin's proximity. The other man leaned even closer.

"I ain't lacking in the dick department," Kevin continued. Caffrey watched, stunned, as his coworker tugged on the meaty, leftward-leaning prize in his dress pants for effect. "But after half an hour in the single digits, last year the little fucker looked like a cocktail weenie."

Caffrey laughed. Inwardly, however, he was screaming at the tops of invisible lungs. He'd just agreed to shuck down to the barest minimum and streak through the heart of the city! Hell, he didn't even own Speedos, though in his underwear drawer was a pair of red flannel boxers with a single button on the front, a Valentine's Day gift from an ex that he'd never worn. The damn things were perfect for the Banana Dash, which had in the past half decade, according to the advertisement, raised over a million dollars for Boston's homeless.

Caffrey hated the cold. The idea of running a mile through the Common in his underwear—in effect, streaking for Santa—ranked right up there with the scrape of teeth on his dick during a blow job. The hardest part, though, would be having to endure the twin images of Kevin Lyons and Jason Starkman standing as close to naked as a man could get without wagging his dick openly in the frosty air, and even with the wind chill, Caffrey knew his dick would likely stiffen up and stay there, an uncommon public spectacle more notable than a bunch of guys jogging through the Common in their shorts.

He was lucky to have been seated at his desk when Kevin approached him. Caffrey's dick had started to swell while he was agreeing to run the Banana Dash and now leaked precome into the tented crotch of his pants, mercifully out of sight.

"I'll have the heat cranked up and the coffee on," Caffrey said, the smile on his face so rigid, he worried it would freeze there permanently, lockjaw disguising his true feelings of equal part horror and arousal.

"Kick ass, dude. We're meeting at ten, off the Beacon Street entrance between the Frog Pond and the Soldier's Memorial."

"Good deal. I'll be there," said Caffrey. Kevin made a pistol out of his forefingers and thumbs, aimed them, then strutted away, leaving Caffrey with a racing heart and precome running down his balls.

He forced his eyes off Kevin's retreating ass, clad squarely in his dress pants, and down to his own crotch where, to his shock, Caffrey saw the telltale stain of wetness that betrayed his guilt. When his dick was safely down again, Caffrey grabbed his jacket off the back of the chair and used it to cover his crotch. He locked himself in the head and jerked off to thoughts about the two men, trying to ignore the promise he'd made to join them for Saturday morning's big foot race.

For the rest of the week, the weather reports tormented Caffrey. One Boston news channel predicted an Arctic chill in the teens, but with sunshine. Another offered the hope of a warming trend—into the mid-twenties, if all the stars aligned. The consensus was, the day would be sunny or partly sunny, seasonably cold—perfect for running a one-mile mini-marathon around the Common in your underwear to raise money for the homeless.

Caffrey's home, a block from the Common, was a modern, two-bedroom townhouse where he retreated after long workdays at Derryfield & Sanborn, where he sometimes brought home men and sucked their cocks (his favorite activity, sexual or otherwise), and where he often jacked off over thoughts of the two choicest studs at the company whose dicks he wanted more than any others on the planet.

He'd left his red flannel boxers on the table atop the flyer Kevin had dropped off at his desk the previous Monday morning. Caffrey had tried to avoid looking directly at the shorts, fearing they would burn his retinas if he did, the underwear equivalent of staring directly at the sun during an eclipse. Every time he walked past the table, he caught a flash of red from the corners of his eyes, a reminder that the clock was ticking, that come a very cold Saturday morning, he would be stripping down to his skivvies to jog around the Common with Kevin and Jason.

For months, he'd refused offers to join them at a local sports bar for a round of beers after work. Over the previous summer, they'd invited him to baseball games at Fenway Park. He'd always quietly backed out, fearful they'd show with a pair of hot girlfriends, or worse, try to set him up with an easy fuck, and his secret would be made public. And now, he'd agreed to run a mile in the cold with them, about as naked as three men could be.

He couldn't sleep. As the week wore toward the weekend, Caffrey would shoot awake in the darkness to find the pillow soaked in sweat and his hard dick fucking the mattress, a few pumps short of blasting his load. He lost his appetite. The dread of going to work, of being near them, grew strangulating.

All because of those damned red boxers, and everything they represented.

•

On Saturday morning, Caffrey stared into the big mirror over the bathroom sink and told himself the torture was over. He shot his best mean look at his reflection, saw his green eyes narrow, caught a flash of perfect white teeth through his trimmed goatee and mustache. He was twenty-nine—if he didn't want to run the damned Banana Dash, he didn't have to, and that was the end of that tune. 'Nuff said. Fuck it. He'd write out a nice, fat check to the race's organizers, and checkbook charity would have to suffice.

Even so, he pulled on the damned red boxers and dressed in layers before heading out into the cold.

•

The brisk December air burned in his lungs. Caffrey's already-pounding heart began to race steadily faster after he turned onto Beacon Street. The Common rose before him, its skeletal trees and monuments framed by gray sky. The pedestrian path glowed with sharp flashes of red color.

The red, he discovered, belonged to dozens upon dozens of pairs of men's underwear, men's bathing suits, Speedos, even a few thongs worn by loud, half-drunk exhibitionists. It was insane, exhilarating. It was—

Caffrey stepped from behind a quartet of runners to find himself staring at the mostly naked god-bods of Kevin and Jason.

He'd often wondered how the two men looked out of their dress clothes. He already knew Jason's arms were hairy, not overly muscular, just right; and had once seen a tuft of brown chest hair at the top of his undershirt at the end of a day when he'd loosened his tie and undone the top button. Caffrey figured it was more than likely that the lower half of his body matched the top.

Jason, who stood six feet tall, was jogging in place dressed only in ass-hugging red Speedos and an old, run-in pair of sneakers. His legs were as perfect as Caffrey had imagined: solid, hairy, and amazingly sexy. Even Jason's bare ankles, visible above the cut of his sneakers, had the power to ignite fires deep in Caffrey's guts.

Jason was bare-chested. As Caffrey forced his feet into

motion and shuffled closer, rounding the other man's body, the front side of Jason Starkman came into view. For the first time, Caffrey saw his V-shaped torso, the ample hair across the pecs cutting down his abdomen in a solid T-shaped pattern. A line of fur cut horizontally across the top of his waistband. Unable to resist, Caffrey forced his eyes lower, into the meaty terrain of the bulge at the center of the tight red fabric, and, to his shock, he was able to trace the outline of Jason's flaccid cock, the clear shape of it from head to root, down to the obvious fullness of two fat balls. The chill had done little to shrink their impressiveness.

Jason recognized him and called, "Dude!" Caffrey's gaze shot up to Jason's handsome face: his pale-blue eyes; square jaw; and short, dark-blond hair cropped almost to the scalp. Caffrey saw that he was wearing a baseball cap with a set of felt reindeer antlers set over it. Another rush of heat surged through him.

"Love the horns," Caffrey said with a chuckle.

Without warning, a hand gripped his shoulder. Caffrey turned into the firm grip, and in the time it took to suck in a deep breath of frigid air, his eyes registered the fullness of Kevin Lyons's mostly naked body. He was wearing only a pair of dark-red crotch-huggers, boxer briefs that looked as though they'd been sewn into place on his tight body, white crew socks, and expensive-looking cross trainers on his big feet. A red Santa hat capped his brush-cut, but even more charming was his glowing red reindeer's nose. That playful, boyish expression melted the last of the ice inside Caffrey.

His eyes briefly wandered up Kevin's arms, over the bulge of his biceps and the tattooed link of chain inked around the thickest point of their circumference, into the dark thatch of his pit hair, and up to his grinning, unshaved face. Then Caffrey's gaze skied down the slope of the other man's chest. Kevin's pectorals weren't as hairy as Jason's. Two tiny, dark, stiff nipples capped the other man's bare flesh. Going lower, Caffrey wandered the treasure trail of coarse fur that cut Kevin down the middle.

Once his gaze went there, Caffrey couldn't help but notice the rest. More lush hair lined the elastic waistband of Kevin's boxer briefs, and beneath that ...there it was, the thick, mysterious outline that had mesmerized Caffrey on so many occasions—only now, a mere thin layer of cotton separated him from seeing it clearly. Kevin's quads and calves were solid and hairy. Caffrey's gaze vanished into the snowy whiteness of the other man's socks.

Kevin's voice struck like a slap to the face and mercifully pulled Caffrey out of the spell. "What the fuck's up with this?" he said, giving Caffrey's winter coat a hard tug.

Caffrey avoided Kevin's eyes, his gaze instead falling upon a nearby group of young and old Santas who were stretching, doing push-ups or jumping jacks, and generally psyching themselves up for the run. Trim bodies and overweight alike had blended together into a panorama of reds and flesh tones. "I—I don't think I can do this, guys."

"The fuck you don't," growled Kevin. "Strength in numbers, man. Off with the wool!"

To Caffrey's shock, Kevin yanked the coat free of his shoulders. A second later, Jason had tugged his shirttails out of his unbelted cargo pants.

"I don't know," Caffrey started to argue. He tried to struggle, but then Kevin pulled him into a reverse bear-hug, and as the feel and smell of the other man's naked warmth possessed him, Caffrey ceased resisting. Jason fumbled down his zipper, and Caffrey thanked his lucky stars he'd worn the damned red flannel boxers after all.

•

Caffrey ran in a daze, only partially aware of his surroundings or the fact that he was jogging through the Common, in December, dressed only in red flannel boxers, socks, and sneakers. The cheers from the crowd of supporters, his location on the pedestrian path, even the knowledge that his clothes were safely bagged back at the registration booth, all of it existed out of focus. Much closer and clearer were the two men jogging a yard ahead of him.

"Come on, you lamer," teased Jason, tossing the words back over his left shoulder.

Caffrey, who was in the best shape of his life, fired off a salute with his middle finger. His eyes latched onto Kevin's hard, square butt, perfectly showcased by his dark red underwear. A thin line of sweat infused the top of his boxer-briefs, just above the ass-crack. Caffrey's naked skin registered the bitter cold, but he barely felt the chill. Fresh perspiration had broken across Jason's back, so near he could touch it, smell it—

Lick it.

The cold air didn't shrivel Caffrey's cock, didn't suck his balls deep into his abdomen as he'd expected it would. Instead, like the two studs he struggled to keep pace with, he was sweating, the heat of his cock keeping him warm. He was aware of its fullness, bouncing under the scant cover of a thin layer of flannel. Caffrey's stomach ached. Hell, his balls did, too, mostly because he continued to savor the flex of Kevin's hairy leg muscles, his ass, the sweat on Jason's back and the image of his bare ankles, protruding out of cover of his sneakers. To Caffrey's embarrassment, the tingle in his boxers told him he'd gotten half-stiff.

The Banana Dash passed in a distortion of time and space that made seconds feel like hours and yards like miles. But then it was over, or so the deafening cheers told him. Caffrey looked up and saw that above Kevin's ass, above Jason's antlers, they'd reached the finish line.

●

Caffrey's hands were shaking so badly by the time the three men reached his townhouse that he nearly dropped the keys to the front door. It took him two tries to open the lock, but when he did, a wall of hot, comforting air billowed out to greet them. Caffrey welcomed Kevin and Jason into the front room and quickly closed the door.

Kevin stretched, while Jason crossed his arms in a huddle. "Nice place, dude," Jason chattered.

"Thanks. I put on the coffee before I left, so it's pretty fresh. Most important, *hot!*"

"You got any beer?" This from Kevin.

Caffrey tipped a look in his direction to see the other man doing a slow three-sixty around the room, soaking in the surroundings, his glowing red reindeer's nose aimed up at the vaulted ceiling, his bare chest visible through his unzipped coat. The two men had brought backpacks, presumably filled with warm clothes, but as yet neither had made a move to dress. Kevin caught Caffrey looking and added, "Believe it or not, I could use a cold one."

"I'll take the coffee, light, extra sugar," said Jason.

Caffrey dropped the cargo pants, shirt, and undershirt he'd worn down to the Common on the nearest easy chair. "Coming right up. Make yourselves at home."

When he returned with a bottle of beer for Kevin and Jason's coffee, Caffrey found the two men seated on the sofa in the front room dressed the same way they'd run the race: footgear, underwear, and hats, their jackets and backpacks tossed onto the pile of Caffrey's discarded clothes. Caffrey handed each man his drink. "Warm enough?"

"Sure," said Jason. Kevin grunted his agreement.

Caffrey poured himself a cup of coffee, black. "So you guys do this thing every year?" he offered.

"Yup," said Kevin. "Where else can you streak through the city like a caveman?"

Caffrey laughed nervously and guzzled down a huge swig of java. The coffee hit his stomach with a mildly painful jolt. "It was crazy seeing all those dudes running around in thongs and shit. Seemed to be a lot of hot chicks supporting them, though. I guess the ladies dig a dude who'll run a mile in blue-ball weather for charity."

"I didn't notice the chicks," Jason said. He reached down and fondled the lump at the bottom of his crotch, accessing it through the leg band of his Speedos. For a brief and blinding instant, Caffrey caught a flash of crotch hair and loose nut sac. "Sure got the blue balls, though."

"Yeah, it was fuckin' cold enough," growled Kevin. Caffrey watched him knock back a mouthful of suds, mystified by the manner in which Kevin held the beer bottle the way all masculine men do, with two fingers wrapped around the neck, gripping it like a cock. "What about you? Your dick die of shrinkage?"

Caffrey didn't realize the comment was meant for him until Kevin tipped an obvious look at his crotch.

Before he could answer, Jason aimed a thumb in Caffrey's direction and said, "Apparently not. Dude, you've been dripping like a leaky faucet since we left the Common."

Caffrey's eyes shot fully open. He glanced down, and there it was, damning proof of his guilt: the same overly normal flow of precome that had plagued him his entire adult life.

"Fuck," he huffed, standing. "I'll be back in a sec. You guys want anything else, help yourselves," he said, starting across the room. But on his way past the sofa, Kevin seized Caffrey by the wrist.

"How 'bout a hot, deep blow job to stop the shrinkage?"

At first, Caffrey thought he'd imagined the statement. Shaking free of Kevin's grip, he forced his eyes down to the two men: one had yanked his Speedos to the side, baring his fat, hairy balls; the other had just snaked his hand deep into his boxer briefs.

"Why do you think we really brought you along with us?" Jason asked. "To warm us up! So get over here and suck our dicks, man."

A dream—it had to be! The two ex-college jocks Caffrey had serviced repeatedly in his thoughts were seated in front of him, offering up their bodies. If it wasn't a dream, then it was a taunt, a trap designed to reveal him for the cock lover he was.

Caffrey could almost have believed it was the kind of

hazing perpetrated by hostile frat boys, if not for the proof offered up by their dicks. The root of Jason's was visible through a dense forest of hair, mightily hard, a thick pink column prevented from rising fully upward by his Speedos. The hand locked in a choke-hold around its midsection couldn't disguise its excitement.

And Kevin's cock—those skin-tight maroon boxer briefs tented at the left in a way that showed that Kevin's rod was as hard as Jason's, stiff and expecting to be sucked.

Caffrey whistled a breathless expletive. It was true. It was real!

He dropped to his knees in front of Jason, slid a hand along the other man's hairy right leg, and lowered his face into his crotch. Each shallow breath filled Caffrey's senses with a mix of clean athletic sweat and the natural mustiness of a man's balls. His lips zeroed in on the target, and as he first kissed and next licked Jason's nuts, a firm tug of his hand pulled Jason's cock out of his Speedos.

Caffrey gave it a firm stroke. It was as impressive as he'd imagined all those times, at least seven inches, maybe a bit more, a good handful around with a fat, square-ish head, the piss-hole already gummed up with precome. Caffrey sucked on Jason's balls, savoring their maleness, before moving higher. The head of the other man's cock and the first few inches of purple shaft vanished into his mouth. Salty, masculine funk teased Caffrey's taste buds.

"Aww, fuck—!" the other man groaned above him.

In a trance, part of him still convinced he must be dreaming, Caffrey reached between his legs, struggled the fly's lone button open, and fumbled his dick out of his boxers. He didn't need to spit in his palm for lubrication, and never had. Caffrey's cock head was slick with wetness. He jerked his dick in one hand and toyed with Jason's body—balls, legs, and ankles—with the fingers of the other.

A deep, musical voice shocked him out of the daze. "Hey, fucker, how 'bout sharing some of that over here!"

Caffrey glanced toward the far side of the sofa, and

Kevin's narrowed eyes locked with his. He spit out Jason's erection and shuffled a yard over to the region between the other man's legs.

Kevin.

Caffrey studied the sculpt of his chest, the image of his legs, one kicked straight out, the other slightly bent at the knee. He gripped the top of Kevin's underwear and pulled it to his knees, then his ankles, finally off his big, sneakered feet. Waiting on the upswing were a set of nuts that matched Jason's in size and looseness, and a long, veiny cock that stretched all the way to Kevin's belly button.

Fuck, how I've wanted this, thought Caffrey.

Half closing his eyes, he buried his face in Kevin's balls, inhaling their raw, powerful smell, tasting them, sucking them one at a time. From there, he slowly took Kevin's cock between his lips and didn't stop until all of it was in his mouth.

•

Caffrey couldn't recall the exact details of how he landed on his knees with both men standing over him with their dicks in his face at the same time. Somehow, Jason's Speedos, like Kevin's boxer briefs, had come off, along with socks and sneakers. He knew he'd licked the sweat from under their armpits, from between each man's toes. He'd eaten their assholes with gusto. Those details he vividly remembered.

The two men fucked his face, each growing more verbal, more agitated. Even a skilled cocksucker's mouth could only accommodate so much dick, but that didn't stop Jason from trying to force in the bulk of his shaft.

"Suck it, dude. Suck my hairy cock to the balls!"

Kevin's hand on Caffrey's shoulder tensed. "Fuck, your prick is making mine feel so good…"

Their tools, rubbing together in Caffrey's mouth, quickly reached the verge of shooting. Kevin busted first, spraying a load of sour come across Caffrey's tongue, his deep, masculine howls filling the townhouse.

Jason squirted before Kevin finished fully unloading. Caffrey gulped, and somewhere amid the chaos and cacophony of moans, he shot his own wad across the two men's bare feet.

Kevin collapsed on the sofa, his spent cock still erect. "Damn, son, that was fuckin' amazing!"

"Yeah," Jason agreed. He extended a hand at his best buddy. Kevin low-fived it.

Caffrey licked his lips. "I've wanted this forever, dudes."

"We know, and we've been trying to get you to give us some service, fucker," Kevin said.

Stunned, Caffrey tipped his gaze from one man to the other. "You have?"

"Yup," Jason said. "And you keep blowing us off. We'd better not have to wait till next year's run to get some more of this."

Fresh pins and needles tingled over Caffrey's naked flesh. "Whenever you want it, I'm ready."

A swarthy smile broke on Kevin's face. He ogled his cock, squeezing a pearl of spent come out of its straining head. Caffrey watched it ooze down his shaft and catch in the hairs of his balls. "Oh yeah?"

"How bout now, dude?" grunted Jason. "I could ride that mouth again."

"I'm up for it," Kevin agreed.

Caffrey smiled and wiped his mouth on the discarded pair of red flannel boxers that had started it all. A few seconds later, he was on his knees again, making good on his promise.

SIGNET AND SILK

J. J. MASSA

I stood at the copier, running a hand through my hair and sighing. My job wasn't all that strenuous, but it was *very* tedious. One of the female partners had just laid an assignment on me that would take most of the afternoon. Being an intern in a big law firm sucked sometimes, even though it was great for my résumé. I had another year left in law school and I needed the credentials.

The file room was small and felt pretty warm. More so because I kept thinking about Pierce Anders's silk boxers. You're not supposed to look when another guy's standing next to you in the men's room. He's supposed to stare straight ahead and so are you. No eye contact and definitely no looking.

I broke the rule. Discreetly, I hope, but I broke it. I looked to the right while Mr. Anders stood there taking a piss, just a quick glance. I didn't see what his elegant hand was holding, only the shine from that signet ring he always wears, and his blue-green silk boxers, the same color as his eyes. Oh, man!

Even that tiny peek sent my heart galloping so hard my chest hurt. Now, I couldn't think of anything else. My mind was spinning with images of the dark-haired, hard-muscled lawyer wearing nothing but those silk boxers, and maybe a sexy smile.

They would be soft at the waist, a caress against the dark hair of his taut thighs, and a whisper brushing over his cock. When he was soft, the silk would cradle him, the tight dark curls pushing the sleek fabric; when he was hard, the silk would feel so smooth, so intimate against his hot flesh.

I had to grab the copier, I felt so light-headed. A loud grinding noise told me that I must've hit a couple of buttons in my attempt to steady myself.

"Shit," I spat, pulling my foot back to kick the annoying hunk of plastic and misery.

"Huh-huh-huh" came a rich, deep chuckle, right above my left ear.

A firm hand landed on my right thigh—the one that had been poised to dent the copier. I looked down and my breath lodged in my throat. A signet ring ... Pierce Anders.

"Sir," my voice sounded hoarse. I cleared my throat. "Sir, I wasn't ..."

"Shh," he whispered. "You've been bad, haven't you? I saw you looking at me in the partners' urinal. What were you doing in there?" A husky chuckle as his left hand began to tease at the button at my waist. "Besides the obvious, I mean."

Oh, god, I thought my heart was racing before! Now it was like a runaway train. "I was ... I had to go," I hedged.

He didn't need to know I'd been hoping to get a glimpse of him. He didn't need to know he was my secret crush.

Deftly he'd worked the button free, his nimble hand dipping into my plain cotton boxer briefs. "Well, what do we have here?" Those elegant fingers were teasing my hard cock. "It's hard and it's soft, and it's for me, isn't it?"

He'd known all along! I slumped back against him, busted. He'd seen me look, probably even seen me watching for him.

"Yes," I confessed pointlessly. "It's hard for you."

The hand at my thigh rose to my waist, unzipping and pulling my boxer briefs and pants down past my hips. I was completely exposed, and as hard as the steel frame of that stupid copier.

"Lean forward, baby," he murmured, both hands resting on either side of my waist.

I wanted to melt on the spot. Maybe he called everyone that, but it sounded so affectionate, so personal. Nobody had called me that, ever. I leaned forward.

I heard the rasp of a zipper and then the rustle of fabric.

One hand moved to grip my throbbing, burning cock, and the other began to stroke my ass cheeks.

"Oh god," I moaned. This was better than any of my daydreams. I'd so hungered for this man, wanted him so bad.

A long finger made its way into my crack, pulling my cheeks apart, stroking my hole. "This is mine, too, isn't it, baby?" he asked, "and this." His right hand slid down and cupped my balls, rolling and fondling them.

"Yeah, all of it," I croaked. "Whatever you want."

"That's what I want." He leaned in, the unmistakable feel of silk and a hard cock underneath sliding across my parted cheeks. "That's what I want, baby," he repeated. "All of it. And I want it now."

"Mm," I groaned. I couldn't say anything more. I could barely get that out.

"Yeah." He stroked his silk-covered cock against me again. "You like silk, baby?" he asked.

"Yeah," I got out. "Silk."

He reached under my tailored dress shirt, finding and fondling my hard nipples. "I like these, too," he purred. "They *are* part of the package, hmm?"

I felt the touch of skin on skin, and a bit of wetness. He'd taken his dick out of the boxers and was rubbing it between my cheeks. I felt the warm precome, slick, wet. Oh, god. I couldn't hold back a little moan.

His hand trailed back down to ghost over my cock again, lightly touching.

"Yeah." My voice sounded so husky, raspy. "'S yours, all."

"So good, baby," he murmured, his voice smooth, sexy.

I felt a fingertip push against my hole, out and in again, deeper. Where had he gotten the lube? Deeper it moved in and then out again and back in, slick and smooth, and so fine. It was amazing. This was Pierce Anders finger-fucking my asshole in the copy room, stretching me. Oh, god, what if someone walked in?

I swayed, clutching at the copier again. His upper arm

tightened around me, the hand on my cock squeezing a little, his thumb stroking my dripping slit. I heard a tearing sound of paper, a low sound of him spitting something, a little fumbling behind me.

"It's okay," he soothed me, like he was calming a skittish cat or something. That voice could talk the leaves off the trees, it was so smooth. "You're my baby now, I'm going to take good care of you." I felt his cock push against my entrance; I bent over farther, offering more, all his. He stroked my cheeks, thumbs pulling me wide. Anybody walking in would see me, open, my ass spread for Mr. Anders's cock. "Now I'm gonna fuck you," he told me. And then the wide, round head was pushing into me. He'd slipped a condom on.

"Yes," I begged. I wanted this so bad. "Yes, please."

Deeper, deeper he pushed, opening me wide, filling me with that huge organ that I hadn't even seen, hadn't even touched with my hands. It felt so big, so hard, so damned good.

Finally, he was all the way in and resting against me. "How do you like that, baby?" he whispered in my ear. "Silk."

He hadn't pushed the boxers off! He had pulled his cock through the opening. When he began to move, every thrust brought that soft, sexy silk against my ass. His steel-hard cock, ramming into me, stroking my hot spot deep inside, and light, sensual silk caressing my ass.

"Uh, uh, oh," I moaned, aching.

He'd been holding my cock, just lightly. Now he reached down, cuddling my balls.

"You're close, aren't you baby?" he whispered in my ear. His voice was tight. He was close, too.

"Yeah," I breathed. "Yeah, wanna come." I sounded like a Neanderthal, but I couldn't help it.

"In a minute, you come when I tell you to." He sounded hard, gritty, commanding. That did it. Shit! I think that's when I fell in love.

"Yessir," I choked, so stiff, my dick would break off if it hit the copier.

"That's right," he growled, pumping into me hard. Suddenly his thrusts were short, jerky. "Now, baby, come in my hand. Right fucking now!" he hissed.

On cue, sparks shot up and down my spine, my balls painful with heat. It felt like I was coming from my toes, up out, painting the side of the copier and spilling all over his hand. At the same time, I felt his cock jerk deep inside my clenching ass.

One arm wrapped around my chest, the other hand held tight to my cock, he licked my ear, kissed at my neck, nipping and sucking. The arm around my torso moved up, cupping my cheek, turning my face to his, those sensuous lips covering mine, taking them in a hard, sucking, dominant kiss.

Finally, he eased back, his big cock slipping out of my ass. I heard him peeling off the condom, fabric rustling, zipper hitching closed. I hadn't moved, was still leaning on the copier, arms spread, braced. Then, surprising the hell out of me, he pulled my briefs and pants back up, reaching around me to tuck, button, and zip.

He stayed there a minute, hands caressing my chest through my shirt. "You ever want to do that again, baby, be at my office at seven-fifteen, hmm?"

I couldn't speak. A click told me he was at the door. I hadn't heard him close it, much less lock it. I whirled around.

"Yessir!" I croaked.

His handsome face relaxed and he gave me a hint of a smile coupled with a sharp nod. Then he was gone. It took me five minutes to remember where I was and why. The rest of the afternoon crawled.

I was at Mr. Anders' office at seven-fifteen, though.

DIRTY LITTLE BOXER BOY

RYAN FIELD

During my freshman year of college I took a part-time job as an attendant in a small tanning salon. A rather unfortunate place with depressing brown carpets, but it was good, clean work that allowed plenty of time to study between customers, most of whom were middle-aged women with too much time on their hands. I would have preferred a part-time job in a men's clothing store, helping guys choose the right socks and underwear (I'd always been into loose boxer shorts—something so hot about the way they fall on men), but the tanning salon was close to the dorms and the job didn't require much thought. Aside from all the female customers, it wasn't a bad gig at all, except for the fact there was often too much free time. The months of September and October were slow; I was lucky to have two or three customers per day. And it was almost unthinkable to see a great looking guy in his early thirties decide to sign up for a month of tanning before a trip to Belize or Mexico.

But that's what happened. It was a rainy Monday morning when Rick walked into the empty salon. I'd been studying for a chemistry quiz when I looked up to see standing before me a tall guy with short, black hair, wearing a navy jogging suit. His appearance was military; short dark hairs stuck to his temples with perspiration, five o'clock shadow in an almost greenish color and strong hands that moved in graceful motions when he spoke. He'd obviously just come from a morning run.

"I'm interested in tanning for about a month," he said. "I'm a doctor, going to Belize on research, and I don't want to burn down there. I've never done this sort of thing before.

Do you think I can get a decent tan for the trip?"

I instantly dropped my chemistry notes and began to explain the tanning process to this hot guy. He had a rugged look, but his soft brown eyes reminded me of a puppy dog's. Though his jogging suit was loose as it hung from his tall, rigid body, I knew there was really good stuff underneath. I liked the power he gave me: a young college student who knew nothing (except maybe how to suck dick to perfection), explaining something to a mature man of the world.

When I was finished with the sales pitch, and I knew he was going to sign up for a month of tanning, I then said, "You really should buy a tanning lotion. It will help you get a better tan, and it will moisturize your body. It's really an important factor with indoor tanning." I honestly did believe the lotions helped, too.

"Can you recommend something?" he asked. "You seem to have a great tan. I want what you use."

"I use this," I said, pulling a basic tanning lotion from a display on the counter. "It's not expensive and it does the job, as you can see." I stretched out my tanned arms. I tanned only about once a week, but I had the kind of skin that absorbed sunlight; just one twenty-minute session made my ass as soft and brown as someone who'd done five of the same sessions. The way I looked was the main reason the owner of the salon had hired me. Though born and raised on the East Coast, people always said I had a West Coast surfer look.

"And I just apply this like any other tanning lotion?" he asked, handing me his credit card so that I could finalize the transaction.

"You try to get it all over your body," I said, noticing that the head of his cock made a slight outline on the fabric of his jogging pants. "Even on your back."

When the tanning sessions were charged to his credit card, and he'd filled out a customer record sheet, I told him to follow me to the tanning booth so that I could show him what to do. Though I was clearly attracted to him, it was all very businesslike.

Until he asked, as I was about to leave him alone in the tanning booth, "Hey Buddy Boy, do you think you could help me apply the lotion? So I don't make any mistakes."

"Sure," I said. "No problem. I'm not that busy today."

He was about to get the massage of a lifetime; of that I was certain.

He removed the sweatshirt, exposing a well-defined chest slightly covered with a rough carpet of jet black hair. In the center of his breastbone was a black fluff that formed a narrow line of hair leading all the way down his lean abdomen, as though pointing in the direction of his dick. He then kicked off his running shoes and proceeded to yank off his damp sweat socks. As I stood there, watching him strip (he wasn't self-conscious at all), I held the tanning lotion with no expression on my face. I wasn't sure where this was leading. But then, when he quickly yanked his sweat pants down and pulled them off, revealing a rumpled pair of white cotton boxer shorts, I nearly fell to my knees. His legs were hairy and long and muscular and I wanted to bury my face in the white boxers...to lick them and sniff them and chew on them. I could see the outline of his rather large cock resting just beside the front opening. To an underwear pirate this was a dream: loose, well-worn boxers begging to be sniffed and licked.

"I think I should put the lotion all over your body," I said, trying not to sound too excited, "to show you the right way to do it."

"If you say so, Buddy Boy," he replied, ready to yank off the white boxers, too.

"No," I suddenly shouted, hoping I hadn't sounded desperate. "Don't take off the boxers. Leave them on for the first few times you tan. You don't want to burn in places that haven't been exposed to the sun before."

"Good thinking," he said, placing his large hands on his waist.

Though it was the truth, and I didn't want to burn his cute ass, my only thought at the moment was to keep him in those sexy boxer shorts as long as possible.

"Just stand still and relax," I told him as I poured tanning lotion into the palms of my hands and knelt down in front of him. I slowly began with his large feet, working the smooth lotion between his toes and then up to his ankles with both my hands. I gently massaged (I wasn't spreading it...I was slowly working him toward an erection) his legs, making sure it got past the body hair and into the skin.

"Damn, Buddy Boy," he said. "This feels so good. I should have come here a long time ago. Do you do this for all the customers?"

"No way," I said, laughing. "You're the first one ever."

"How old are you? And what's your name?" he asked.

"Nineteen. Joe," I replied. "Now, you lie down in the tanning bed and I'll finish massaging the lotion on your body. I want to cover every inch of you, and it's much more relaxing if you're lying down."

When he was flat on his back in the tanning bed, I decided to strip down, too.

"I don't want to get lotion all over my clothes," I said as he watched me rip off my white T-shirt and kick off my jeans. I took everything off—shoes, socks, and underwear. I wanted to be on my knees with my back arched, my ass in the air, and my legs spread as wide as possible.

"You've got a great body, Buddy Boy, and I see that your tan is even in all the right places," he said, as he reached up from the tanning bed and ran the rough palm of his left hand slowly down my ass. Then, with his thick middle finger, he slowly began to circle the opening of my ass. By that time my cock was rock-hard.

I knelt down, while he continued to work his finger into my hole, and began to massage lotion onto his strong thighs. He must have been an avid runner; his thighs were like rocks. Not an ounce of flab anywhere.

"Now, just close your eyes and relax," I whispered, my

legs spread as wide as I could spread them, his finger now all the way up my ass. "I'm going to apply some lotion all the way up your legs, so that if the sun's rays go through your boxers you won't get burned."

"You're the expert, Buddy Boy."

I poured more lotion into the palms of my hands and then slowly ran both hands up under the white boxers. I massaged lotion way up, into his groin area, while his large hairy balls rubbed against the front of my hands. As I did this I noticed that his cock was growing larger by the moment. Suddenly the head began to pop through the front opening of the white boxers. Then, rather quickly, an eight-inch erection was popping through, pulsing with each movement I made.

"Is that okay?" he asked as he looked at me and then down at his huge hard dick, slowly finger-fucking me into a delirious state of submission.

I smiled. "Don't worry. I'll take care of that, too."

I buried my face in his white boxers. They were slightly sweaty from his morning run, and smelled like nectar from the gods. I licked the white cotton, working my tongue through the front opening, past the base of his hard cock, so that I could release his large hairy balls too. I sucked them both up into my mouth, and slowly pulled them through the opening. For a moment, when his cock and his balls were sticking out of the opening, I took a quick look at them. To me, nothing is sexier than seeing a huge dick and a large set of sweaty balls sticking out from a pair of white boxer shorts.

Slowly, while my hands clutched the white cotton on his shorts, I began to lick my way up the shaft of his dick toward the head. A large cock head, by that time dripping with precome.

Suddenly, just as I took the entire dick all the way down my throat and was about to begin the first sucking motions, a voice rang out, "Is anyone here?"

The voice was familiar. A woman customer who never

missed a day of tanning.

But I thought fast. "I'm back here, Barbara, with an electrician. We had some trouble with your favorite tanning bed. It'll be fixed in an hour or so. Why don't you come back then."

"Oh, okay," I heard a voice shout. "I have some errands. I'll come back."

With his cock still standing and ready to burst, a finger as far up my ass as he could get, he whispered, "Good thinking."

"Just relax," I said, grabbing my own cock so I could shoot a load too. "This will only take another minute or so. You're ready to explode."

"Tell me about it," he moaned. "I'd love to fuck you."

"I wanna finish you off like this," I said. "I really wanna suck you off."

"Well how is this?" he said, as he slowly shoved two more fingers up my ass.

"Fucking fantastic," I moaned.

I returned to sniffing and licking his boxers for a moment. And then began some serious sucking motions on his dick. Not just licking, or moving my mouth up and down the shaft. That does nothing to a man. I sucked hard and fast, jerking my own cock the entire time. In no time he reached a point where his juice was ready to shoot. You can usually tell during a good cock-sucking session when someone is ready to shoot a load because his legs start to wiggle, and his toes often curl.

"Ahhhhh," was the only sound he made as he shot a full load of come right down my throat. I felt it hit the back of my throat.

I shot one too, all over the side of the tanning bed, while he fucked me with three fingers, never missing a beat.

Though he pulled his fingers out after we came, I kept his cock in my mouth for a while, not ready to release it until I knew he'd been completely drained and was ready to lie back and enjoy a relaxing tanning session. I didn't torture him, knowing that the head of his cock would be sensitive after shooting a load. I simply kept it in my mouth, slowly sucking each last drop of his come. I wanted to feel his meaty dick slowly go down against my tongue, and then gently suck his balls back into my mouth so that I could roll them into a state of complete relaxation. I knew from the way he gently caressed my head that he really liked this.

"That was fucking fantastic," he whispered to me, as I released his floppy dick and neatly packed it back into his white boxers, where it was safe and sound. Then I gently kissed the opening of the underwear, pilfering one last sniff for the road.

"I enjoyed it too," I said, stepping back into my jeans. "Especially the white boxers. I love all boxer shorts, but white ones really get me hot."

"Fuck, Buddy Boy," he said, "I especially liked the way you drained me dry."

"You tasted like candy," I said. "Your come is very sweet."

"Damn!"

"Now, you relax and enjoy your first tanning session," I told him. "I've got to get back to the front desk before someone else comes in. And you need to get some rest. You've had two workouts today ... a long run and a good suck-off."

About twenty minutes later he returned to the reception counter, where I was folding a few small towels. "Did I get any color?" He lowered his running pants so that I could see his black pubic hairs.

"It's too soon to tell," I said, "but you should see something in about an hour, after you take a shower."

"Cool," he said, now acting slightly awkward. "Should I come in tomorrow?"

"Oh, yeah," I said. "I think you should come in every day until you go to Belize."

"I think so too," he said as he headed for the exit. "I'll see you same time tomorrow."

"Great," I said. "And, don't forget that you probably should wear a pair of boxers the first few times."

"Oh, I won't," he said and laughed. "Tomorrow I'm going to wear a pair of light-blue ones that are really loose and baggy. I'll wear them for a while, so they won't be too fresh and clean."

I licked my lips. "That sounds perfect."

"See you tomorrow," he said, as he jauntily headed out the door.

•

When he was gone and I went back to clean his tanning bed, I noticed that he'd left his white boxers hanging from a hook near the door. Obviously, he intended for me to have them. I slowly lifted them from the hook, placed them to my face and inhaled deeply, still in shock that I'd managed to fulfill one of my sacred fantasies that morning. How many people go through life without ever doing what they crave sexually? So many times I'd been with guys who were wearing underwear that I wanted to devour, but I always held back for fear they'd think I was peculiar.

As the weeks passed, Rick returned for his tanning session every day of the week, always wearing slightly used boxer shorts (he once wore a sweaty jockstrap, and though I enjoyed chewing on it while he fucked me, I told him that I still preferred boxers). I quickly learned that he was strictly a top man; it was never a problem for either of us. He fucked my brains out and I couldn't get enough of his cock. Sometimes he'd leave the boxer shorts on, with his cock popping from the opening, while he fucked me over the top of the tanning bed. And then sometimes (I liked this the most) he'd lie on his back while I spread my legs and sat on his large cock, covering my head with his dirty boxers. I'd ride his dick while I chewed and sucked the fabric. He seemed to enjoy the fact that I was so into his underwear, and always left a pair for my collection when the fucking was finished. But he liked fucking me the most, claiming that my ass felt like velvet around his cock. He never used a condom (we'd both been tested, and swore monogamy to each other), never had to pull out and jack off to come, and always shot a full load up my ass, whether I was riding his cock or was bent over while he nailed me to a wall or a floor or a door.

When it was time for him to leave for Belize, even though we both knew it was only temporary, neither of us was happy about it. But he swore to e-mail me, and to send letters daily. We didn't know about the future, and didn't want to discuss it; there wasn't time to do anything but fuck (and sniff boxer shorts), and we both knew that relationships aren't formed on that alone. We'd deal with that when he returned from his trip. As a going-away present I went down on my knees and I sucked him off while he finger-fucked my ass, just as we had done the first time, and we promised to keep in touch.

Well, a week passed and I didn't hear a word. He didn't answer my e-mails and I began to assume that it was just a passing fling. And then one afternoon a package was delivered to the salon, addressed to me, with a Mexican return address. I quickly opened it and found a rumpled pair of white boxer shorts and a small note that read, "My e-mail's been all fucked up, and it won't be working until next week, but I wanted to send you something so that you won't forget me. Have fun with these. I'm going to jack myself off tonight while I think about you sniffing them. I'm mailing a really sweaty, smelly pair next week ... Love, Rick."

NEVER TAKE IT OFF
LYNNE JAMNECK

The underwear she wears makes me want her to fuck me.

She knows this. Still, it's not the reason she wears it.

My girlfriend's gorgeous. She's toned and muscled. She's a butch with balls.

When she goes shopping for underwear the men all look at her, but curiously. It's because she takes such pride in what she wears beneath her clothes that I find her so attractive.

Sometimes I watch her when she doesn't know, like through the crack in the bathroom door, because she never closes it properly. Sometimes I think she's onto me.

When she's finished her shower and she's all dried off she lets the towel drop to the floor. She stands there, with her back to me, naked. Even her ass is muscled. I tease her all the time—it's because she likes to fuck so much. So hard. She laughs that deep laugh and tells me to stop being a tease.

When I first met Lex, I thought it was weird, with the baby powder. Now I can't imagine her smelling any other way.

The baby powder goes everywhere, covering her entire body. It makes her look like Michelangelo's David, the statue. She pats down all the extra powder, between her thighs, or on her neck, on her belly. Then she takes the unopened plastic packages and she sits down on the edge of the bath to open them.

Lex buys new underwear the first of every month. That's how I know when to watch.

It's always white. I find the color contrary, because when she puts it on it makes her look virginal. Not in a sexual way, just her being. She looks clean. Cut to perfection. Every angle and every line in place.

It's always a wife beater. You ever see Robert DeNiro in *Taxi Driver*? I think that's probably where the name came from.

The vest goes on first.

Lex has perfect breasts, neither big nor small. They make my mouth water. She loves me touching them, unlike her cunt. When I suck her nipples, she yields.

Today Lex is not wearing a bra. She can get away with it. Besides, once she's on the construction site, the vest she wears disguises everything.

She turns around and I can see the dark areolas through the thinly ribbed material. I swallow hard. I have to keep myself from standing up.

She bends over to pick up the other package, then stands upright a little cocky. That's why I sometimes suspect she knows. She's not the type to be vain without an audience.

She wears tight Lycra boxers. The way the material clings to her makes me hot. When she pulls them on it's as if her body fuses to the material, every muscle perfectly in place.

She stands in front of the basin and squirts toothpaste on her brush. While she cleans her teeth I look at her shoulders, how relaxed they are, and the sinews in her neck. When she leans over me at night, in bed, they flex and extend to keep up with the rest of her.

Quietly, I keep watching.

●

When Lex comes back from work it's almost eight o' clock. She works late, now that the sun's up longer. I bring her a beer, placing a cold Stella Artois in her hand where she sits on the couch. With her legs apart like that and her feet firmly planted on the ground, I can see what she has in mind. Lex wipes her mouth and calls me closer.

I straddle her lap and her lip curls. She smells of cold sweat and sawdust. Her hands are kneading my ass and the thought of how rough they are makes me wet within seconds.

We fight and laugh in between undressing. When Lex sees the black bra and panties I'm wearing, her face turns serious. She pushes me onto the couch, on my back, and starts undoing her belt and unbuttoning her pants. I'm already naked.

Lex never takes her underwear off when she fucks me.

I don't mind.

The way she feels beneath the stretch of the material, the flex of her muscles and the coolness of her skin makes me burn.

She stands by the foot of the couch, chiseled in white. There's a bulge in her boxers. It screams with intent. Lex pulls up a chair, lights a cigarette, and swallows a mouthful of beer.

She looks at me like there's a dare involved, but I know what to do. I sit up, my naked ass on the leather couch and my hand on the bulge in her crotch. The hard of her cock and the soft of the underwear makes me whimper.

In no time at all I've freed her from the constraint of her underwear and I'm going down on her. Lex's mouth clams up when I'm blowing her. It's like she can't talk, like she's mute. Every now and again, when my cheek rubs against the boxers, rubbing the soft against her skin, a low grunt will stick in her throat and her fingers will pull at my hair. I hear her swallow beer hard once again before she pulls me off her and tells me to lie the fuck down on the couch. All of a sudden she can talk again.

When she fucks me like this, with single-minded purpose, my hands are usually on her ass, willing her on. That way I can feel the tight stretch of her underwear as she moves. When I open my eyes I see her nipples bloom rigidly beneath the vest.

At some point she flips me over and when she enters me

from behind I buck to meet her. She's heavy. The friction of the fabric separating our skins turns desperate. I can feel the wetness of sweat pooling in the material. Lex holds me down as if she's scared I'll try and run away. When she bucks, her body stiff, her cock still hard inside me, I come with a moan that makes her yell at me. Something rude. I blush just thinking about it.

When I open my eyes again Lex is back on the chair. She looks at me through trailing cigarette smoke. She's still wearing her brand new underwear. Her breasts are a relaxed curve beneath the white, her strong thighs hugged in Lycra.

Her armor makes her look chivalrous. Because that's exactly what it is. Lex is tough and mean but inside she's butter. She's vulnerable, just like the rest of us. Every time I see her like that, through the crack in the bathroom door, decked out in white, in new cotton, I'm reminded of that. It sounds silly, but her underwear tells me exactly how she feels about me. That's why I'll never insist she take it off.

THE POLITICS OF GRAY

MARCUS JAMES

My name's Rex. I'm twenty-two and I have an underwear fetish. Now I'm not ashamed to admit this; actually, I love it. Anytime, anywhere, give me a guy in skivvies and I'm hooked. I'm on my knees worshiping him like I'm at church receiving communion.

Now my fetish does have its, um … discriminating tastes; in fact, it's very specific. I like my men in briefs, low-rise, designer, brand-name, and especially character ones like Batman, Atom Boy, etc. Then there're boxer briefs; I like those low-rise to mid-rise. Green purple, red, yellow, orange, all of these colors are out of the question. Color depends a lot on my attraction. If I go home with a guy and he's got the wrong color on, I leave. It's that simple.

Also, I can't stand men who wear nothing at all; if they free-ball then I'm gone. I like the tease, the forbidden secret, the thing that reveals everything but the last bit.

I don't understand my attraction for guys in undies; it's been with me since I was a kid. Discovering those hot boys in the locker rooms, half-naked lean bodies and great equipment, lingering just behind colored cotton, held in place within a snug pouch. The slightest thing making them quiver and push against the stitching, trying to get free.

Clothes shopping has become a test of will, thanks to this need, this lust for underwear. I remember once—quite recently, in fact—I was walking through Macy's and came upon the underwear section. Against my better judgment I dared it, I tested my resolve, and it kicked me in the ass.

I found myself in a garden of undies, undies of all kinds:

mid-torso'd manikins with godlike bodies, like statues of gods, clothed in tiny little briefs, white, black, and gray, each color of underwear representing the purpose of the deity. White was for innocence, losing virginity; gray was for making love, for lingering in bed afterward and grinning dumbly at one another, and black, oh black ... Black was lust, orgies, white parties, hook-ups, gay-pride month in hot, perspiring after-hours night clubs; it was dangerous, rough, blindfolds, teeth, and blood. Black was what I knew the best, though gray is what I longed for and white had been very brief.

Before these godlike manikins were shelves and shelves of packaged underwear with beautifully shot photos of homoerotic models with erect nipples and thick pieces; like sacrifices, like lambs laid out before these gods. I got hard, I had to adjust myself, I had to wipe the sweat off my forehead and palms. I couldn't avoid it.

Like a heroin addict needing his next fix, I grabbed a package of Calvin Klein low-rise briefs and ran to the dressing room, shutting the door and locking it behind me, ready to indulge. I looked in the mirror, my eyes large and my hair falling over them, tainted with perspiration.

I kicked off my shoes, undid my jeans, threw off my shirt, and sat down on the bench, spreading my legs and caressing my nine-incher for just a moment over my own pair of little gray Gap briefs. Then, as if unable to control the craving any longer, I dropped my underwear to my knees, ripped open that package of briefs, and closed my eyes; slipping the tiny black polyester-cotton-blend brief over my stiff cock, I began to stroke it.

I was in another place. My mind raced, the map of my brain like a movie screen, and on this screen was a clip show of those models in briefs, of hands tugging on stiff cocks under that cotton pouch, of those god-statue-manikins coming to life, of developing flesh, of moving hands, moving legs, and throbbing cocks. It was a divine threesome and I got to watch.

The fabric tantalized my cock, teased the shaft, and excited the head; the sweat moved down my stomach, my abs. I slipped my other hand down and tugged gently on my cleanly shaved balls, knowing I needed to stop, not knowing how, and then ...

Boom! I shot my load, over and over again into the soft fabric of those briefs, felt the hot, pearly substance seep out of the micro nooks and crannies of the fabric, saw the stain, and for a moment I didn't care. I couldn't move, I was spent. I left in such a rush that it must have looked as if someone was trying to kill me. The briefs stayed in the dressing room, along with my sacrament. (Now keep in mind this wasn't the first time that this had happened; it's just the most recent.)

I've seen a shrink about this, a sex psychologist, and she tells me all of the time that it's normal, everyone has their kinks—I just have to learn to control mine. Looking at her in her expensive chair with her tiny body clothed in a tight Donna Karen skirt and Marc Jacobs stilettos, her silky blond hair full of wild curls, and she chewing on a pen like I would suck a dick, it always makes me wonder: *What's her kink?*

Now we've talked about gray—gray the color, Gray the god, gray the shade of underwear that gets me harder, quicker, than anything else. The underwear of making love slowly, of warm, glittering, knowing glances, of sly smiles and teasing grins—the pair I want most of all. Let me tell you about gray.

Gray is a young man named Adam. Adam is a guy I work with. Adam is a model, an underwear model. Adam is six foot three, taller than me by a couple of inches, with caramel-colored skin and messy black hair, the kind of hair that works for any photo shoot that he has to do because it can be styled in any look that's needed for the shot.

His butt is like a bubble, but a firm bubble. His legs are strong, his chest lean, and his arms are solid with muscle, nice biceps that he flexes my way on more than one occasion.

I want him; I want his lips, lips that move into a smart grin, lips like cushions, and eyes dark, endless, like his mystery.

Every day that I stand next to him at the bookstore where we both work at in San Francisco's infamous Castro district is torture, a semi of emotions that I can't escape. It runs me over every day. We talk about music, which he loves; we talk about art and books we have read; we talk about sexual things, things that make me nervous, though I don't show it.

We pass innuendoes with each other. I tell him that I'm known for my blow jobs (which I am), and he grins slyly and raises his brows in a fashion that says I'm piquing his interest; this even includes Adam adjusting his crotch. You'd think this would be a good sign, but it isn't. In just as direct and swift an action he grows cold, distant, and treats me like I don't even exist. Sometimes he'll go stack books all day instead of stand with me, leaving me to deal with everyone at the counter.

Adam can leave me feeling empty, like I don't even want to exist. If he found out what he does to me, there's a good chance he'd just leave me be and treat me as if I am nothing more than a bother. Sometimes I think he already does.

He runs me into the ground and then picks me up with a smile, a look, a nice word, a secret that lives beneath it and is meant only for me. But then at the end of the day he leaves, and I lock up for the night and head back home, feeling everything tear up inside of me. My bus ride home is spent crying silently and listening to Tori Amos.

Adam pushes me to black more times than I would like to admit. On my nights off I go to several dance clubs in the Castro, get drunk, and prepare myself as the metaphorical sacrifice. In these clubs with hot, shirtless men with taut, sweaty bodies, eyes that look on everyone with lust, tongues that move across lips into mouths and taste the salt of flesh, I submit. Like a pack of wolves has worn me down, like a killer has brought me to my knees, I give in to black.

Sometimes with one, sometimes with two, three, even

four, all of them wearing black. Tiny black briefs or mid-rise boxer briefs, I give in to them and forget about gray, I curse gray, I blaspheme gray, and then, come the next morning, alone in my apartment with a rough hangover, I pray for Gray's forgiveness and wish that I can be white again.

•

"Hey Rex?" I turn to Adam, see him staring at me, moving closer to me, his voice baritone, just shy of a tenor. His dark eyes sparkle behind smooth glasses and his tongue slides across his bottom lip.

"Yeah?" I watch him move closer, the distance filling between us, growing smaller, and soon I'm cast in his shadow.

"I've got this gig coming up at F.C.U.K. on Saturday. It's just a small show, but if you want to come, that would be cool. I've got an extra pass to give to someone; you'd get backstage and everything." He hands me the cardboard pass slipped inside the clear plastic glove, looped with a black lanyard, and I'm shaking, my knees are buckling, and I'm grinning like an idiot. It's like you're in elementary school and someone hands you your very first valentine.

"I'll ... I'll be there."

"Good." And then he walks away, back to the books, back to his stacks. I watch him and catch a glimpse of black underwear—well just that elastic band with "2(X)ist" stitched in white across it. That night I jerk off for twenty minutes, shooting load after load until I'm exhausted, thinking about that flash of band and flesh.

I thought, *Hey, this is going to be different, he's given me a backstage pass and everything for Saturday. This week is going to be a good week!* I was wrong. He never once talked to me and mumbled a "Hello" only after I said "Hi" first. He even began to flash that secret smile to others, randoms that walked into the bookstore, people that suddenly seemed more important than me.

•

Saturday came and I wasn't sure if I would go. I was going to back out, but something inside me tugged; it was the ultimate torture, it was Adam modeling, looking even more beautiful than usual. I had to go because I had to inflict more pain on myself. We always come back to what drives us, our kinks, or, better yet, our addictions.

F.C.U.K. was full, maybe a hundred or so, all of them with passes, all of them exclusive, even some celebrities. I won't name them, but we all know the usual crowds.

Hip club music pulsed through the speakers, including Juliet's "Ride the Pain," "Temptation Waits," by Garbage, and other such sexual dance hits. Cameras were getting ready for their call to duty, and I moved to the back, where all of the models were gathered.

"Adam." He turned and looked at me, showing no sign of happiness in seeing me.

"Oh, hey, Rex, you made it." No "Glad you made it," or "Hey, happy you're here"; it was just "Oh you made it." His gaze seemed cold, distant, reserved, and I knew then that I should leave.

"Yup." He nodded and stood, wearing a pair of jeans, a black T, a cool deep-red–collared shirt with black stars all over it, and a black velvet blazer. He slipped dark aviator shades on his face and walked away, not even telling me he'd be right back. "Fuck this." I grabbed a pen from my pocket, grabbed a piece of paper that was sitting on the table and began to write:

"I can't do this anymore Adam. You push and you pull and yet you never give one way or the other. I don't know what to do because being around you hurts, more so than you will ever know, more so than I could ever tell you. Guys are dangerous; I think you're dangerous; extremely dangerous.

"You fill all of my seconds, but I can't do this. If this snaps something inside you at all, then, boy, you better treat me better, because I'm just going to go away. I want you more than the stars in the sky or the sun, but I can only take so much and that's it, I'm there. I'm already there."

I folded the paper, wrote his name on it, and laid it on his table, preparing to slip out.

"Hey, I'll see you out there, 'kay?" Adam had that grin again, that smile, and I nodded dumbly, especially after I realized that he had just emerged from behind a curtain wearing nothing but low-rise gray briefs.

Seeing him there—his body, his chest, his stomach, no six pack but still flat, his strong legs exposed, and that nice, thick cock tucked in that pouch—God, I was beginning to pop one right then and there.

"Okay. Bye." It wasn't until I slipped out that I remembered the note. I was fucked, I knew it, and not in a good way.

Eagerly I watched him move down that runway, confident, grinning, and moving like a god among mortals. He was gray on earth, he was like my fantasy, he was that manikin turned flesh. Then he looked at me and frowned ever so slightly, before winking to me, slipping his thumb under the band of those hot gray undies and pulling them down only slightly, exposing the beginning of cock, his eyes looking from me to his crotch and back to me. I was so hard that it hurt. He was gone in an instant.

"Hey, Rex!" I turned to see Adam looking at me, keys in hand, dressed in blue jeans and a white T, a duffel bag thrown over his shoulders.

"Uh-huh?" he moved closer to me, and all I could think about at that moment was his muscle of a cock in those tiny gray briefs. Oh gray …

"Can I give you a lift?" I looked at him and I nodded, not prepared for what was going to happen.

●

We're standing outside my apartment and he looks at me as if expecting me to invite him in, but I'm not sure if I will—but I don't have to; he follows me in anyway.

"Well, this is my place." I say, standing in the living room with my arms outstretched.

He grins and steps closer to me. My breath has become heavy and what I think is going to happen doesn't; instead he pushes me forcefully on my couch.

"What the fuck!" He laughs and shakes his head, moving closer to me, looming over me, and for the first time I'm scared of a boy, I'm scared of him.

"All right, listen to me, Rex, and listen good." He's almost yelling. "I like you, you spastic naïve klutz; I've been trying to get your attention for weeks and weeks now, but you never make a freakin' move! You play back, get all interested, then you fucking pull away! God that's why I get weird with you!"

I can't believe this, this admission, and so I stand up and push him back, acting more on my anger, my rage, than on anything else.

"Yeah, well, I like you too, you fucking jerk!" Adam reaches for me, grabs me, and throws me on the bed in my loft space, and I know where this is going.

We kick our shoes off and Adam traces my face with his hands for only a moment before gripping me by the back of my head and kissing me. Those lips, those fucking beautiful lips! God, I've wanted them for so long and they're just as soft as I thought they would be. Our breath is hot as it passes between us, our tongues wet and one rubbing against the other.

My fingers find his shirt and I slip them under the hem, pulling it up off of his body, exposing that wonderfully smooth, warm, firm chest. He removes my shirt and I push him onto his back, straddling his jean-covered crotch. I can feel his firm, hard cock grinding against the tight of my ass, his pelvis moving rhythmically as I smile and bend down, placing my hands on his chest and biting down gently on his nipples, teasing them, grinding against him.

Adam lets out a sigh as I maneuver my way down to his crotch; I hunger for it, that cock that's so desperate to get out.

My tongue follows the middle of his chest, stomach, that torso. His flesh is salty and warm, and, God, I want that cock.

I undo his jeans with my teeth and pull them down, revealing tiny black briefs with red-hem lining and the Thunder Cats emblem, tented by his hard cock. I'm a little disappointed with black, but it makes sense: his forcefulness, his dominating presence, his archetype is black—yet I had hoped for gray.

He looks at me with those dark and sparkling eyes, that knowing grin, and I'm hooked; I couldn't have pulled away even if I had tried. I slide my tongue down on the Thunder Cats emblem and I trace the cat head with my tongue, its entire design, and again he sighs and his cock quivers and I know that's my cue.

I don't remove the undies. Instead I reach in and pull that hot stiff one right out. I look at it, its perfection, its slight slick of precome, and I go down. I close my eyes and work with the rhythm that beats in my head, I work his shaft gently, then roughly, then gently again. I pull it out and run my tongue along the side of the shaft. I make my way up to the mushroom cock head that begins to swell and I flick my tongue fast on it. I move down to his balls and I move them in my mouth while jerking him slowly. He laughs in pleasure, laughs like a kid getting told a great secret, and I then move back onto his cock.

He's in one of the hottest pairs of underwear that I have ever seen, ever touched, and I'm so hard that it hurts, it's painful, I need to come, I need to let it out before I die from it.

I undo my jeans and he watches eagerly. I pull off my underwear and he's ready. From my wallet I remove a condom and slip it on his aching cock, pinching it and leaving enough room for his load. He smiles and then sighs as I slide down on him, fitting him inside me.

I go to work, moving up and down on his shaft, moving my hips in a clockwork motion, then back to up and down, and he's enjoying every bit of it. He curls his fingers around my own stiff one and begins to jerk me off; he's doing it perfectly, and before I know it I'm blowing my load, shooting my jism all over his chest, the glistening milky substance on his caramel skin, and just as the sweat is moving on us, glistening in the afternoon light, as Goldfrapp plays on my stereo, Adam comes. He moans and I can feel it, the heat of it, feel it fill that condom, and it feels like I'm in heaven.

I fall to him and we laugh.

"You know I got your note," he says to me, naked, underwear still on, and he's sweaty and smells like boy.

"Oh, you did…" I shy away.

"Yeah, one of the assistants found it and stuck it in the hem of my underwear…" Why was he still here, why was he still talking to me? Black isn't known for that, black doesn't stick around for tea and conversation.

"Oh."

"Yeah, I read it and it made me sad, but it also woke me up." I smile, and he leans down and kisses me gently on the forehead.

"I liked that underwear …" I muse, and he grins.

"Good, 'cause, uh"—he leans over the bed to his duffel bag and pulls open the zipper—"they let me take one thing with me and I picked the underwear. I liked it, though I've never worn gray before, but I saw the way you looked at it and I figured that you'd like it too."

He showed them to me and I smiled as he pulled off his Thunder Cats underpants and slipped the gray ones on instead. He opened his arms up and I moved into him, against him, and he fell asleep. I had landed a gray!

I bet my sex therapist will like this, I think while lying there with Gray.

Still, I wonder, looking at her as I always do, if everyone of us is a sexual pervert, then what in the hell is her kink?

WHOSE PANTIES?

ALISON TYLER

Marco is a musician and a model. He has long, straight black hair and dark-blue eyes that always remind me of the color "cornflower blue" in a crayon box. He's sinewy rather than slender, with corded muscles on his arms, a strong back, and a flat stomach that the *Baywatch* dudes would kill for. We met near the Santa Monica Pier. I was on my morning run, and he was taking his surfboard off the roof of his car. I had just panted up a hill, and was cruising toward my slowdown when I saw the bumper stickers all over his car: 106 GHOULS. One of my friends had dated a member of that band, and I stopped to ask if he knew the members.

He nodded, smiling at me until I asked the next appropriate question: "Are you one of them?"

It turned out that he was the one who had dated my friend years before, when both were new to the Hollywood rock-and-roll scene. I'd been piqued by her stories about him, her tales of his sexual prowess. Now, with him standing directly in front of me and giving me such an evil smirk, I felt drawn to find out for myself. I made the first move, inviting him over for breakfast when he finished surfing. I pointed out my apartment building, gave him the number, and jogged off, feeling his eyes on me as I sprinted to the corner.

I'd gotten cleaned up by the time he arrived, and he, still in his wet suit, asked if he could shower while I finished getting breakfast ready. I heard him singing over the sound of the water, recognizing his voice from tapes I'd heard at Kimberly's house. He sings for a hard rock band, but he can conjure a soothing lullaby sound when he wants to. I could tell he was serenading me, and I wondered what he would wear when he got out of the shower. Would he put his wet suit back on? Or wear a towel?

Images of the man showering were alive in my head as I poured orange juice into glasses to make mimosas. He strode into my living room suddenly, surprising me. That's what Kimmie had said about him? That he was always full of surprises. He wasn't wearing a towel. He wasn't wearing his wet suit. He wasn't wearing the robe from the back of the bathroom door.

He was wearing my black lace panties and a pair of my stockings. Both had been hanging up in the shower. I didn't know what to say or do. I'd known from Kimberly that he was wild. It's what had attracted me to him. I've spent too many nights being bored by lovers in bed. Marco was definitely not boring ...

"I hope you don't mind," he said, moving toward me, that evil-seductive grin still on his face.

I shook my head. "No, knock yourself out." I wondered what he would do next, and I realized I was wet, wondering.

"I couldn't resist," he said, sitting on the edge of my couch and staring at me. My apartment is small, with the dining room and living room together, separated only by the sofa. My hand was still on the forgotten orange juice container, my entire body frozen in place.

I watched as he ran his fingertips along one of the stockings. His legs looked good, sexy. His body was very pale against the black silk. I took a step toward him, thinking that I wanted to take the place of his hands, wanted to run my fingertips along his legs.

"There's something erotic ..." he started to say, looking at his reflection in the mirrored panels around my fireplace, "something so sexy about lingerie."

I got up my nerve to walk all the way to his side, and once there I settled myself next to him on the couch. His cock was positively protruding against the silk panties, and I could see the full outline of it pressing to be free.

I reached out and stroked him lightly through the silky material, and he leaned back against the couch and sighed.

This whole encounter shocked me. I couldn't believe how turned on I was at seeing this man in my underwear. I was dying to kiss him through the silk, to run my tongue along the seam at the back of the stockings, to kiss his cock and balls and ass through the panties. Rather than analyze these desires, I acted on them, having Marco spread out on the rug and then setting myself free to do what I wanted. I started with his toes, licking them through the silk stockings. Then I carefully moved up his legs.

My stockings were the garterless kind that stay on by themselves. Marco has legs that many women would be jealous of, and he looked so fucking hot in the lingerie that I couldn't control myself. I bit at him through the silk, not caring about any runs I might make. When I made my way up to his cock, the head of it was poking out of the waistband.

"Naughty boy," I said, mouthing the tip of his tool before moving back, knowing exactly what I wanted to do next. "Get over my lap." I sat up on the sofa and let Marco drape his body over my knees. His cock pressed against my thighs, and I could feel more of the sticky precome on the head of it. I ran my hand over his silk-clad ass and then spanked him, thrilled by the feeling of power and pleasure and pain. My hand stung from the blows, but I didn't go too hard, just enough to make him squirm and rub his cock against me.

I slipped the panties down to see his reddened ass and then I pushed him off my lap, back onto the rug, and started kissing him, parting his cheeks and diving my tongue into his asshole. I was ravenous, crazed, and I fucked him like that until he rolled over and grabbed me, stood, and pushed me over the sofa, thrusting his cock into me from behind.

Feeling the stiffness of him inside me was divine, and the silkiness of his stocking-clad legs against my naked thighs. The way I came, the way I shuddered and screamed his name, was surreal. I caught a glimpse of us, of our reflection, in the mirror around my fireplace, and we looked transported, unearthly.

After we both came, we collapsed together on the sofa. I leaned my head against his chest and confessed to knowing him, knowing that he liked things in the extreme. I confessed my curiosity. He smiled his devilish smile and stroked my hair away from my eyes. Then he kissed me and cradled my head in his hands and said, "I was curious about you, too." And I suddenly knew that Kimmie had told him about my track record, and that maybe, just maybe, he'd parked on top of that hill on purpose.

Because I've heard it said that in L.A. there simply are no coincidences.

FRENCH CUT
THOMAS S. ROCHE

You don't wear lingerie. It's not that you have anything against it, it's just not something you do. Your underwear is practical stuff: all-cotton jockeys, sports bras, the occasional pair of boxers. I've never see lace gracing that beautiful, slim body of yours, never seen a Wonderbra caressing those firm breasts or a French-cut pair of panties on your pussy when we undress for the evening or to make love. You show a distrust of anything girlie, really, but clothing is where your sexy androgyny shows itself the most. You sleep in my threadbare old tie-dyed T-shirts, long enough to reach midthigh on your slight frame, and I'm not even sure you know the meaning of the word "stockings."

It all makes sense, really. You're a natural girl. No meat, just tofu, legumes, the rare slab of salmon. No alcohol, just a few puffs off a joint when you're in the midst of your once-yearly party phase. No coffee, just herbal tea with, now and then, a dollop of honey when you're feeling really naughty. No chocolate, just a sprinkling of carob chips mingling with nuts and berries in handfuls of savored trail mix. For you to wear lingerie would be as strange as a French whore downing a jug of Odwalla and a handful of chlorophyll and superfood tablets.

Which is why it grabs me when I see the lacy white thong riding up above the waist of your hiking shorts. I can't take my eyes off it as I hurry to keep up with you on the difficult trail. For the first few minutes I want to tell you, want to sneak up behind you and whisper in your ear that I've noticed. But I remember your lecture, when we started hiking together, on wearing sensible underwear and cinching your belt tight enough that it doesn't slip down over your hips. I know there's a reason you've broken your own cardinal rules, and something tells me I'm going to find out.

We're close to the summit now, the isolated spot you've told me about where we can see the whole Golden Gate spread out below us like an Impressionist tableau. I follow behind you with my cock tingling in my pants, hinting at a hard-on that wants so badly to come into being as my eyes linger on the French lace of your thong.

It happens, finally, when you stop and bend over to pick up a pinecone.

"Look," you say. "It's perfect." You've got a natural appreciation for pinecones—they're the seeds of the evergreen, though normally the reproductive potency of this one wouldn't have such an effect on me. Now, though, it causes my cock to grow hard in my shorts, quickly and painfully so that I have to shift and tug at my jockeys.

Because when you lean forward I can see down your top—and see the hint of lace deep in your cleavage, the low-cut bra embracing your gorgeous breasts.

"Uncomfortable?" you ask, smiling, looking up at me, still bent over, cradling the phallic pinecone suggestively.

"Not at all," I say.

"Too bad," you tell me. You toss the pinecone off the trail and launch into a tawdry sprint, your hips swaying more than a hiking instructor would like.

Breathing hard already, I jog after you.

●

We reach the rocks sheened with sweat, your tank top so damp that when you slip off your backpack I can see the straps of the bra, tempting me even more. I follow you up the last bit of the trail, out onto the plateau of rocks and dirt sparsely covered with scrub.

"Isn't it gorgeous?" you ask, sweeping your hand over the breathtaking view of the bridge, the ocean, and the bay. You bend over and start rummaging through your backpack; the thong climbs high, your hiking shorts falling farther down so I can see the curve of your ass.

"Gorgeous," I say.

You take out the blanket and spread it on the dry brown grass. You take out two plastic wine glasses, set the small, cloth-insulated lunch box on the edge of the blanket, and stretch beautifully in the slanted morning sunlight.

"It's awfully hot," you sigh. "Don't you think it's hot?"

"Sizzling," I say as I come toward you.

"Only one way to cool down," you tell me, as you reach for the buckle of your belt.

I stop in my tracks, watching as you unfasten your belt and slide your shorts down your smooth, tanned legs. The skimpy thong you're wearing plunges so low I can see the top of your blonde hair, and there on the front of it, rimmed by lace, is a little pink heart.

You kick off your running shoes, slide off your socks, and reach down to pull up the sweat-soaked tank top. When you pull it over your head, I see that the bra matches the thong, a girlie push-up that makes your slight breasts look two cup sizes larger. The cups are so low-cut that they almost reach your nipples, which have gotten quite hard and are sticking plainly through the transparent sprinkling of lace. On the cups themselves is a pair of pink hearts, flawlessly matching the one on your pussy.

"I just love to undress out in nature," you tell me, smiling as you see my eyes drinking in your lace-clad body. "Don't you?"

I take the hint, dropping my backpack and stripping off my sweaty T-shirt, then kicking off my shoes and pulling down my hiking shorts and underwear as one. Your eyes linger over my erect cock, pointing toward you and slightly inclined like a come-hither finger begging.

But I'm the one coming to you. You lie down on the blanket, stretching deliciously out and turning from side to side so I can see both the infinitesimal string between your buttocks and the tiny patch of heart-adorned lace that covers your pussy. You smile flirtatiously.

"I went shopping yesterday while you were napping," you say. "I don't know what came over me."

I join you on the blanket, pressing my lips to yours and feeling your tongue surge into my mouth. My hand finds your nipples, feels them harden still more under my touch, and the feel of them poking through the girlish lace excites me even more than I expect. Your fingers curve around my hard cock and you smile when our lips part.

"I'm hungry," you whisper. "Are you hungry?"

"Starving," I growl.

"Good," you tell me, and roll over, away from me. I reach out to touch your ass, fascinated by the unfamiliar way the lace thong looks against your tan.

You unzip the lunch box and take out a small plastic baggie, frosted with condensation. You roll against me, pushing me onto my back and climbing atop me.

"Say aaaaaah,'" you tell me. "And close your eyes."

I do it, opening my mouth. The cold morsel I feel between my teeth shocks me; when I bite, I taste the mingling of forbidden dark chocolate with the taste of strawberries.

"Oh, wow," I mumble, my mouth full.

"Shhhhh," you say. "Just taste. Keep your eyes closed."

I savor the taste of it, ripe and rich and invigorating. I hear you chewing, and when you kiss me, your lips taste of chocolate and strawberry. "Keep your eyes closed!" you laugh.

I feel you shifting atop me, reaching out to the lunch box. You place a chilled orb in my mouth, and when I bite down I taste the overwhelming sugared juice of a cherry. You kiss me, hard, your tongue slipping in and lapping at the syrupy confection.

"One last time," you say. "Sit up a little. Keep your eyes closed."

I hear the twist of a screw-top, the faint glug of liquid. You place the rim of the plastic glass in my mouth, and your hand on the back of my head, telling me when to tip. Red wine floods my mouth, and I feel it dribble warm onto my chest even as I recognize the aromatic flavor—Merlot.

"Messy, messy," you say, bending down to lick the droplets of wine off my chest. Your tongue remains against my skin as you lick up to my throat, then kiss me, your mouth tasting of sweet chocolate, fruit, and wine. You take a drink yourself and curl up on top of me, the soft lace of your bra caressing my face as it darkens from the droplets of red wine still slicking my lips.

"I would have brought a cigar," you tell me, "but that would have been going too far."

I'm overwhelmed; I have to have you. My mouth finds your nipple through the lace and I bite gently, suckling it into my mouth. You gasp softly as my tongue deftly pushes the lace down so I can get to the smoothness of your erect bud. Then you're moaning, as my hands cup your ass and gently tug the lacy crotch of your thong out of the way.

"If I'd known chocolate and wine would have this kind of effect on you," you sigh as I guide you onto my cock, "I would have done this months ago."

Then you're not speaking, you're moaning, as I feel the head of my cock parting your lips, feel you sliding down onto me, hungry with need, my shaft filling your cunt as my mouth teases your nipple. The lace against my cheeks feels strange, erotic—but that's not the reason I want you, nor is it the chocolate or the wine that's intoxicated me. It's the feel of your cunt around my shaft, the desperation with which you slide my cock deep into you.

When I grasp your buttocks and roll you over onto your back, the wine goes flying and spreads a dark stain across the blanket. Neither of us pauses, even as the bottle tips and a glugging stream of Merlot begins to pool under you. I slide into you deeper, your legs going easily up onto my shoulders as I pick up the bottle and empty it over your breasts.

"My new bra," you breathe, only able to mock despair for the faintest instant before my cock reaches its deepest point inside you and you thrust up against me, your lips opening wide. I lick red wine from your breasts as you clutch me tight, your hands running through my hair, your body meeting mine with each hungry thrust. By the time you're ready to come, I've reached out and snatched another chocolate from the baggie.

"Open your mouth and say 'aaah,'" I tell you, and my thumb teases open your lips just far enough to slip the treasured chocolate cream onto your tongue. You take the whole thing in one bite, your eyes closed as you savor the sensations. I'll never know if you actually come at the very moment you taste the chocolate, because you're one of those girls who comes so hard and so long that isolating your moment of pleasure is next to impossible. But the twist of your body and the arch of your back tells me that it's close enough for lovers. I fuck you harder as you chew the cream and swallow, your moan rich and thick around the textured confection.

Then I shut my eyes tight, on the very brink of orgasm, and I should expect it—but I don't.

Somehow, without missing a beat, without lessening your own pleasure, you've managed to reach out and snatch a lemon creme from the baggie, even as it opens and the chocolates scatter across your belly. Your fingers pop the creme into my mouth and its taste fills me at the instant I come, orgasm and sweetness blending in an instant as I thrust deep into you, feeling myself clench far inside your body. When I feel your legs descending from my shoulders, your thighs caressing my sides, I settle on top of you and feel the squish of chocolates between us, coating your skin and mine in the melted ooze of indulgence.

My tongue licks the chocolate from your breasts, feeling only a small tinge of sadness as I look at your ruined bra. You unhook the bra and squirm out of it, then reach down and slide off the thong, looking distastefully at it as I see that the chocolates and wine have run down, staining the pink heart with our jealously guarded vices.

You toss the lingerie into the brush, leaving them for some lucky hiker to puzzle over. You smile up at me, your face and breasts moist with wine and melted chocolate, looking, somehow, even more lascivious than the skimpy lace did.

"See?" you sigh. "I never should have let that lingerie salesgirl talk me into this. What have I been telling you? Chocolate and wine are filthy habits." You snuggle up closer to me, as our skins slide together with the mixture of drink and debauchery.

And when I kiss you, I taste them both. Sweet, like you, and just as forbidden.

ON THE BIAS
JULIAN TIRHMA

Standing behind me, Curt fingers the end of a purple ribbon twining out from the bottom of the corset. In the cloudy, too-small mirror, I see her cat smile, no teeth showing.

"What about this one?" Curt asks.

This is the fourth corset I've tried on, and that's after a few "bustiers" (whatever those are), two teddies (another horrible name), and a matching set of bra and panties. I try not to frown as I stare at myself, all hooked, tied, and cinched into this contraption.

"You like it, don't you?" I swish my hips a bit, convincing myself it's sexy.

She tries to remain objective. After an hour of squeezing into this fitting room with me, the flashes of brown nakedness in-between the moments I'm stitched in bands of tight, itchy satin ringed by useless frills of black lace, she's ready to give up. "I'm … it's a little too … it sits too high on your waist, doesn't it?"

I nod vaguely, already searching for the bow that hides the clasp that begins the long process of unraveling skin from stay.

Ignoring her supplications, I pull on overalls and a yellow tank top. That's it. No more department stores. No more lingerie shops on Hollywood Boulevard. No more malls. If she wants me to wear lingerie on our fake-honeymoon weekend, she's gonna have to weave it herself.

It's not that I hate lingerie. It's just that there is something that turns me off about silk, satin, ribbon, lace, embroidery, see-through, primpy numbers that jut across my breasts, cut into the sweet line of my ass, and detract from the triangle of my cunt. And the colors—black, of course, but also candy pink that makes my skin look sallow, a "nude" that looks like I slapped on a giant Band-Aid, and deep magenta, the kind your mom would have been given for her Valentine's Day present in 1973.

When Curt asked if I wanted to go on a fake honeymoon at a real hotel and pretend we had never had sex with each other, I was all for it. We booked the room, bought the champagne, and got someone to take care of our animals. It wasn't until Curt suggested we wear special fake-honeymoon outfits to lose our fake-virginities that the problem started.

Wandering through eight floors of parking lot, it was like Curt read my mind when she said, "Why couldn't you get a seamstress to make something that's exactly what you want?"

•

The next afternoon I took off from the doggie wash early and headed up to Altadena to meet with a seamstress, Ms. Patel. Over the phone, I hesitated to tell her what I needed sewn, but I hinted that I was going away for my honeymoon in a couple of weeks and realized I needed some special clothes.

I was expecting someone like a woman who took in the sleeves of a bridesmaid's dress a few years back. She was dowdy, midwestern, with mouse-brown hair and little pink glasses to see the stitches. During the fitting she kept saying things like, "Your best friend getting married will be such an event in your life! I mean, it makes you think about getting married yourself."

But this lady ... she was my age. A warm amber scent enveloped me when I walked into the hallway and stood where she had just been standing. She was Indian with long, thick hair I couldn't tell was dark brown or black under the yellow candelabras. She smiled with big, green, friendly eyes and scratched her neck.

"I'm Manjari. You set your parking brake, right? This

steep hill has been known to coerce some cars into the ravine." When she spoke with her lilting, almost-British accent, I felt as if my voice was too warbley or coarse to join hers in echoing off the hand-painted Mexican tiles.

A quiet dog followed us up the curve of a staircase into the alcove that serves as a sewing room. It smelled a little like my grandmother. Thread has a smell, like laundry and hay. And little scraps of cloth smell mustier, like a library and mimeographs. Even plastic buttons smell like newborn baby scalps.

"So, on the phone you said you wanted something for a honeymoon? Did you want to look at any magazines or pattern books for ideas?" She sat on a rickety whitewashed chair piled with pillows, leaving me standing by the ironing board.

I liked how she kept the identity of the garment unnamed.

"I'm not a designer or anything, but I thought maybe I could draw what I had in mind." I couldn't look her straight in the eye, so I perused the boxes and baskets piled on shelves.

Manjari moved a bag of stuffing and a tin of zippers to find some scratch paper. A stubby pencil hung from a string tied to a drawer handle so it wouldn't be lost.

Thankfully, she went to get us water so I could sketch alone. I drew a few curves for my body and started looping it with swaths, buckles, dotted lines for hems, crosshatching to show pattern. I heard the ice clinking in the glasses as Manjari returned, balancing a fingerbowl of lemon slices as she came up the tile stairs.

She gently set them on a side table, her eyes glued to my drawing. Her manner didn't change as she got the idea for what I wanted, so I just started talking as naturally as if it were another bridesmaid's gown.

"The top part, here," my finger trailed the thin line showing a strap, "I wanted out of something really soft, but this fabric here," I pointed to a panel down the front of me, "can be a bit stiffer."

She leaned over my shoulder, taking a sip of her water without lemon, and squinted her eyes. Considering the options, she suggested, "So, raw silk straps and garters, but a leather bodice?"

I stared at my own drawing to keep from meeting her eyes.

Taking my silence for disapproval, she tried again. "Feathers and patent leather?"

"I'm thinking soft like a chenille corduroy, and stiff like a jacquard."

Manjari took another long sip of water, chuckling into the glass. Then she fondly picked up the piece of paper and held it up alongside me, as if envisioning how the garment will hug me, drape me, buckle me up.

•

When Manjari leans over me, her hair comes out of its loose knot and tickles my calves and the tops of my feet. Her nose is level with my scabbed knees, her long lashes just inches from my bristly legs.

With the tape measure, she gently circles one ankle, then the other. In-between each measurement, she scratches some numbers and letters on a yellow pad. She measures the distance from my thighs to the ground, around each upper arm, something from my collarbone to my cleavage, my sides where a zipper might go. I'm amazed at how she can catalogue my body like this, with math, those light pencil markings mine and only mine.

During this process, she says nothing besides directives. "Lift the arm a bit." "Place your feet as far apart as your shoulders." "Take a deep breath. Hold it." "Tilt up your chin for me."

Her soft dry hands are as cool as the blue plastic measuring tape. They flutter purposefully over the downy fur on my lower back, across my thighs like a switch, along the tender skin that shows my pulsing blue veins.

It isn't warm in the room, but I begin to sweat. Because I'm wearing such loose underclothes, just a cotton undershirt and boxers, she has to press to get an accurate measurement. My top sticks to my back, my boxers ride up as she tugs them to my "natural waist." When she encircles me with the tape, her nose at my bellybutton, she must come close to read off the measurement. Then she drops the tape slack so it shimmies along my navel and dangles at my thigh.

It seems like it teases me as it goes, a snake on a tree, trailing along every branch.

Inevitably, Manjari reaches the end of her column of numbers on the yellow pad. Snapping her tape measure into its cylinder, she looks up expectantly. I put on my T-shirt as she finds an incredible book of fabric samples underneath a cat bed.

"Most seamstresses don't have anything like this, but I happen to sew clothes *and* reupholster antique chairs, so I covet my upholstery samples." Manjari flips the swatch book so the colors blur.

Greedily I leaf through the swatches, finding what I like more by texture than color. Deciding what I want more by the name of the color than the actual shade. Butternut. Saffron. Elderflower. Wax. Entrada. Copper Kettle.

After running my finger over the few inches of glued square, I flip over the card to read what kind of fabric I've chosen. One lustrous chartreuse is chintz. Another looks like Renaissance velvet, dusty gray. I find shantung silk, lavender matellasse, silver damask, blood-orange twill.

When I find one I especially like, Manjari unclips it from the ring and pins it to my shirt so I can see how it looks. After the whole roll has scattered its woven spectrum across every surface in her sewing room, I'm left with a handful of the ones I want. Transforming her measurements into a list of how many yard I'd need for each sample, she sends me off.

Saying good-bye at the door, shuffling our legs so the dog

wouldn't escape, she plays with her tape measurement.

"As soon as you get me the fabric, I can start sewing. Meanwhile, I'll make a pattern out of tissue paper."

"I'll go shopping in the next couple of days. Maybe we can do a fitting next weekend?"

"Sounds good. If I'm not here when you bring the stuff, you can stash it on the side porch around that way."

My hand lingers near hers when I hand her my check for the deposit. She shyly takes it and stuffs it in her pocket. I resist the urge to burrow my nose in her amber-scented hair, and transfer my affection to the dog.

Rubbing behind his ears, I'm extra sweet. She tells me, "Ralph really likes you, too."

•

When I ring her bell a few days later, no one answers. Ralph peers at me through the window as if to say, "Manjari is going to be disappointed; she's not here." So I go back down the steps and follow a dirt path past a real wheelbarrow to find the back door. Its blue paint flakes off to show underneath layers of pink and beige. One of the paned windows has busted, so it's closed off with a rectangle of cardboard and tan packing tape. Later, I realize that it's probably a warm-season doggie door.

There's a little bench, like for a mudroom, which just fits on the stoop. Instead of setting the bag underneath it, I take a seat. Ralph has followed me to this door, too. I scratch the window where her nose touches, and we make twin smudges.

•

This time the sewing room is much neater. In a picnic basket, she's housed all my supplies. A little stool with three legs stands at the center while the tall worktable has been dragged to the side. She pushes the frilly, Swiss dot curtains aside to let some filtered light in, showing every surface free of dust.

Carefully, as the pattern pieces are still pinned to tissue paper, Manjari unfolds long strips and round sections. Having never seen a piece of clothing in so many pieces, I'm confused how it will fit together. They crinkle like a first-grader's construction paper Pilgrim costume.

"It might be hard to visualize, but remember this is just the first fitting. It's for me to make sure it will all go together and feel comfortable." Manjari sticks multicolored ball pins in her mouth and motions for me to get undressed and stand on the stool.

Since she's really fitting the thing as it would be worn, I realize I have to be absolutely naked. She has a space heater blowing in the corner, so I don't have the excuse that I'd be too cold. As she busies herself with unpinning certain segments, I quickly pull off every stitch of clothing and jump on the stool.

Goose pimples erupt and my nipples harden. She pretends like she isn't looking at me, but I know that she's aware of the moment all my skin is exposed to the open air.

The raw wood of the stool tickles my feet. I press my knees together and close my eyes.

I feel Manjari's fingers at my collarbone first. Something slips over my head and she whispers to herself, "Watch the pins." Next it wraps across my breasts and gets clipped into place. When she's at my hips, I have the courage to open my eyes. A few pins remain in her mouth, and she still manages to lick the tip of a white pencil so she can draw dotted lines on the fabric. I guess these mark where to cut or where to sew.

She has propped a full-length mirror in front of me, leaning it against the sewing machine. I can see the shape of the garment now, swooping yet sharp. Delicate yet Gothic. Elegantly sparse yet elaborately decorative. The memory of the fabrics comes back to me. Then I realize that Manjari has made embellishments.

Instead of two straps, they are double ribbons, with a circlet around my neck like the finest collar. As she separates the tissue from fabric, there's a cutout appliqué on the bodice that shows leaf-shapes of my bare olive skin. Between the corset and garter belt, she fashioned crisscrosses of brown webbing, the kind that goes inside seat cushions. At the end of the dangling garters are tiny crimson tassels with gold threads. When she gently turns me around, I peek over my shoulder to see the way the bottom laces around my hips with raw silk cord, a greenish gold.

When she has it all together, it looks more finished than what I expected. She's pinned the bodice so tight, I glimpse cleavage beneath the unhemmed edges. Stooping behind me, she reaches between my legs to find some dangling strips that are supposed to be clipped together. Instead of regular underwear, or even a G-string, she has created an unusual design to keep my pussy exposed. She's run *two* lengths of rosy brocade between my legs with a narrow space left in the middle.

To measure the pieces properly, she must brush her hands on the inside of my thighs, twisting my hair in her rings and narrowly missing my lips with her pins. Their sharp tips make me as nervous as her twirling hands make me melt. I'm still tingling when they leave to retrieve long, shimmering gloves out of the picnic basket and feed them onto my arms. She explains they'll have a little button to keep them in place above the elbow.

"I can't even believe what you've done in a week. And with such strange fabric…"

Talking through her teeth, she replies, "It was fun. I love to do projects like this, something different."

She turns me back and forth, repositioning things, tugging them into place. Everywhere her fingers go leaves a hot trace like the dotted lines of the white chalk. She draws out where she wants to bind me, to brace me.

My toes curl around the stool. She says, close to my ear, "Pretty good, but not quite perfect. Some parts still need an adjustment here and there."

From behind again, so I can only half see her reflection in the oval mirror, she only makes the crudest effort at disguising her caresses. One warm, burnished hand slides under the matellasse that cushions my breast, dancing her fingers over my left nipple like the way she feeds fabric to the pedal of the sewing machine.

Kneeling on her soft cotton looped rug, she can look up between my thighs. Both hands reach up into me, staining the rose brocade a darker pink. She makes little circles on my clit like it's a loose button she must mend. Her other hand crawls up my cunt, nestled there in fur and cloth so soft and smooth she wants to upholster her sofa with it.

Her index finger is hard and weathered, like her own thimble, and I like the contrast of something worn and scratchy on my liquid bubble clitoris. Meeting those flicks are cushioned thrusts inside my cunt, her fingers blunted by folding over themselves, eager to form a fist. Three, then four of her slender fingers fit, and I can imagine that I'm dripping down her palm into her gold bracelets.

When my stomach tightens impulsively, two pins stick me in the thigh. When I try to relax, leaning back, three more stab me around the shoulder blade. Correcting for this, I scrunch up something at my left ribcage, and then I'm pricked from the glove slipping down my arm.

Manjari doesn't seem to care if I'm in perpetual discomfort. Her face rests against my ass, like it's a puffy, toile throw pillow. Even without burrowing, I'm sure the pins are trailing light tears down from her eyes, lipstick along her mouth, or dewdrop earrings. They won't penetrate the skin, though. They linger, pressing against it, teasing fate.

FATE AND GRAVITY

JUSTIN TYLER

Jackson Croft. Twenty-five years old. Five-ten and 145, give or take a pound or two. Blond hair, hazel eyes, dark lashes so long they nearly lay on his cheeks when his eyes are closed. Skinny, smooth, and terribly pretty. A dangerous combination for any young man walking into the Brass Lantern Pub on "Boxer Twister" night.

•

Jackson was newly divorced, his four-year marriage to a daddy's-little-girl debutante a dismal failure. He honestly thought he'd loved her, at least at some point. As time wore on, he made the discovery that she truly loved only one thing: Daddy's money. She'd used it to control Jackson, making all of their decisions unilaterally. Where they lived, what they ate, the type of car he drove, what he wore, the type of work he did, the friends he was permitted to associate with, how often they had sex and what position they did it in.

He'd been suffocating, so Jackson did the logical thing, the one thing he knew would hurt his wife the most. He had an affair with one of her best friends.

It just so happened to be her best *male* friend.

Jackson made a discovery about himself during that time. Although he thought he still liked women, as sexual creatures if not as human beings, he knew for certain that he liked men. Due to his good looks, his outgoing personality, and a sexual appetite and repertoire that just seemed to come naturally to him, Jackson had a great deal of experience with sex when he met his wife-to-be. He had always enjoyed sex, and he'd thought that making love with his wife was the end-all and be-all.

Until he slept with Drew Shore.

Well, they hadn't exactly slept. It was more like five solid hours of fucking each other senseless; actual sleeping had not been involved. Jackson learned quite a few things about himself that night. He learned that getting fucked in the ass was the best thing he'd ever felt since discovering jacking off as a kid. He also learned that he had a hell of a lot more control over his own gag reflex than he'd demonstrated during dentist appointments.

He also learned that *he* was the one in control, despite the physically submissive position of being on one's hands and knees. With a sensual arch of his back, a subtle toss of his blond head, and a well-timed, sexy moan, Jackson played Drew like a finely tuned fiddle.

Jackson's wife learned that no amount of money could buy the look she saw on her husband's face, or the sounds he was making when she caught him and her best friend together in her marital bed. She also learned that she *wasn't* the end-all and be-all.

Late that night, Jackson had moved back into the basement apartment of his sister's house, where he'd lived from the time he'd graduated high school until his wedding day. He then spent the better part of the next year making up for lost time. The gay community in the large mid-Atlantic city was fairly concentrated, and he became a fixture in the town's so-called gay ghetto. Gone was the shyness and lack of self-esteem that his relationship with the controlling debutante had created. The young man who walked into the clubs on Friday and Saturday nights was brimming with confidence, and fairly oozing with sex appeal.

Jackson was pretty—he goddamn well knew it by then— and he'd used it to his full advantage. Every head turned when he walked into a bar or dance club, and it was a given that he wouldn't have to leave alone if he didn't want to. On the day he received his final divorce decree in the mail, there was only one gay club in town that he hadn't yet visited, or, rather, conquered. He'd purposefully avoided it, as he was a bit leery of its reputation for things getting a little wild and crazy right there on the premises. Getting naked and intimate with other men behind closed doors was one thing; doing it in semipublic was another matter entirely.

•

Jackson crumpled up the divorce papers and threw them into the fireplace, watching as the sparks were sucked up into the flue. He poured himself another shot of Petrone tequila—his third since fetching the mail—and downed it quickly. He stopped to check himself in the cheval mirror one last time before leaving his apartment. With his slim build, fair skin, and blond hair, you just couldn't go wrong with basic black. Jackson grinned at his reflection.

Yeah, he thought, *I'd do me.*

Jackson locked his apartment door, then jumped into the driver's seat of his silver Mazda RX-8, the only tangible property he'd come away with in the divorce. He shifted the six-speed into gear, and the car pulled away from the house with a perfectly tuned roar.

He was finally going to visit the Brass Lantern Pub. It was Thursday night.

"Boxer Twister" night.

•

Jackson had grown up hearing his mother tell stories about the red-velvet-rope treatment at New York's Studio 54 in the seventies, where bouncers with trained eyes only allowed the most beautiful, well-dressed people into the establishment. He thought that it was rather silly, and that perhaps his mother was even exaggerating the story a bit to make the times sound more glamorous. That is, until he stood between the red velvet ropes outside the Brass

Lantern Pub, dance music blaring from within.

From his vantage point, he saw a burly, brown-haired bouncer with a bushy mustache and long beard motioning furiously in his direction.

"Yo, blondie!"

Jackson was surrounded by men, most of them under the age of forty, all of them gay, and the majority of them very well dressed and quite attractive. Scanning the area surrounding him, he cringed when he didn't see another blond in his immediate vicinity. He looked tentatively at the bouncer, raising his eyebrows questioningly.

"Yeah, you, princess!" the bouncer bellowed. "The blond in black—up front!"

Oh shit. Jackson grimaced. *I'm not even in the goddamn building yet and I've already got a fucking nickname. From somebody who looks like a cross between Santa Claus and a Hell's Angel, no less.*

Pardoning and excusing himself with an apologetic smile, Jackson edged his way through the crowd to the front of the line.

"Well, what do you know, princess," the bouncer said with a gruff voice and a hint of a kind smile. "The boss said to let you in."

"The boss?" Jackson inquired curiously.

The bouncer nodded to a remote swivel camera mounted on the side of the building, aimed down at the roped-off sidewalk. Jackson followed the man's gaze and nodded.

"Ah," Jackson acknowledged. "Lucky me."

The brawny bouncer snorted a laugh, the kind smile a lot more obvious to Jackson this time. "I doubt you ever have any problems getting lucky."

Jackson smiled wanly. "They're going to eat me alive in there, aren't they." He phrased it not as a question, but as a resigned statement of fact.

"Yep," replied the bouncer, grinning. "Don't worry, princess. If things go too far for you in there and you get uncomfortable, just cry 'uncle' and I'll bail you out."

Jackson exhaled sharply. "That's good to know, man. Thanks. What's your name, anyway?"

"Everyone calls me Uncle." The burly man winked a sparkling blue eye.

Jackson laughed, his nervousness quelled for the moment. "I'm Jackson. It's a pleasure to meet you, Uncle."

"Likewise, I'm sure," the big man replied warmly. "Now, go on inside and have a good time. I've got your back."

Jackson nodded and took a deep breath, letting it out slowly. "It's not exactly my back that I'm worried about."

Uncle chuckled. "Relax, princess. Another shot or two of Petrone before the game starts, and you'll be just fine."

"Jesus, it's that bad that you can tell what *brand* it is?" Jackson breathed into the palm of his hand and sniffed, reaching into his blazer pocket for the pack of cinnamon Tic-Tacs he'd stowed there.

"I've been doing this a long time," Uncle said, grinning. "If you'd been drinking wine, I could tell you the vineyard and year. Now, scoot. Fifteen minutes until game time."

•

Once inside the club, Jackson made a beeline for the nearest bar and ordered a double shot of Petrone. He knew that the liquor would taste funky, chasing the handful of Tic-Tacs he'd eaten after leaving Uncle and the velvet ropes, but he didn't give a shit. He needed the Dutch courage far too much to be bothered by something as trivial as having a clean palette for the rare Mexican firewater. Downing the tequila and cinnamon combination with a sour face, Jackson decided that at least one more double shot was in order. Although he'd had three before he even left his apartment, the shock of being singled out in line had pretty much scared the buzz out of him, and damned if he was going to go through with this "Twister" thing sober.

Before he could ask, another double of Petrone had already been poured for him. As Jackson reached for his wallet, the bartender waved his hand.

"This one's on Uncle, princess," the barkeep giggled. "He just radioed back and told me to tell you to relax. So, relax!"

"Oh my *God*!" Jackson groaned. He leaned his elbows on the bar and covered his face with his hands. "What the fuck am I *doing* here?"

"Well," the bartender offered with a grin, "in about two minutes you're going to go over there"—he pointed to a doorway to the left of the bar—"and relinquish everything except your boxers to our exceptionally lovely and trustworthy cloakroom attendant." A pretty, young, brunette woman smiled and waved at the bartender from her post. "Don't worry, princess, she's a die-hard lesbian. Talk about the perfect melding of person and job ..."

Jackson picked up the large shot glass, saluted the cloakroom girl and then the barkeep, and polished off the tequila that Uncle had so kindly provided. He placed the glass carefully on the bar, turned, and made his way to the cloakroom, dumping out another handful of Tic-Tacs en route. He figured the very least he could do for his fellow "Twister" players was to not knock them over with his tequila breath.

•

Jackson was extremely grateful for the significant amount of liquor coursing through his veins. Otherwise, he'd have been a lot more nervous than he was, and he'd have certainly been a hell of a lot colder. The only thing now separating him from the air conditioning blasting through the crowded club was a pair of red silk boxers, with satin appliqués of orange and yellow flames licking up the sides.

He stood on the sidelines with a piece of paper that the pretty cloakroom lesbian had given him in exchange for his clothes and shoes. On the paper a large number 6 had been inscribed with a black Sharpie.

The master of ceremonies, a slight, effeminate man around forty years of age, began speaking into a microphone on the edge of the Twister playing surface.

"Ladies—if any—and gentlemen! Welcome to the Brass Lantern Pub's notorious 'Boxer Twister' night!"

A raucous level of cheering and applause erupted from the assembled crowd—all male, as usual—at the announcement.

"For those contestants new to our proceedings," the emcee continued, looking straight at Jackson, "here are the rules. This is a double elimination tournament. The winner of each match goes on to play the winner of the subsequent match, and the loser of each match plays the subsequent loser, with the winning 'winner' and the winning 'loser' meeting in the final. Don't worry, we know it's complicated. I'll make it easy and just call your number when it's your turn to play."

The crowd chuckled loudly with a generous smattering of applause.

Jackson blanched, doing the math. *Oh shit*, he figured out, *double elimination ... that means I'm in the third match. I think I need another drink ...*

"Now, the rules for Twister itself are just as God and Milton-Bradley intended," the emcee went on. "There are four colors on the playing surface, and four corresponding colors on the game spinner: blue, red, yellow, and green. The spinner is further divided, within each color, into right hand, left hand, right foot, and left foot. So, if the spinner lands on red, left foot—well, hopefully you're all bright enough to figure that out. Oh, and we did indeed petition Milton-Bradley to add another ... appendage to the spinner, but alas, they were reported to be reluctant to tarnish their family image. Either that, or they simply couldn't figure out how to fit that in with the whole right-left thing."

The bar patrons laughed uproariously. Jackson broke out into a cold sweat and high-tailed it for the bar.

The bartender saw him approaching; he smiled and

poured another healthy glass of the imported tequila.

"Thank you," mouthed Jackson, grabbing the glass and swilling down its contents, "thank you." He reached down as if to grab his wallet from his pants pocket, embarrassingly recalling that he was wearing only his bright red, flame-adorned undies.

"Catch me later," grinned the barkeep.

•

As Jackson stood fidgeting on the sidelines, he became much less nervous as the second match progressed. The first match had actually been quite tame, merely a game of Twister like you'd see in anyone's family room except for the fact that both participants were dressed only in their boxers. The second match, between contestants three and four, wasn't any different. No untoward touching or groping as Jackson had expected to see, just a quite ordinary game of Twister, with a lot of laughing and giggling and not much else.

Jackson was feeling quite relaxed, partly from the vast amount of tequila he had consumed and partly from the surprisingly chaste nature of the first two Twister matches of the evening, By the time his number was called by the emcee, Jackson was not only very much at ease and a little more than slightly drunk, he was feeling a bit randy. He was actually hoping at that point to infuse a little bit of excitement and heat into this otherwise staid event.

"And now, for your viewing pleasure," the emcee announced with a lecherous grin, "may I introduce contestants numbers five and six! Please enter the playing field, gentlemen!" Jackson blew out a breath and walked out onto the plastic Twister surface to take his place beside the master of ceremonies. He was feeling pretty damn good until he saw movement in the crowd and another young man began his approach toward the plastic mat. It took a concentrated effort for Jackson to retain his cool when his opponent walked across the floor to join him.

The preceding contestants had been attractive, yes, but this guy was goddamned, drop-dead, fucking *gorgeous*.

Contestant number five was in his early twenties, probably a year or two younger than Jackson and perhaps an inch or two taller. Just as fair and just as slender, but that fucking *perfect* sort of smooth, muscled skinny that was both masculine and god-awful pretty at the same time. He wore a pair of plain, black silk boxers that contrasted wonderfully with his pale complexion. Straight, sleek, shiny, jet-black hair rested lazily between his shoulder blades in the back and teased at his forehead with shaggy, razor-cut bangs in the front. His eyes were almond-shaped, green and dark and haunting, like a pine forest in a scary movie, framed by perfectly sculpted eyebrows and black lashes so long and thick they almost looked uncomfortable. The boy's lips were plush, pouty, and perfect enough to make whoever America's current supermodel was envious beyond belief.

Jackson, despite his earlier reservations, was extremely glad that he was wearing relatively loose-fitting boxer shorts. His dick had gotten rock hard the moment he saw the black-haired boy walk across the floor, and he was quite grateful for the modest coverage that his flame-decorated boxers provided.

The hooting and cat-calling from the crowd had begun the moment that Jackson had walked onto the Twister plastic, and it had only increased when his raven-haired opponent joined him. The emcee, grinning like the Cheshire Cat, tapped loudly on his microphone to regain the attention of the crowd.

"Gentlemen! Gentlemen! It would appear that we have a rare event unfolding before us here tonight at the Brass Lantern Pub! For the first time in over two years we have a preliminary match featuring two Twister virgins!"

The din of the crowd was nearly deafening with applause and cheering, whistling and cackling. Jackson looked at his opponent nonchalantly and shrugged; the black-haired boy shrugged back and smiled broadly.

Jackson returned the smile pleasantly. *Holy God*, he thought, continuing to smile, *all of a sudden I don't think I'm the one that Uncle is going to have to rescue...*

The master of ceremonies raised his hands to quiet the gathering, and finally the noise died down enough for him to speak.

"On such a momentous occasion," the emcee announced, "I think it's only right that proper introductions be made. Your name?" The emcee put the mike in front of Jackson's face.

"Hello. I'm Jackson, and I'm suddenly *very* happy to be here."

Jackson's comment was greeted with loud applause, and a fair amount of whooping and hollering.

"And you are?" the emcee inquired of the black-haired boy, moving the mike toward him.

"The name's Trevor, and I think five is my new lucky number," the dark-haired newcomer replied in a clipped, British accent. He looked over at Jackson and grinned. Jackson met Trevor's gaze and smiled back.

Holy shit, Jackson mused, *all that and a sexy accent, too. I'm a fucking dead man.*

The crowd went berserk.

●

"Player five," the emcee announced after spinning the dial. "Left hand, green."

Trevor walked across the plastic Twister surface and decided on the green spot closest to the center. He squatted down and placed his left hand firmly on the green circle. He looked over toward the emcee and nodded, his move complete.

"Player six," said the emcee, waiting for his spin of the dial to come to a stop. "Right foot, red."

There were sixteen red circles on the oversized Twister

board, but only one of them held any interest whatsoever for Jackson. He walked from the edge of the plastic tarp to place his right foot on the red circle to the immediate right of where Trevor's left hand rested on the green circle. Jackson looked down at the squatting British boy and grinned, then turned and nodded to the master of ceremonies to acknowledge that his first move had been decided upon.

"It would appear we have a bold strategist among us, gentlemen," the emcee grinned slyly. He walked to the center of the playing surface and raised the microphone to Jackson's face. "And your line of work?"

Jackson smiled and leaned into the microphone. "United States Marines, Special Tactical Unit."

The audience applauded generously with a collective "ah" and the emcee fanned himself dramatically, lowering the mike to the black-haired boy's level. "I hate to say it, but I think you're in trouble, girlfriend. And what do *you* do for a living, pray tell?"

Trevor tilted his head to lean into the mike, speaking clearly with his musical accent. "I can't tell you, exactly. Suffice it to say that I'm a code-breaker for a government agency, on loan to your wonderful country at Her Majesty's pleasure." He looked up at Jackson and smiled sweetly before continuing. "My job is to know what the enemy will do, before they do it."

A loud chorus of "oohs" erupted from the crowd, along with an appreciative round of applause.

"Have mercy," the emcee cooed, fanning himself even harder. "Perhaps we should have played Battleship tonight instead of Twister!"

The audience clapped loudly and cheered. Jackson grinned down at Trevor, and the black-haired code breaker looked up and smiled, winking a green eye surreptitiously at him.

Jackson melted. The game was definitely on, but he and Trevor were no longer the unsuspecting pawns: the voyeuristic crowd was.

The master of ceremonies spun the dial. When the arrow came to a stop, he announced Trevor's turn. "Right foot, yellow."

Without raising up from his squatting position, Trevor slid his right leg out to the side, brushing his naked foot against Jackson's bare right heel before bringing it to rest on the nearest yellow circle.

Just the fleeting touch of a bare foot against his, but it made Jackson shiver from toe to head nonetheless.

The emcee wasted no time in spinning the Twister dial. It was Jackson's turn to move.

"Left hand, blue."

Jackson couldn't help but smile at his good fortune. As fate would have it, there just happened to be a vacant blue circle right between Trevor's squatting legs. The audience recognized the luck of the draw before Jackson even twitched a muscle, and his movement toward the blue dot kept time with the staccato clapping from the crowd. The blue circle in question was just slightly in front of Trevor, so Jackson simply couldn't help but nestle his left forearm up and into the boy's crotch en route to his final destination.

Now bent over to allow his hand to touch the Twister mat, Jackson found that his head was nearly resting on Trevor's shoulder. He heard the boy moan quietly when his arm wedged up between his legs, and he definitely felt something happening there, the same thing that had happened to *him* the moment he'd seen the gorgeous young man approach the playing field.

Without any further discourse, the emcee spun the dial for Trevor's next turn. "Left foot, blue." The audience catcalled and whistled, anticipating the position of the only logical move.

The closest blue circle that Trevor could reach with his left foot was immediately behind him. He raised himself up carefully, ass in the air, and firmly planted his left foot behind him onto the blue dot. A compromising position, needless to say, but he didn't mind entirely, considering his opponent. At this point, the Brit just wanted the bloody game over with so he could drag the beautiful, sexy, blond-haired American out of the building and into the nearest apartment, hotel, car, or alley, whatever venue might be most convenient.

Another spin of the dial and it was Jackson's turn to apply strategy. "Left foot, yellow."

Ha.

Without an instant of hesitation, Jackson stretched his left leg straight out toward the yellow dot underneath Trevor's body, between the black-haired boy's left foot and left hand.

Only six moves into the game, and already the players were in an extremely precarious predicament, with the crowd cheering them on. Being behind Trevor and holding the proverbial "high ground," as it were, it would have been very easy for Jackson to skin Trevor's boxers off his ass and down his legs right then and there. As much as he felt compelled to do just that, he wanted more than that from the boy, and he didn't necessarily want an audience in attendance. So, using his American military training and his natural, logical reasoning, he decided to put the final decision in Trevor's court.

Jackson leaned over and rested his chin on Trevor's right shoulder, his full weight borne on his left hand in the blue circle just in front of the other young man.

"You have two choices here, boy," Jackson whispered breathily through black, silken hair. "You can stand strong and we keep playing this child's game for a crowd of strangers until we're exhausted, both of us being very competitive sorts. Or, you can collapse underneath me right now, and we both surrender, go back to my apartment, and see what happens from there. I leave the choice up to you."

Jackson felt Trevor's naked shoulders shudder beneath him, his back rising and lowering with every breath as the boy considered his alternatives. Also having been trained in the military, Trevor didn't take but seconds to weigh the pros and cons of his current situation, and he didn't second-guess his decision for an instant once it had been made.

Trevor let his arms and legs buckle beneath him, his chest hitting the plastic surface of the Twister pad hard. Jackson toppled heavily onto the boy's back.

The emcee blew a whistle, announcing the end of the third match of the night. "And the winner is number six, Jackson! In the loser's bracket, we have Trevor! Gentlemen, please keep your ears open for your numbers later in the evening. Everyone, please give a welcoming round of applause to our newest competitors!"

The assembled crowed applauded wildly as Jackson and Trevor collected themselves from the plastic mat. With Trevor's hand grasped firmly in his, Jackson leaned over to whisper into the emcee's ear.

"We're both forfeiting. Thanks for the introduction."

The master of ceremonies smiled. He covered the mike with his hand and leaned into Jackson's shoulder, whispering back to the blond. "I love being a matchmaker even more than I love being an emcee. Play safe, and please know that you're both always very welcome here."

Jackson grinned and pecked the emcee on the cheek, and pulled Trevor by the hand away from the playing surface. On their way to the cloakroom to reclaim their clothing, Jackson literally bumped into Uncle's imposing figure.

"Leaving so soon, princess?" Uncle asked with his customary kind smile.

"I got sort of distracted," Jackson replied, smiling in Trevor's direction.

●

The drive home was nothing short of agonizing.

Jackson's Mazda was a six-speed, so his left hand was occupied with the steering wheel and his right with the stick shift. Trevor's right hand had engaged itself with channel-surfing the one hundred–plus satellite radio stations on the console, leaving his left hand with nothing better to do than to torment Jackson's corduroy-clad erection.

Jackson's apartment was only seven miles from the pub, but never had such a short distance seemed to him like such an eternity to drive.

●

As he fumbled noisily with his keys at the front door to his apartment, Jackson felt Trevor's lithe, warm body pressing up against his back, the boy's breath rasping in his ear.

Please fit, please fit, PLEASE FIT, Jackson pleaded silently with the key in his hand. Finally, the lock cooperated and the door swung open.

Jackson quickly closed the door behind them, the only ambient light in the room being the dim glow of the tropical fish tank in the far corner. Trevor was in front of him, the boy's hand pressing against his chest, backing him up. Jackson somehow managed to make it to the stereo controls, reaching down and behind himself to press the start button on the CD player. He had at least left something decent, something sexy on the five-disc changer when he'd last played it.

Loreena McKinnot's "Marco Polo," an Irish instrumental track with a sultry Middle Eastern undercurrent. Music just doesn't get a whole hell of a lot sexier than that.

Before the second measure had begun to play, Trevor was all over him. Jackson sighed and quietly squealed as Trevor touched him, the boy's hands skirting his shirt up and over his arms and head to bare his chest. Short, manicured nails skated down Jackson's skin from his shoulders, teasing at his nipples before warm palms caressed his flat stomach.

A brief moan escaped Jackson, quickly swallowed up by lips so soft, so warm and moist and so very perfect, that the mere touch of them was an almost painful thing to bear. Warm, slender-fingered hands wrapped around his waist, moving their way up his back in firm, slow, erotic, concentric circles. Jackson thought he was going to die happy just from the sensation when he heard a voice, soft and beautifully accented, close to his ear.

"My God," Trevor whispered quietly to him, "you are the softest, softest thing I have ever felt. I can barely breathe."

Jackson wrapped his arms around the black-haired boy, pulling him closer to him, so close that not even the thinnest sheath of paper could have been slid between them. Before he could utter a word in response, the British boy spoke to him again.

"You are so amazingly beautiful," Trevor said, still not able to catch his breath and still whispering softly into his ear. "So beautiful. So soft. So perfect. Jackson, I never, ever cry. Please tell me, why are there tears in my eyes now?"

Jackson didn't have an answer for him. He had never been one to cry either, yet his own vision was blurred by tears. He was experiencing emotions that he'd never experienced with another person before, feelings he hadn't thought possible.

"I can't even think straight right now," Jackson whimpered. "Make love to me, Trevor. I really don't care what you do—what we do—just love me, however you want to. Okay?"

The bed was only a few feet away from them, but they couldn't even manage to make it that far. They fell to the floor together, slender legs and arms akimbo in a crumpled, hopeless, helpless heap upon the carpeting. As their bodies hit the floor, they kissed. And if ever, ever there was such a kiss that spoke of love and loss, and hope and need, and longing and want, then that was the one.

Shoes were hurriedly kicked off, and clothes were struggled off and flung about, and by virtue of fate and gravity Jackson ended up on the bottom of the pileup. Trevor lay on top of him, no less a willing prisoner of the same fate and gravity. Jackson leaned back and raised himself up on his elbows, and Trevor got up onto his knees, pressing his face into his lover's chest, nipping at firm muscle and laving his tongue over hardened nipples. Trevor licked and kissed his way up Jackson's chest and neck, his mouth coming to rest again on lips just as full and warm as his own. Their tongues sought and found each other, their kiss deep, wet, hot, and utterly soul-damaging in its intimacy.

It struck them at the same time that they were both left wearing only the boxers they had adorned so purposefully for that anonymous game of Twister earlier in the evening. In as little time as it took for them to recognize that they were still wearing them, the silk garments were removed, half shimmied off by the wearer and half pulled off in a frenzy by the other.

With their boxers strewn haphazardly on the floor surrounding them, Trevor and Jackson were naked, wrapped tightly in each other's arms. With no preconceived notions or planning in regard to who was to be top or bottom, it just so happened that the gravity spill had landed Jackson on his back with Trevor on top of him. That's the way they remained.

No preconceived notions or planning. Merely the random chance of fate and gravity.

Trevor gently rolled Jackson onto his stomach, laying himself fully out on the other boy's back and legs. The British boy stretched and pressed himself gently into his lover, closing his eyes, rejoicing and reveling in the feel of every inch, every centimeter of the warm, pale skin that touched his own. Jackson reached forward, opening the floor-level cabinet where the CD player was, the same place he'd stowed an unopened plastic bottle of lube, something he'd never needed to use in his own home but kept there anyway, just in case. He reached back until his hand met Trevor's and placed the plastic bottle in his lover's hand without so much as a word. That silent transfer was all that was needed in the way of permission, of acceptance.

Jackson heard the snap of the plastic lid, the sound of it

just as erotic to him as the music that was playing, as the breath that was tickling at his neck. He heard the sound of the slick gel being rubbed quickly between hands, warming his heart as he knew the fluid was being warmed up for him. He sighed as he felt Trevor's hand slide between the cheeks of his ass, both the hand and the liquid soft and warm to the touch. His legs spread apart, opening himself willingly, wantonly, lovingly.

Trevor nestled himself into Jackson, his cock hard, harder than he'd ever imagined it could be. He pressed the head of it against Jackson, moving against him, pushing himself slowly into his lover's body. The thick ring of muscle protested and Jackson moaned, partly from the hurt itself and partly from wanting to take the hurt so badly from this exquisitely beautiful man. Jackson breathed and relaxed, and the sting subsided, his muscles softening and giving way to his lover's entry. Trevor reached underneath him, gently prodding Jackson up onto his hands and knees.

Trevor, who never, ever cried, felt hot tears rolling down his cheeks, simply because he'd never seen or felt anything more beautiful, more lovely, than this man on his hands and knees, giving himself to him so willingly, so completely. As his lover's cock entered him fully and filled up all those empty spaces from the inside, Jackson's back arched, his blond head was tossed back, and erotic, primal sounds escaped his lips, this time and for the first time not of some preplanned, controlled performance but because his body and his soul truly felt it and simply reacted. In fact, Jackson had never felt so *out* of control of himself in his life, and for that one, blissful moment, he really didn't care.

Jackson had experienced a lot of sex in his adult life, but this was honestly the first time that he'd ever really made love with someone, the first time that he'd truly given up everything that he was, or had, to someone else. He could feel, for the first time, everything; the man pushing his hard cock in and out, inside of him, the warm, soft hands drifting lazily up and down his arms, the long, silken hair teasing at the skin between his shoulder blades, the hot, wet tears dripping slowly onto the small of his back.

Everything. He felt *everything*.

Trevor came deep inside of him, soundlessly, the silence of his orgasm so much more erotic than the forced, fake noise that Jackson usually associated with the event.

Jackson shuddered and came as well, staining the carpet beneath him without so much as a single touch to his own cock. His lover's wordless climax had been enough to send him over the edge, and he'd never felt more fulfilled, or more like a man than he did at that moment.

●

No doubt about it, it had happened quickly and unexpectedly, they both admitted to each other many years later. A completely chance meeting in a totally random place, both of them looking for one thing and finding something different entirely.

This ... *this* was the end-all and be-all.

This was love.

PANTY PLAY
TANYA TURNER

Even as I stepped out of the cab, my coat gaping open just enough to let everyone in on my little secret, I heard the whispers. It was my party, after all, so I let the trails of "Is she wearing her underwear?" and "Did I just see her nipple?" float by. To get publicity as a writer, I knew I had to do something to make a scene for my debut novel's book party; otherwise I'd just be one of umpteen new authors on the shelves, getting perhaps five minutes of fame until next week, when a whole slew of competitors came down the pipeline. Since my novel was called *Panty Play*—a play on the protagonist's name, Carrie Panter—I decided to go all out with the party. I instructed guests to dress as sexy as possible, and for my part, I had gone above and beyond.

I'd chosen an extremely skimpy bit of wispy black and purple material to cover the parts of me that were absolutely essential to cover, leaving plenty of skin to be freely ogled. The top featured lace trim along the edges, but then went sheer, with tons of little polka dots all along the fabric. You could see my nipples beneath them—well, you could see the star-shaped pasties I'd put on to cover them up, to draw more attention to them than had they been bare. The top flapped open in the middle, flashing my bare stomach and leading the way down to the matching black underwear, covered in elaborate lacy designs that didn't actually let you see through them but gave the illusion that if you looked hard enough you might. I wore thigh-high fishnets that left a little gap, enough to get a glimpse of my pale thigh. I'd let my long, black hair fall simply down my back, the ends hovering in the space left between my top and undies. On my feet I wore purple alligator-skin slingbacks, playing up the purple tones in my outfit. I had a feeling most people were going to go wilder for my new look than for my book, but that was fine with me—after all, all publicity is good publicity, right?

As I stepped out of the limo, though, I wasn't quite prepared for the number of cameras that started going off, along with hoots and whistles, as I let my black trench coat gape strategically open. By the time I reached the door to the club, my cheeks were starting to redden, not from the cold but simply from knowing my entire body was on display. I almost felt like I might've been better off naked, but I quickly looked down at myself, smoothing a hand down my hip and toying with the waistband of the panties. Then I took a deep breath and opened the door. Once again, I was in for a shock! What must have been three hundred people were crammed onto the dance floor of the nightclub. I'd left the decorating up to my friend Ray, because that's his specialty, and he'd chosen to adorn the walls with various kinds of panties in all different shades. I looked up and saw thongs, bikinis, tangas, boy shorts, lace, silk, cotton, running along every wall. Above and below were posters with my book cover, featuring a woman's darkened silhouette, her privates covered by a simple white pair of panties. After over two years of nonstop writing and revising and editing, of wondering if anyone would give a damn about Carrie and her capers, here they were, people who actually did care, who might even take my book on the subway with them and devour it while other riders craned their necks to see what *Panty Play* could be about.

I looked around to see various fellow writers, editors, artists, and performers already getting the party into full swing. No one was laughing at me or my book, as I'd feared; in fact, small crowds were gathered around ogling the panties, and I heard one guest wonder out loud if they'd be party favors. As I walked in, everyone seemed to go quiet, waiting for me to take off my coat. I entered, passed my coat to a friend, and almost collapsed. Instead of my usual nerves, I felt a calm settle over me. I'd been working out for months in preparation for this day and had gone over every aspect of my appearance dozens of times. As I strutted through the crowd, wearing next to nothing, all I heard were "oohs" and "ahs." I could feel my nipples thrusting forward, poking against the sheer fabric of my top, demanding their own audience. I beamed a big smile out to the crowd as I strode to the bar, gaining confidence with each step.

My publicist and I had developed several games for guests to play love onstage, including Guess What Kind of Panties I'm Wearing?—the prize being a basket full of assorted panty goodies. We made our contestants either show a smidgen of their actual underwear or draw it to the best of their ability. When I looked around, I noticed several couples nuzzling up, men whispering into women's ears what kind of undies they'd like to see on them, and I clocked a few guys and one smoldering woman checking me out. I felt like my nipples were doing the talking for me, so I mostly remained at the table signing books, my legs crossed, my whole body warm with excitement and adrenaline. I sipped ice water to stay cool, not wanting to sweat in my beautiful new outfit. Toward the end of the night, my old friend Rudy sauntered by. I hadn't seen him in at least five years, though we'd kept in touch via e-mail. He'd seen me rise from scribblings for tiny magazines into full-fledged best-seller status and grabbed my arm to tell me he'd seen my book splayed across the front window of our favorite bookstore. As his fingers brushed my skin, I felt my body relax into his touch even as arousal overtook me. I crossed my legs tighter, feeling the press of the fabric against my slit. Rudy had always done this to me, and for the life of me, now I couldn't recall why we'd never gotten together. Certainly, it wasn't for lack of interest on my part.

"And Lisa, baby, you've never looked better. I remember the shy girl I met who wouldn't even try on anything that didn't come past her knee, and look at you now," he said, his eyes dipping down to my bared cleavage while he scooted his chair closer. Just then, someone came up and asked for a book to be signed. I wrote her name and added my usual inscription, "Have fun with your panties—don't do anything I wouldn't do in them!" then scrawled my name. As I did, the pen almost went dipping up the page like a hospital readout as Rudy's hand crept along my leg. It was safely under the table, so nobody else could see, but his wide, warm palm and powerful fingers sent a surge of arousal all through me. The expression on his face didn't change, but I was sure he had a hard-on.

"Lis," he said when I turned back to him, trying to keep my face composed, "I have a present for you. I want to give it to you now," he said, his voice getting low on the last five words. I didn't know what he meant. Was it drugs? Did he want us to go smoke outside? But when he slipped something soft into my hand under the table, I suddenly got it. I looked down at the lacy bundle in my hands. It was a pair of red panties, soft and delicate, with crystals adorning the front patch in the shape of an L. "I know you can't put them on right now, because everyone would see," he said, but maybe you can just hold them in your lap. He eased them out of my startled, relaxed fingers and nonchalantly wedged the monogrammed panties between my legs. I moved just enough to allow him entrance, letting him ram his hand hard up against my pussy lips. All night I'd been churning, wet and hungry, in the heightened state I always succumb to at parties; added to this was the dose of narcissistic pride that seeing my book cover blown up into extra-large glamour all around the room gave me.

I pressed back against him as best I could, also pressing my shiny red lips together so as not to have my mouth hanging open as he massaged me through two layers of panties. A young woman came rushing up to the table. "Hi, Ms. Squire, I'm a friend of Vaughn's and I just wanted to tell you I loved your book. I hope you're writing a sequel! I'm doing a story for my college paper and there's just one thing I have to ask you. What's your favorite kind of underwear?"

I smiled at her, risking opening my mouth, hoping that moans of arousal wouldn't come pouring out involuntarily. My nipples were already proudly beaded pebbles, thrusting themselves at anyone who approached as Rudy's fingers pushed against my slit, slamming the fabric against me. I wondered how I'd ever get up; they surely had to be soaked with my juices by now. "Well, I really can't pick just one; I have so many special pairs. But I did recently get some panties that hold a special place in my heart. They're light as air, red, sheer, and very sexy, and the letter L is spelled out in crystals across the front. They're perfect," I said, trying not to cough as Rudy boldly slipped his fingers beneath the waistband of my original black panties, somehow working his fingers against my wet folds even though my legs were clamped together. I really for the life of me had no idea why we'd never done this before.

"Those sound beautiful. I hope they bring you lots of fun times," she said. She then gave me a smile and a wink as she sauntered off. I could barely look at Rudy; what I wanted to do was close my eyes, but I couldn't grant myself that luxury until every guest had left. When Rudy slipped his fingers out from between my panties, I sighed, disappointed even though I knew it was necessary.

"Let me give you a ride home," he said, looking at me with those intense blue eyes like we'd just spent the day strolling around the shops after brunch. He wiped his wet fingers on my inner thigh, and I pressed my legs tightly together, trying to trap him there. He escaped, along with my gift. "Why I don't I take these with me so they don't get lost?" he asked. I nodded up at him, too weak for a verbal reply.

I began the process of saying my good-byes. Most people were gone, but the ones who remained were my close friends, and even I felt a little self-conscious about telling them I was slipping off to be with my lover, so I kept mum even as my pussy pounded. I was sure that my lust was written all over my overly exposed body, but I found that wearing lingerie as your outfit gave you a certain amount of leeway; people were so awed at your audacity, they didn't really notice the details quite as much as they might catch muffled hair or flushed cheeks. Not wanting to be caught staring, they missed the way I held my legs tightly together, my hard pink nipples pressing against the sheer fabric. Or if they did notice, they didn't say a thing.

Finally we were in Rudy's car, racing uptown—well, as much racing as we could do. That's one thing about New York, there's traffic any time of the day or night. "Touch yourself for me," Rudy said, his eyes still on the road. I unbuttoned my coat, letting anyone who cared to look see my skimpy outfit—and my hand slithering down the front of my panties. But when Rudy joined me in some very seductive panty play, whipping out the red pair he'd bought me and surreptitiously stroking them along his hard dick while he drove, I was simply stunned. How could he drive and jerk off at the same time? When he instructed me to hand him my panties, there was no way I could refuse. I stepped out of them, my scent suffusing the car as I quickly repositioned my coat so we wouldn't get arrested. Now he held both pairs in his lap, his eyes on the road and with only one hand on the wheel as I pleasured myself. By the time we pulled up at his place, I was so far gone that I was practically humping my hand. He parked, and then reached for my hand to let me stroke his cock with the aid of the panties. I was jerking us both off at once, and he didn't seem to mind getting closer and closer until he lost it, his come oozing out and soaking his pants, both pairs of panties, and my hand.

We made it upstairs, and eventually stripped, making love the traditional way, with his cock slowly sliding in and out of me, hitting all the right places. But somehow, our sex wasn't quite as urgent as our furtive traffic gropings. We lounged around, letting the night blend into the next day as if we didn't have a care in the world. When I finally awoke, he pulled me close and kissed me deeply. "I just have one question for you, my darling." I thought he was going to ask why we'd broken up, or when we could make love again, or what the future held, but instead, he said, "Will you sign this for me?" and handed me a copy of my very own book.

I took it from him, holding the pen he offered me against my lips until inspiration struck. "Rudy, you give good panty and you always will." And I meant every word.

THE OL' BADA BING

SIMON SHEPPARD

Okay, for whatever reason, I've always been partial to big, husky guys, especially the ones who seem kind of rough on the surface but have a trace of sweetness, maybe, underneath. So when I saw him at that stripper bar, my dick went up like a cop-car antenna. Not everybody would have shared my opinion, I guess, but I thought, *One of the hottest guys in Jersey.*

And I guess I caught his attention, too. He smiled at me, a twinkle in his eyes that I could see halfway across the room, and gestured at his whisky, then at me, a move that clearly meant *Can I buy you a drink?*

Within moments he was beside me making small talk, and after a while he said the semi-inevitable: "Hey, why don't we get out of this place, go somewhere more private." It wasn't a question, really. More of, well, a command. And hell, I could do without the near-naked broad twirling around a pole. There was another pole I was considerably more interested in.

So I drove to his place, following his big-ass Lincoln Navigator through the night. Nice house, large place, quiet as a tomb. He waited for me at the door, then disarmed the security alarm as we walked inside.

"This way," he said.

"Hey, I don't even know your name."

"That's okay. Does it matter?" He said it with a smile, but his tone was still, well, a little ... I don't know...

The bedroom was—like the rest of the house—big, nice, fancy in a slightly overdone way. I didn't give a fuck about the decor, though. I wanted this guy, whatever his name was, whatever his bedroom suite looked like. I stood right in front of him, so close I could smell the fading booze on his breath.

He smiled, so I reached up and stroked his cheek. He stepped forward, pressed himself against me. I could feel his hard-on. Already. Fuck, yeah.

I put my lips to his, but he pulled away.

"Hey," he said, "no kissing."

A disappointment, but one I could live with. Instead, I reached down and squeezed his crotch. Yeah, nice big piece of meat. He kind of humped my hand.

"Hey," he said, "don't you want to get undressed." It was, again, not really a question.

He backed up, slipped his knit shirt over his head. Nice, big, hairy chest, meaty tits, just the way I like 'em. He was down to his boxer shorts now.

"Whatsamatter? You change your mind?"

"Not at all," I said. "I'm just a little slow. I was … admiring you."

He slipped his shorts off. "Well, maybe you should get naked." His uncut dick stood up smartly beneath his hot, sizable belly. "So's I can suck your cock."

I didn't need to be persuaded. I stripped down to my socks and stood there stroking my hard-on, and looking, I hoped, seductive. The guy dropped clumsily to his knees and stuck his face up against my crotch. His tongue flicked over my cock head. He looked up and smiled. "Feel nice, buddy?"

I nodded. He, for his part, slipped his lips around my cock head and started nursing. It felt great, fucking great. He reached up to stroke my chest, and that's when I noticed what I might have subliminally seen but ignored before: The guy was wearing a wedding ring. He hadn't even bothered to take it off. Well, no big surprise. No big whoop. He might have a wife, but he sure could suck dick.

After a few minutes of deep-throating, his mouth let go of my hard-on. Looking up at me with that glint in his eye, he said, "Hey, buddy, want to try something?" This time, it really was a question.

"Sure," I said. "I guess." I figured if I didn't like whatever it was, I could always leave.

He lumbered to his feet, walked over to the bed, and bent over. His meaty ass cheeks parted enough to expose a furry streak of jet-black hair. Fucking hot. He reached under the bed and pulled out a suitcase, tossing it onto the mattress. It had one of those numerical locks. He whirled the dials and opened the lid. From where I stood, I still couldn't see what was in it.

"So you're okay with this." A statement again.

"Depends."

"You're okay with it."

"Yeah, I guess."

He pulled something out of the suitcase. It was black, silky, and frilly. A pair of women's panties. His expression was just plain weird now, a combination of little-boy-caught-doing-something-wrong sexual excitement and—somewhere—a veiled threat. But his dick was still rock hard. Rock hard.

And, hell, so was mine.

I stood there. He stood there. Finally, he said, "Well, go on. Tell me to put them on."

"Put them on." I'd never done this sort of thing before. I bet it sounded like I lacked conviction.

"Say, 'Put them on, cocksucker.'"

"Put them on, cocksucker." I tried to sound more masterful.

"Bitch."

"Huh?"

"Say 'Put them on, bitch.'" His face bore a "Do I have to explain every little damn thing to you?" look.

"Put them on, bitch." Now, I thought, I was really getting into it.

He sat on the edge of the bed and pulled the panties up over his gnarled feet, powerful, hairy calves, thick thighs, and wriggled them up over his straining cock. He stood up, looking faintly ridiculous and—to my immense surprise—

very sexy.

His palms running over the silky undies, the man said, "I'm your sexy bitch" And he was.

He turned and reached into the suitcase again. The shiny black fabric caressed the generous curves of his butt. I just couldn't believe how exciting this was.

He'd pulled a matching brassiere from the suitcase. He held it to his face, rubbed it over his stubbly cheeks. Meanwhile, my hand had found its irresistible way to my cock.

He looked up at me and held out the bra. "Would you help me put this on?"

Well, I've always been—if nothing else—a gentleman. He turned around and pulled the bra straps over his meaty arms. I let go of my cock, and pulled the bra the rest of the way up, fastening it over his broad back.

"Mmm," he said. "Put your arms around your cocksucking bitch." When I did, he rubbed his silk-clad ass against my straining erection. I'd never done anything remotely like this before—hell, I'd never been with a *woman* wearing panties before—but it was turning out to be big fun. Not *despite* the undies. *Because of* the undies.

He pulled away from me and lay on his back on the king-sized bed, next to the open suitcase. The sight of this big, tough Italian in lingerie, his cock head just peeking over the waistband of his increasingly damp panties, was more than a bit ludicrous. It was also—astonishingly—very, very hot.

He reached into the suitcase. "Want to put these on your little whore-girl?"

I'd never touched a pair of garters before, but I pulled the frilly black pair up to his meaty thighs. Still lying back, he pulled a pair of black fishnet stockings over his big legs and clipped them into place. He looked up at me with an expression that somehow combined innocent eagerness and thoroughgoing depravity.

"Ooh, Tony," he cooed, licking his lips like some second-rate porn actress, "fuck me."

My name's not Tony, but that didn't matter. I jumped onto him and pinned his wrists to the mattress, dry-humping his panty-clad crotch.

"You fucking slut!" I sneered. Where had *that* come from?

He thrust his hips upward. "Fuck yeah... but call me Doctor Melfi."

Huh? "Doctor"? What was *that* about? "Who's he?" I asked.

"It's a she, you idiot. Go on, tell Doctor Melfi what a whore she is."

We lay there, cock against silk-wrapped cock, my face right next to his. "Doctor Melfi," I obligingly hissed, "you are such a fucking cunt."

The doorbell rang.

The man in panties froze.

The doorbell rang again, long and hard, followed by pounding on the door that sounded loud even in the bedroom.

"Shouldn't you get that?" I asked.

The man's voice was a hoarse whisper. "Don't say a word. Don't move a muscle, or I'll ... "

I began to get the feeling I was in way over my head.

The pounding stopped, but it was another five minutes before the guy said anything. During those long moments, I had visions of guns in the dresser drawer, of the door being broken down, of being led off naked to the New Jersey Pine Barrens. Not pleasant imaginings, and I was ashamed to note that I still had a hard-on. But none of those things happened, and the man in panties spoke at last. And what he finally said was: "Lick my clit." I had the feeling I shouldn't refuse.

I slithered myself down so my face was right in his crotch and sucked at his still-stiff dick through the precome-soaked black silk. It tasted like salty fabric. Meanwhile, he kept up a line of nonstop porn chatter.

"Oooh, yeah, Daddy, I'm your little pussy-bitch, your hot wop cunt, your little guinea gash."

Now, I myself am as Italian as Chef Boy-Ar-Dee, so what first seemed merely irritating became downright offensive. I scooted up, stopping for a minute to rub my face on his chest, against smooth silk and thick fur. When my cock reached his mouth, I fucked his face. That, if nothing else, shut him up.

I thrust in hard, and he sputtered and choked a little bit, but he was able to take it all. Yeah, he was a pretty damn good cocksucker, all right. I reached way down and squeezed his meaty tit through the black bra, and boom, I couldn't help it, I shot my load down his throat. I was exhausted, so I rolled back on the bed, panting, but eating my come had only made him more excited. He pulled his panties up so his cock was completely covered again, and jacked himself off through the frilly silk, going on and on about Melfi and wop and whatever. And then he shut up, his eyes rolled back in his head, and little oceans of come started soaking through the panties, pearly white against black silk.

He caught his breath for a second, then sprang to his feet. Reaching back, he managed to unbuckle the bra and pulled it off, using it to wipe off his belly. "Hey, pal," he said, "I'd invite you to stick around for a shower and a drink, only what happened at the door, the knocking and that, I think that was my business partners. You better go."

I didn't need convincing; I was already pulling on my clothes.

When we got to the front door, he handed me a pad and a pen. "We're gonna see each other again, right." It was, again, not so much a query as a command. "I really can't give you my phone number, so you write yours down."

I made something up.

He opened the door, looked around as if to make sure the coast was clear, and said, "That was great. I'll be seeing you. I'll call you soon."

•

But his call didn't come, of course. And whenever, over the next couple of weeks, I thought about what had happened, I was sure I'd done the right thing not to give him my real number. I figured that fucking around with a wise guy in ladies' lingerie should probably be one of those once-in-a-lifetime things.

I was watching some DVD one night when my doorbell rang. There stood two nattily-dressed men with pompadours: Guidos, I guess you could call them. One was tall, one was short, and they both looked like the kind of guys you wouldn't want to meet in a dark alley. Right off, I figured that I knew who had sent them. I was right.

"Our boss wants to see you," the shorter one said. "Now."

And who was I to refuse?

A GRACEFUL REVELATION

RASHELLE BROWN

Late one evening last spring while I was at the library scanning the titles in the "legal briefs" aisle, a girl ran into me. Hard. She was carrying a pile of books and apparently had been scanning titles herself, though I don't know how anyone can read when she's walking that fast.

I'm a suspicious woman by nature, always on guard at some level, and so in the moment before we collided the keener instincts of my animal self kicked in and I braced myself and leaned into her. She sprawled backward, the pile of books flying out onto the floor around her. For a moment I was mad, still on the defensive, and I glared at her. But then I saw her—harmless, scared, young, and staring back at me through glasses that had gone out of style three years ago.

"I'm sorry!" she said, a loud whisper, really. I watched as the initial shock became embarrassment and she looked as though she might cry.

"It's okay," I said quickly, trying to sound sincere and caring—anything to make her not cry. I extended my hand to help her up, but she had already busied herself with picking up the books around her. The binding on one of them had come loose and when she picked it up hundreds of pages fluttered out onto the floor, spreading themselves in an arc around her. Had she lain down and put her arms out to the sides she could have made a kind of odd indoor snow angel.

This upset her immensely, and now she did begin to cry, only she was laughing, too. When her mouth curved upward into a smile, something in me stirred. She was attractive, in is Lane sort of way. She was messy—dressed in jeans that were a bit too big and a T-shirt that would have long ago been condemned to the rag pile in my house—but there was something more. The eyes behind those glasses were more than shy or embarrassed. The face beneath that mess of spiraled hair held a potential that I could almost see. I crouched down.

"Let me help you," I said, scooping up loose pages by the handful. A library worker emerged in the aisle, and gave us a disgusted look. Just as she drew breath to speak, I cut her off. "We've got it," I said, with the authority my power suit lent me, and the woman nodded, dropped her eyes, turned, and left without a word.

"Thank you," the girl said, sniffing away the last of her tears. "God, what a crap day!" She changed positions then, getting onto her hands and knees to get the last of the loose pages in front of her; her T-shirt shifted a little, and I caught a glimpse of something. It was blue, satiny, wide-banded, and two-toned. A blue-gray floral pattern barely distinguished itself atop a midnight background. That something inside of me stirred a little more vigorously as I realized that this was her bra strap. I followed the line of it down with my eyes and could just make out a surprisingly ample swell pressing out against the large T-shirt that hung like a sheet from her frame.

Why would you dress that way? I was thinking when she saw me staring, realized what I was looking at, and dropped the pages too quickly to readjust her T-shirt. I was equally embarrassed; our eyes simultaneously dove and our hands followed, both grabbing the same stack of loose papers on the floor.

Her hand brushed mine and I felt its warmth. She jerked her hand away and ventured a quick, upward glance at me, her eyes almost totally obscured by thick, unruly rivulets of hair. I removed my hand from the papers and she reached to pick them up. Then, slowly, I placed my hand atop hers and ran my fingertips along the back of it. I watched red circles form on her cheekbones as I did this, and I felt a stirring heat within myself as I had this one thought: *Is she wearing matching panties?*

She held my gaze for a brave second, then dropped her eyes, but she did not pull her hand away.

Emboldened by this, I asked, "What's your name?"

"Grace," she said quietly, still looking at the floor.

"It's nice to meet you, Grace," I said, almost seducing myself with the tone of my own voice. "I'm Catherine."

Now she pulled her hand away, the stack of papers firmly in its grasp. "It's nice to meet you, too." She got to her feet, then stooped to pick up the other books and her T-shirt shifted again.

"Let me help you carry those," I said, taking some of the books from her. She juggled her share of the stack into one arm and adjusted her collar immediately.

"Thank you," she said.

We walked to the counter and placed the books in front of the same woman I had earlier chased away. The woman studied the pile of papers and the broken binding and shook her head. "You'll have to pay for this," she said to Grace.

Grace began digging through her backpack. "Hold on," I said. "She's not liable for the damage to that book. She hasn't even checked it out."

"What are you, her lawyer?" the woman asked, irritated but avoiding my eyes.

"Well, I'm *a* lawyer," I said, "and she doesn't have to pay for it. Besides, I know for a fact that you have a full-time staff person whose only job is to make repairs to books. I'm on the Board."

Unaccustomed to dealing with those who questioned the authority of her scornful looks and loud "Shhh's" the woman was at a loss. "Very well," is what she finally came up with; then she turned her attention back to Grace. "I suppose you'll be wanting to check the rest of these out?"

"Yes, please," Grace said, handing over her library card. When the transaction was finished, Grace loaded the books into her backpack and I followed her out.

"Thank you so much, that looked like an expensive book," she said, meeting my eyes, but crossing her arms over her breasts. "Are you really a lawyer?"

"Yes," I said. "And you're welcome. Where are you going now?"

"Oh, I don't know. Back home, I guess. I was going to study here, but they close in twenty minutes, and besides, after *that* ..."

I laughed. "Where do you live? Can I give you a ride?"

She seemed to consider these simple questions for a very long time. "It's not that far," she said at last. "I usually just walk. I live in one of the converted Victorians over on Pine Street."

"That's right on my way," I lied.

"Well, okay," she said. I felt a little like a teenage boy coaxing the junior high girl into my sweet ride.

"How old are you?" I asked.

"Twenty-two," she answered. "How old are you?"

The question caught me off guard, but I answered anyway. "Thirty-three." She said nothing.

I pressed the button on my keyless remote and the dome light came on inside my Mercedes.

"That's your car?" Grace asked.

"Yes," I said. I had never felt better in my life.

Inside the car, Grace seemed to relax a little. I had the classical music station playing low on the radio and told her she could change the station if she liked. "I like this," she said, and I believed her.

I drove slowly, willing all the stoplights to turn red. "Do you have a roommate?" I asked.

"Two," she answered. "Three of us share a studio."

"Wow, that's gotta make studying pretty tough."

"Yep," she said. "Unfortunately, I think they're both home tonight. It's finals week."

"What are you majoring in?"

"Marketing," she said, then quickly added, "I want to

work in the nonprofit field."

"Hmm," I said. "What's the money like in that?"

"Well, not very good. But I'm not that interested in money."

"That's because you're young," I said. She said nothing in return, but I could instantly feel the mood change in her. My mind raced for something else to say. I had nothing, so I lied. "Actually, I do quite a lot of pro-bono work."

"Really?" She sounded more interested than skeptical, so I went with it.

"Yes. Last year I logged a lot of hours with the H.R.C." Now not only was I lying to her, but I was fishing for information—did she know what the H.R.C. was?

"The Human Rights Campaign?" she asked excitedly. "That's incredible. I would *love* to land a job with them."

There it was, then.

"You know, you could study at my place, if you like," I said casually. Before she could respond I added, "I'm going to be working late into the night anyway."

"Oh, I don't know. I mean, you barely know me,"

"Nonsense!" I said, patting her thigh (it was very firm). "We're a couple of like-minded women. Besides, what better way to get to know one another?"

She didn't consider for very long. "Okay. I'll need to run in and get some things, though."

"No problem," I said, pulling to the curb outside 507 Pine Street.

It was an agonizing seven or eight minutes sitting in the car, waiting for her. I was almost certain that she would come down empty-handed and tell me she'd changed her mind. But finally she emerged, her bulging backpack over one shoulder.

She swung herself into my leather bucket seat and I noticed that she had fixed her hair a little. She was dressed the same, though, and this excited me.

I drove quickly in the opposite direction to my small manse on the outskirts of town.

"My place wasn't exactly on your way," she said, looking at me with a shy smile.

"It wasn't exactly close to the library, either," I countered.

The cocoon of the car made me bold and giddy. I wanted to reach for her, to feel the firmness of her thigh again—to run my hand upward and inward just to see what she would do. But that might spur things on too quickly, and here was something new: I didn't *want* this to happen quickly. I was, before that night, a patent hedonist for whom there was no pleasure in delaying gratification. Patience was not a word in my vocabulary. Everything came to me easily, and so I took it as it came. But here was something I wanted to wait for, to prolong and draw out to its very last possible moment. So I restrained myself, and in doing so, my longing grew.

It had begun to rain some minutes before, and as I pulled up the driveway I saw her trace a trickling drop of water down the window with her finger. The simple sensuality of the act drew a groan from me and I could tell she heard it. She dropped her hand and did not look at me, embarrassed by her knowing.

"This is a big place," she said quietly.

"I know," I said, feeling something other than my usual pride. It was another imperceptible change in me, but real and undeniable.

I led her through my house in the usual grand-tour manner, turning on lights and proclaiming the title of each room as I went, but it now felt shallower and more transparent with each step. The vaulted ceilings, the three bedrooms, the huge cherry-paneled office, the gourmet kitchen, the sixteen-foot split-rock fireplace—they all conspired against me somehow. Grace remained silent.

We ended in the great room. I lit the fire with the press of a button and dimmed the lights using the same remote. I motioned to the sofa, "Make yourself comfortable," I said. "Can I get you something to drink?"

"Just some water," Grace said, setting her backpack on

the floor. The top wasn't quite zipped shut and I saw an article of clothing inside. So she was prepared, at least, to spend the night. I regained a bit of my confidence.

"I'm having bourbon on the rocks," I said. "Just water for you?"

"I thought you were working," she said, smiling slyly.

"I work best after having a bourbon by the fire," I smiled back.

"Bourbon on the rocks, then."

When I returned with the drinks she was fishing the last of several books from her backpack. "You're all business," I said. "You must be a very good student."

"If I make all A's on this round of exams I'll be assured a graduate scholarship," she said, embarrassed to be talking about herself.

"When are the exams?" I handed her the bourbon.

"They start on Tuesday." She sipped the bourbon—a tiny sip—and managed not to wince as she swallowed.

"So you have a few days, then," I said.

"Yes, I have a little time."

It was raining quite hard now, and the sound on the skylights above was delicious. We sipped our bourbon in silence on opposite ends of the sofa and I noticed the thinnest edge of the blue bra running along the outside of her T-shirt's collar. The sum total of it all was too much, I had to do something.

"That's a nice bra," I said, shifting toward her.

The bourbon went down the wrong pipe, though, as Grace coughed gauchely. Her hand flew to her neck and she adjusted the collar.

"May I ask where you got it?"

"I don't know," she said, her voice constricted. This was followed by another hack. "Excuse me," she said quietly, clearing her throat and taking a deep breath. Her whole face was red now. She took off her glasses and wiped at her watering eyes. She took another deep breath.

"You have beautiful eyes," I said, not in the usual Big

Bad Wolf way, but in a tone bordering on surprise. It was a genuine compliment.

"Thank you," she said, wiping her glasses on the bottom of her T-shirt. This made her collar shift widely to the left, and exposed the whole width of the bra strap. I moved next to her. She stopped wiping her glasses and looked at me. She was stunning.

"Would you like some water," I whispered, mesmerized.

"No, thank you," she whispered back.

I moved my hand to her shoulder and ran a finger along the bra strap. It was of superb quality. "You really don't know where you got this?" I whispered.

"There's a little boutique on St. Peter Street," she said. She was looking straight into my eyes and I felt the thread inside me snap.

I ran my finger gently down the front of her shirt, tracing the bra strap to the cup. My finger continued down between her breasts to the underwire and circled slowly to the outside, then across the middle to where her nipple stood hard, ready for me. A low groan, the twin of my earlier one, floated from her lips. She closed her eyes and moved toward me. I took her glass from her and set hers and mine on the floor, then lifted the T-shirt over her head.

Her eyes stayed shut and mine played. I took her in greedily, actively trying to memorize each detail as I went. I put a hand to her other breast and felt that nipple harden instantly. I traced her waistline with my eyes. Her stomach was perfect in its youth, far more perfect than my hour in the gym each day would ever produce. It was trim and firm, but with soft skin and a wonderfully subtle cleft down the middle. I grabbed her nipple lightly between my finger and thumb. She shuddered and whispered inaudibly, "Please."

I brought her to me and laid her back gently. She opened her eyes and they were eyes of desperation, the exact emotion that I, too, was feeling. I unzipped her pants, and she gave a worried look around the room. I leaned past her and fumbled for the remote on the end table and pressed the button that shut off all the lights in the house; I barely made out Grace's "Thank you."

I pulled her jeans down to her ankles and she kicked them off the rest of the way, then, awkwardly, I pulled off her socks. My eyes adjusted to the dark; only the flickering firelight illuminated the huge room now. The matching panties were exquisite. I looked at the pile of rumpled clothes on the floor and back at her—now she was someone else entirely.

The panties were tight, low-cut bikinis with little scallops of midnight blue fringed around the edges. A perfect pair of young, firm legs disappeared into those scallops, and seeing this made my surrender complete. I wanted the life of this girl. I wanted unassuming proportions, and service to others. I wanted the ideals of the young. I wanted to be polite. I wanted to possess this quiet, secret sensuality. I wanted to ask someone, "Please," and for that to be all I wanted.

Grace smiled up at me. "Why are you looking at me like that?"

"You're so beautiful," I said. It was all that I could say.

She unbuttoned my blouse and unfastened my trousers, and I let her. I slipped my clothes off and she pulled me down on top of her. I felt her warmth, her goodness, her longing, and I felt her bra and panties against my bare skin.

I rolled off her, onto my side and touched her softly. I placed my hand on her thigh and ran it upward and inward as I had so badly wanted to do in the car. She moaned freely, throwing her head back. The cool blue satin of her panties slipped over the intense warmth that lay beneath. I ran a finger lightly down the blue scallops of one edge. She reached down and hooked a thumb into the waistline of her panties. I grabbed her hand forcefully. "No! Leave them on," I said. "Please."

JOCK BAIT: A SPIKE THE SKATERPUNK STORY

CHRISTOPHER PIERCE

Wanna hear a dirty story?

I thought so, you perv.

It's about something that happened to me. Something sick, twisted, perverted, totally *fucked-up*.

Listen to this.

I'm twenty-two, about five foot seven, weigh 145 pounds, am skinny and lean. I've always got a baseball cap on backward and my skateboard by my side. I never wear underwear, but I love it on other guys.

Whenever I can scrape together enough dough I buy a day-pass at a gym. Now of course I can't afford to go even for one day to one of those tight-ass high-class gay gyms where everyone that's there stepped out of a goddamn magazine ad. So I gotta go to one of them dirty, cheap gyms downtown, where it's chicks, guys, anybody who don't wanna pay three hundred dollars to work out for an hour and a half.

I don't pay attention to the chicks, of course. Some of them look at me, but I'm not down with that scene, y'know? I'm a cock-sucking, butt-reaming queer all the way. But the guys, fuck, it's hard not to stare. All those freakin' muscles strainin', those sweaty armpits stinkin', and those waistbands stickin' up from the top of their shorts.

Lookin' at the waistbands of the guys' underwear is my favorite thing to do at the gym. I try to guess what kinda shorts they got on. My twisted little brain thinks of all the possibilities: tighty-whities, flimsy boxers, jockstraps, bikini bottoms. I love the thought of those sexy men's cocks and balls all safe and protected inside their underwear, sometimes held tightly, other times floppin' free. Then I imagine what it'd be like to worship those cocks and balls, being on my fucking knees in front of those guys, just sucking like there's no tomorrow.

So the last few times I was at this rat-hole of a gym I noticed these two guys. They were hard to miss. They were fuckin' studs, man, not all mutant-gross-overdeveloped like some bodybuilders, but just nicely muscled. You know what I mean? Butts so tight you could bounce a quarter offa them. Arms with nice, round-shaped biceps that inflated whenever they bent their elbows. Washboard abs. Nice, hairy, sexy legs. Lotta gay guys overdo their chests and arms, get all nice, and forget their legs. Whatcha get there are real nice torsos propped up by skinny-little bird legs. Makes me gag.

But not these two.

Their legs were just as toned and buffed as the rest of them. They had to be military, 'cause they both wore dog tags and had these high-'n'-tight haircuts. They never talked to anyone at the gym, just came in, worked out, and left. But everyone noticed them. The chicks for sure, and some of the guys. I tried not to be obvious when I watched them, but it was fuckin' hard. They never let on that they knew I was salivating over them, they just ignored me like they ignored everyone else.

Lookin' back I guess it's obvious they knew, but at the time I guess my brain wasn't getting enough oxygen to think 'cause all my blood was going to my cock.

So of course what I was most interested in with these military guys was what they were wearing underneath their camouflage pants. Briefs, jockstraps, boxers? I was desperate to know, but I could never get close enough to them to check 'em out properly. And unwanted attention from another guy is a good way to get a straight dude good and angry. I'm a tough little shit but I didn't think I could go up against these two without some serious damage to myself. I've been beat up plenty of times and had no desire to repeat the experience.

But I had to know.

One night I followed them to the showers, which were downstairs in the dirty basement of the gym. There was hardly anyone left at that hour, the place was gonna close soon. So while the two military guys were soaping up under the nozzles, I took a peek into their gym bags. If I'd had any brains at all I woulda realized that there was a big old mirror on the opposite wall. The mirror gave people in the showers a perfect view of the locker area, so they could see if some dumbfuck was messing with their stuff.

So like an idiot I'm kneelin' down in front of their bags like it's Christmas morning under the tree. I reached into one and rummaged around inside. Undershirt, deodorant, CD player, dog tags—jockstrap! The other bag—sweat socks, hip-hop mag, tank-top, toothbrush—jockstrap! With my treasures in my hands I lifted them to my nose and mouth, breathing in what had to be the finest fuckin' odor on the fine fuckin' earth. The double dose of sweat, musk, and piss was so intense I almost keeled over.

I heard the showers shut off, and I stuffed the jocks back in the bags, grabbed my bag and my board and hightailed it outta there. I headed back to my rat-hole apartment by way of the alley behind the gym. That one sniff of the military studs' jocks carried me all the way home where I jerked off until every last drop of come in me had been squeezed out.

So later in the week, when I'd scrounged up enough cash to go to the gym again, I looked for the hot dudes, but they weren't there. I was disappointed but what could I do? When I left the gym and headed out back for the alley, I stopped in my tracks. In the middle of the alley, on the ground, was a jockstrap.

Hmmm ... I thought, *what's this?*

I walked over to it and got down on one knee to examine it. I picked it up and looked at it—it could have been anyone's, but why would a jockstrap be left on the ground behind a gym?

Suddenly everything went dark, and I answered my own question.

Bait.

"What the fuck?" I yelled as I was surrounded by something and closed inside it. Someone punched me in the gut, and I keeled over onto the ground inside the whatever-it-was.

"Got you, faggot!" a man's voice said.

I felt hands grabbing at me through the canvas of what I realized must've been a bag of some kind—a military duffel bag. Those fuckers from the gym—they'd ambushed me and stuffed me into one of their man-sized bags! I tried to struggle but they hit me again, this time not caring where. They punched me in the back, the side, even a few on the face and head.

"Help!" I tried to yell, but the wind was knocked out of me.

I stopped struggling and went limp, and the bag with me in it was lifted off the ground and hoisted over one of the guy's shoulders. He started to carry me quickly out of the alley, and his buddy kept his hands on the bag to prevent me from falling or struggling. As I tried to catch my breath, I noticed something—it stank inside the bag, it was really reeking. Then I felt something else all around me, something besides the canvas of the duffel I was trapped in.

Suddenly I figured it out.

The duffel bag, aside from me, also contained underwear. A lot of jockstraps, to be exact. And I could guess who they belonged to. I breathed in deeply, savoring the stale musky smell all around me. And my cock got fuckin' hard—*I was getting kidnapped and I was horny*. Was this fucked up or what?

I sorta lost track of what was happening after that; I was just grooving on the odor of the military studs' jocks. I must've been carried a ways away to a car or truck, where I was dumped into what felt like the back seat. My kidnappers got in and started up their ride, then drove the hell out of there. We drove for a while. They may have been talking, I couldn't tell from the rushing wind, they must've had the windows open. I wondered what would happen if they got stopped by a cop. I wondered if I wanted that to happen. I wondered if I was getting off on this underwear/kidnap scene.

Soon enough the vehicle stopped and the military dudes got out. I was pulled out of the back seat and once again the bag was slung over one of their shoulders. They carried me inside what had to be a house or apartment, although I figured probably a house 'cause it'd be hard to explain lugging in a man-sized sack with a body in it to the neighbors. They took me inside and brought me to a room, then opened the duffel bag and dumped me out onto a bed—although with all the jockstraps.

"You sons-of-bitches —" I started to yell, but I stopped when I got my bearings and saw what was going down. It was the two military studs, like I thought, dressed in their camouflage pants and white wife-beater undershirts. They were grinning at me. One of them held a coil of rope, the other had a gun that was pointed at me.

"Where's my board, you bastards?" I yelled like an idiot. The one with the rope backhanded me across the face.

"Shut up!" he said.

"You like sniffing our jockstraps, faggot?" the one with the gun said.

"You jerk off thinkin' about sucking our cocks, dream about gettin' butt-fucked by us?" from the other one.

"Well, your dreams are about to come true, you sick twisted little fucker."

I thought about running, but where could I go? I was in a strange place, with two mean motherfuckers onto me, one with a gun for fuck's sake. And my goddamn cock was betraying me, hard in my shorts for the studs to laugh at.

"Knew you'd be into this, faggot. Take your clothes off!"

I obeyed, shucking off my tank-top and shorts. My

pecker was stiff, stickin' up from between my legs. My abductors pointed at it and laughed. Then, while his buddy was pointing the gun at me, the one with the rope tied me up. He stretched my arms out, twisting the rope around my wrists and then tying it off under the bed. Hurt like a son-of-a-bitch. He didn't do my legs, and I knew why. Easy access to my butt-hole.

Now I was getting scared, and I was too stupid to shut up. I started begging them not to hurt me, to let me go, usual crap a captive says to his captor.

"Goddamn it, Curtis!" the one with the gun said. "Do something about his fucking mouth!" The one who'd tied me up, Curtis, grabbed a jockstrap off the bed and jammed it into my open mouth. My nose and mouth were invaded by the scents I'd smelled at the gym, but now I could taste them again—sweat, piss, old come maybe? Curtis took off his undershirt and wrapped it around my head, tying it behind, holding the jockgag in place.

"That'll keep you quiet."

I shut up, starting to go into erotic overload with this scene. Tied up at gunpoint and gagged with a jockstrap by two military studs—was this a wet dream or a nightmare? Could it be both? How could I be terrified and totally turned on at the same time? Maybe 'cause I'm a sick, twisted little fucker, like they said.

But we knew that already.

"How's that, Rick?" Curtis asked his buddy.

"Much better," Rick said, lowering the gun and putting it on the floor. "Now let's get the fuck on with this."

The two studs undid their camouflage pants and let them fall to the ground. Just to make matters worse/better they were both wearing jockstraps. They left them on, just pulling their big cocks out the sides.

"Who first?" Curtis asked.

"Flip a coin," Rick said, tossing a quarter up in the air.

"Heads,"

"Tails. I go first."

Rick climbed up onto the bed and pulled off his undershirt. He roughly yanked my feet apart and inserted himself between my legs. Spitting into his hand, he used it to slick up his cock, which was as hard as mine. Looked like I wasn't the only one getting off on this. He thrust himself forward, poking his dick right into my waiting asshole. It was the worst pain I ever felt in my life (so far) and I screamed into the jockstrap that was gagging me. I clenched my teeth into it as Rick fucked me, turning my poor butt-hole into raw hamburger. While he thrust inside me the dog tags hanging from his neck banged against my neck.

When Rick was ready to shoot his load he pulled out of me. Then he jerked himself off the rest of the way, growling and snarling like an animal. When he came he squirted about six ropy strands of spunk onto my chest, then got off the bed.

"Sorry for the sloppy seconds, man," Rick said to his buddy.

"No problem," Curtis said, "you got him warmed up for me."

Then Curtis did something that was so bizarre and hot that it changed the whole scene for me. Instead of spitting into his hand, Curtis scooped up a handful of Rick's spunk and used it to lube up his dick. No straight guy would do that, and I realized that not only was I not the only one getting off on this, but I wasn't the only gay guy in the room either. It sounds hot to get fucked by a straight guy, but it was somehow even hotter to know that these dudes, these incredible masculine military studs were queer/gay/homosexual, just like me.

But there wasn't time to think about this, because Curtis took his lubed-with-spooge dick and shoved it into my asshole. He fucked me longer than Rick had, and looked right into my eyes the whole time. And somehow I knew that he knew that I knew. When he was done he shot off on me, adding his gooey spunk to his buddy's, which had dried onto my chest. He took his hands and rubbed the come into my skin, smearing its stickiness all over me. It was disgusting and fuckin' hotter than hell.

"All right, party's over," Rick said, picking up the gun again and pointing it at me. "Untie him, but leave the gag in, I think he needs something to remember tonight by."

Curtis did what he was told. I was weak from being fucked so hard and didn't even try to struggle when I was loose. I didn't see what it was that hit me, but something came down on the back of my head and knocked me out. As consciousness slipped away, I could feel them stuffing me back into the duffel bag along with their dirty old jockstraps.

I woke up back in the alley.

I was naked, on the ground, and it was daylight. I was about to freak out when I realized that my clothes were lying next to me, along with my skateboard. I sat up and undid the undershirt that was tied around my head. Pulling the jock gag out of my mouth, I stuffed the undershirt and the jockstrap into the pocket of my shorts.

Then I got up, grabbed my board, and headed home.

Fuckin' crazy night, I thought.

Better than most.

When I got home I took out the undershirt and jockstrap and held them, first against my nose and mouth, then against my crotch. I whipped out my dick and jacked myself off until I came right into the underwear. When I'd recovered I realized a piece of paper was in my pocket that I didn't put there. Unfolding it I saw there was writing on it.

It said RICK & CURTIS, and beneath it was their phone number.

ACKNOWLEDGMENTS

Many thanks to Miriam Datskovsky, Ellen Friedrichs, Heidi Joy Schmid, and Nichelle Stephens for their friendship and support, and the late Hottpants blog (hottpants.blogspot.com) for inspiration. Thanks to Christopher Pierce for being so on the ball when my mind was swimming with underwear stories, and our editor, Shannon Berning, for trusting us with this project.

Christopher Pierce extends heartfelt thanks to his coeditor, Rachel Kramer Bussel, and Shannon Berning and her colleagues at Alyson Books for the opportunity to coedit the Fetish Chest series.

ABOUT THE CONTRIBUTORS

ZACH ADDAMS, a Native Californian, has published erotica and nonfiction in various web publications and such anthologies as Violet Blue's Sweet Life series and Alison Tyler's Naughty Stories series. He often finds himself returning home with fewer clothes than when he left.

TENILLE BROWN's fiction is featured online and in several print anthologies including *Best Women's Erotica 2004*, *Chocolate Flava*, *Naughty Spanking Stories from A to Z*, and the forthcoming *Amazons: Sexy Tales of Strong Women and Glamour Girls: Femme/Femme Erotica*. She keeps a daily blog on her website, www.tenillebrown.com.

RASHELLE BROWN lives and writes in beautiful Hastings, Minnesota. Her work has appeared in *The Lesbian News* and *Brew Your Own Magazine*. Her own underwear (unfortunately) consists mostly of drab cotton briefs and sports bras. But hey—everyone can dream!

LEW BULL is a teacher by profession who has published academic articles and has coauthored a textbook on business English. He has recently completed research on the use of gay languages and gay identities, which he is hoping to get published. He has been in a gay relationship for the past twenty-eight years, so it can be done!

PAUL CHAMBERS often thinks very naughty thoughts during his workday, but so far, no one else has noticed.

ANDREA DALE lives in Southern California within scent of the ocean. Her stories have appeared in *Best Lesbian Erotica 2005*, Fishnetmag.com, *Dyke the Halls*, and *Sacred Exchange*, among others. Under the name Sophie Mouette, she and a coauthor saw the publication of their first novel, *Cat Scratch Fever*, in March 2006 (Black Lace Books), and they have sold stories to *Sex on the Sportsfield*, *Sex in Uniform*, *Best Women's Erotica 2005*, and more. In other incarnations, she is a published writer of fantasy and romance. Her website can be found at www.cyvarwydd.com.

RYAN FIELD is a freelance writer who lives in Bucks County, Pennsylvania. His short stories have been published in collections and anthologies, and he is working on a novel.

KRISTIE HELMS is a Boston-based writer whose first novel, *Dish It Up Baby* (Firebrand Books) was a 2004 Lambda Literary Award finalist for Debut Lesbian Fiction. Her work has appeared in *The Utne Reader*, *The New York Press*, and *Genre* magazine. Helms's essays have also been featured in *I Do/I Don't: Queers on Marriage*, which was awarded the 2004 Lambda Literary Award for Nonfiction Anthology, and *Pinned Down by Pronouns*, a 2003 Lambda Literary Award finalist for Nonfiction Anthology. She holds a bachelor of science degree in journalism from Murray State University in Kentucky and studied creative writing with writers Toni Amato and Donna Minkowitz.

T. HITMAN is the nom-de-porn of a professional writer who chooses briefs over boxers while routinely working on stories for numerous national magazines. He is also the author of several novels and nonfiction books, and holds story credit on two episodes of a popular Paramount TV series. Recently he celebrated a decade as a feature writer, reviewer, and columnist at *Men*, *Freshmen*, and *Unzipped* magazines, but contrary to reports, he rarely goes commando while striving to meet his deadlines.

WILLIAM HOLDEN lives in Atlanta with his partner of nine years. He works full-time as a librarian on LGBT issues. He has twelve other published short stories and one unpublished novel. He welcomes any comments and can be contacted at Srholdbill@aol.com.

MARCUS JAMES, twenty-one, is the author of *Following the Kaehees*. He lives in El Paso, Texas, though a native of Washington State. Contact him at www.myspace.com/marcus_james and check out his website at www.marcusjamesbooks.com.

LYNNE JAMNECK is the author of the Samantha Skellar mystery series as well as of numerous short stories that have been featured in a host of anthologies. Her speculative fiction has been featured in *H. P. Lovecraft's Magazine of Horror* and *Best Lesbian Erotica 2003–2006*, and upcoming works are slated to appear in *So Fey: Queer Faery Fictions* (edited by Steve Berman), *First-Timers: True Stories of Lesbian Awakening* (edited by Rachel Kramer Bussel), and *Sex in the System: Stories of Erotic Futures, Technological Stimulation, and the Sensual Life of Machines* (edited by Cecilia Tan). Lynne's blog is at http://publishedwork1lynne.blogspot.com. Drop her a note at samskellar@gmail.com.

STAN KENT is a former nightclub-owning rocket scientist with chameleon-colored hair, and an author of erotic novels. A dedicated voyeur and lover of shoes, boots, and women wearing sexy lingerie in them, Stan has penned nine original, unique, and very naughty works, including the Shoe Leather series. Selections from his books have been featured in the *Best of Erotic Writing* Blue Moon collections. Stan has hosted an erotic-talk-show night at Hustler Hollywood for the last five years. The *Los Angeles Times* described his monthly performances as "combination moderator and lion tamer." To see samples of his works and his latest hair colors, visit Stan at www.stankent.com or e-mail him at stan@stankent.com.

GENEVA KING (www.genevaking.com) has been published in *Erotic Fantasy: Tales of the Paranormal, Who's Your Daddy, Ultimate Lesbian Erotica 2006,* and *Best Women's Erotica 2006.* She intends to publish a collection of her stories, if her professors ever give her enough time to do so.

J. J. MASSA (www.jjmassa.com) writes erotica, erotic romance and mainstream romance. Most of her work can be found at www.venuspress.com

JOEL A. NICHOLS's erotic fiction has been anthologized in *Full Body Contact* and *Just the Sex,* and an excerpt from his novel *Wicked Little Town* won second place in the Brown Foundation Short Fiction Prize in 2005. In 2002 he won a Fulbright to Berlin. He lives in Philadelphia.

NEIL PLAKCY is the author of *Mahu,* a mystery novel featuring the Honolulu police detective Kimo Kanapa'aka. A contributor to *Men Seeking Men, My First Time* (volume 2), and *Dorm Porn,* he is also the editor of a forthcoming anthology from Alyson Press that focuses on gay men and their dogs. He received his master's of fine arts in creative writing from Florida International University and is a professor of English at Broward Community College.

RADCLYFFE has written more than twenty romances, erotica collections, and action intrigue novels. As the president of Bold Strokes Books, she publishes critically acclaimed lesbian-themed works by other noted authors. She is a two-time recipient of the Alice B. Reader's Award and is a 2005 GCLS award winner in both the romance and intrigue categories. Her recent works include *Honor Reclaimed* (2005), *Justice Served* (2005), and *Erotic Interludes 2: Stolen Moments* (2005).

TERESA NOELLE ROBERTS's work has appeared under her own name in *Best Women's Erotica 2004* and *Best Women's Erotica 2005,* FishNetMag.com, and many other publications. She is one of the two coauthors behind the pseudonym Sophie Mouette. Her work under Sophie's name has appeared or is forthcoming in several Wicked Words anthologies from Black Lace Books (U.K.) and in *Best Women's Erotica 2005*. Sophie's first novel is forthcoming from Black Lace Books in March 2006.

THOMAS ROCHE's published stories and articles number somewhere in the high hundreds—he's long ago lost count. His books include the Noirotica series, *His, Hers*, and *Dark Matter*. He lives in the San Francisco Bay Area and is the managing editor of Eros Zine (http://www.eros-zine.com). Visit him at www.skidroche.com and www.livejournal.com/thomasroche.

MINAROSE, a newcomer to the world of erotica, is excited to be published for the first time in this anthology. She enjoys writing sexy stories of all types, but favors the realms of science fiction, fantasy, and all things supernatural. Also a freelance web designer, MinaRose's most recent accomplishment is www.christopherpierceerotica.com. She is always on the prowl for new and challenging projects. MinaRose lives, works, and plays in South Florida where the sun inspires her heated visions. Feel free to visit Mistress MinaRose at www.minarose.christopherpierceerotica.com.

SIMON SHEPPARD is the author of *In Deep: Erotic Stories*, *Hotter Than Hell and Other Stories*, *Sex Parties 101*, and *Kinkorama*. His work has also appeared in more than 175 anthologies, including many editions of *The Best American Erotica* and *Best Gay Erotica*, and he writes the column "Sex Talk." His next project is a historically based treasury of queer porn. He lives in San Francisco, hangs out at www.simonsheppard.com, and has seen every episode of *The Sopranos*.

JAY STARRE has created numerous nasty stories for gay men's magazines and anthologies including *Honcho, Torso, Men, International Leatherman,* and the Friction series for Alyson Books. From Vancouver, British Columbia, he was first runner-up in the Mr. BC Leather Contest of 2002.

JULIAN TIRHMA lives in the heart of Koreatown, Los Angeles, where he writes smut crowded with corduroy, Pentax, hair, knights errant, and feasts. Bringing insights from spurned trysts, depraved petticoats, and embroidered archetypes, Julian emphasizes deliberately ambiguous identifications to elbow the boundaries of queerness. Smut should turn you on, get you off, trick you up.

TANYA TURNER likes to sleep in her sexiest underwear. Her erotic stories have been published in several steamy anthologies. She can be found prowling department stores in search of the perfect panty.

ALISON TYLER, called a trollop with a laptop by the East Bay Express, is naughty and she knows it. Over the past decade, Ms. Tyler has written more than fifteen explicit novels, including *Strictly Confidential, Sweet Thing, Sticky Fingers,* and *Something About Workmen* (Black Lace), as well as *Rumors, Tiffany Twisted,* and *With or Without You* (Cheek). Her stories have appeared in numerous anthologies, including *Up All Night* (Alyson), *Sweet Life I* and *Sweet Life II* (Cleis); and in *Wicked Words* (volumes 4, 5, 6, 8, and 10), *Sex in the Office, Sex on Holiday, Best of Black Lace 2,* and *Sex in Uniform* (Black Lace); as well as in *Playgirl* magazine and *Penthouse Variations.* She is the editor of *Heat Wave, Best Bondage Erotica* (volumes 1 and 2), *The Merry XXXMas Book of Erotica, Luscious, Red Hot Erotica, Slave to Love,* and *Three-Way* (Cleis); *Naughty Fairy Tales from A to Z* (Plume); and the Naughty Stories from A to Z series, the Down and Dirty series, *Naked Erotica,* and *Juicy Erotica* (Pretty Things Press). Please visit www.prettythingspress.com.

JUSTIN TYLER is an author of gay erotic fiction, previously published under various pseudonyms. Justin lives in Baltimore, Maryland, and enjoys dancing and people watching, and is a firm believer in happy endings.

MILA WHITELEY's erotic fiction has appeared in *Come Quickly for Girls on the Go* (Masquerade), *Down and Dirty* (Pretty Things Press), and on the Good Vibrations website. She supports her writing career (and lingerie habit) by working in retail in West L.A.

KRISTINA WRIGHT is a full-time writer living in Virginia. She holds a B.A. in English and is pursuing a M.A. in humanities with an emphasis on women's literature. Her erotic fiction has appeared in more than twenty-five anthologies, including *Best Women's Erotica*, *Sweet Life: Stories of Sexual Fantasy and Adventure for Couples* four editions of the Lambda Award–winning series Best Lesbian Erotica and *The Mammoth Book of Best New Erotica* (volume 5). For more information about Kristina's life, writing, and academic pursuits, visit her website www. kristinawright.com.

ABOUT THE EDITORS

RACHEL KRAMER BUSSEL (www.rachelkramerbussel.com) is senior editor at *Penthouse Variations*, and a contributing editor and columnist for *Penthouse*. She writes the "Lusty Lady" column for the *Village Voice*, and contributes regularly to Gothamist.com, Mediabistro.com, and the *New York Post*. Her books include the Lambda Literary Award finalist *Up All Night: Adventures in Lesbian Sex*, *First-Timers: True Stories of Lesbian Awakening*, *Glamour Girls: Femme/Femme Erotica*, and *Naughty Spanking Stories from A to Z* (volumes 1 and 2). Her erotica has been published in more than sixty anthologies, including *Best American Erotica* (2004 and 2006), Best Lesbian Erotica (2001, 2004, and 2005), and many others. She has also written for AVN, BUST, Cleansheets.com, *Curve*, *Diva*, *Girlfriends*, *Rockrgrl*, the *San Francisco Chronicle*, *Velvetpark*, and *Zink*, and has posed nude for *On Our Backs*. She blogs incessantly at lustylady.blogspot.com and cupcakestakethecake.blogspot.com.

CHRISTOPHER PIERCE's erotic fiction has been published in numerous books and magazines. His first novel, *Rogue: Slave*, has been published by STARbooks Press. Write to him at chris@christopherpierceerotica.com and visit his world at www.ChristopherPierceErotica.com.